PASSENGERS

& Perils

PASSENGERS

& Perils

Matthew Hughes

PASSENGERS & PERILS
By Matthew Hughes

Copyright © 2022 by Matthew Hughes

Ebook ISBN: 978-1-927880-22-7
Paperback ISBN: 978-1-927880-23-4

One

"Conn," Jenore said to me, "there's one more second-class passenger. His name is Todfrey Hamble."

I was looking at the roster of cabin assignments to which I'd been putting the final touches when Jenore had popped her head through the doorway into my working space. "Where am I supposed to put him?" I said. "We're full. I can't –"

She gestured with a small hand to quiet me. "Yalum and I cleaned out that little cabinette that used to be Vullamir's storage, the one we've been using to store games and performances. I put them in the salon's cupboards."

"That's a very small cabin," I said. The tiny room had been devoted to storage of paraphernalia belonging to Lord Vullamir, back when this space yacht had been named the *Martichor* and was the property of the head of a first-tier aristocratic family from Old Earth. I had been glad to see the life masks of Vullamir's ancestors done away with. The "masks" were actually globes that completely covered the wearer's head and contained the preserved "essences" of long-dead relatives. When worn, the masks revived the essences and gave them a half-life whereby they interacted with the senses and mentation of the wearer. I had tried one once, and the effect had caused my skin to creep and crawl.

We had sold them to a collector of curios on Fosdyck's Garden, a secondary world of Novo Bantry, the Grand Foundational Domain from which we ran our charters. Lord Vullamir had no use for the *Martichor* anymore, having accrued the disfavor of Filidor, the Archon of Old Earth, for certain unsavory practices as a leading member of a pernicious cult called the Immersion. Since the space yacht had been thus abandoned on the planet I owned, title transferred to me.

"I showed the cabin to Ser Hamble and he said it would be fine," Jenore said. "He is in a froth to get to Meech's World, and none of the starship lines operating out of here have a direct service there."

Now I was puzzled again. "Meech's World is not on our itinerary," I said.

Another gesture of her slim hand. This one told me the problem was already solved. "It is now. Yalum said we'd divert there, instead of stopping at Yaroslav to top up on energies. Then we can go through a different whimsy that will bring us out closer to Novo Vieste than the one he'd planned to take. We'll actually get there half a day sooner."

I showed her a motion of my own hand, one that signaled surrender. I'd never had to give that hand-sign when I'd been an indentured competitive duelist in Hordam's Unparalleled Gaming Emporium on the gaming world of Thrais. But that was just one of the changes that had led me to my present position as owner and supercargo on the space yacht *Peregrinator*, captained by Yalum Erkatchian and crewed by Jenore Mordene. The former was the only friend I'd ever made, and the latter was the woman I loved.

I heard a noise from the corridor behind Jenore. So did she. She glanced at something I couldn't see then came back to me. "The cultists are coming aboard," she said.

I rose from the table where I'd been working. "I'll see to them."

A small frown clouded her face. "They're a fractious bunch," she said. "Be…neutral with them."

"I will not mention their insanity," I said. I'd learned to overlook the various forms of madness one encounters in dealing with the varieties of humankind spread across the Ten Thousand Worlds.

"And be respectful of their idol," Jenore said. "It seems to mean a great deal to them."

THE IDOL WAS AN UGLY THING: a squat lump of cast metal gone green with age, though more recently it had been clad in a vest and pantaloons of hammered gold. Pot-bellied and hunched over in a crouch, with a lipless downturned mouth and half-lidded eyes, it resembled someone's impression of a toad that was turning into a man, or vice versa—a hybrid that did not appear to be happy about the transition.

The cultists, seven of them, were the leading members of the Ubrachian cult,, which had devotees on several worlds, and had been around long enough to have generated schisms and heretical subsects. Robed and cowled, they filled the corridor of the first-class accommodations, two of them carrying a kind of stretcher made of dark, polished wood, on which the object of their devotions sat like a dissatisfied traveler. The god's worshipers comprised three youngish men, three middle-aged specimens, and a seventh person so aged and wizened—and so deeply enshrouded in a voluminous robe—that its gender could not readily be determined.

Apparently, the process of moving the idol required ritually slow and synchronized footsteps, accompanied by a deep-throated chanting of a mantra in a tongue I did not recognize.

The leader of the coven, Addeus Ing, one of the middle-agers, saw me coming along the corridor toward them and raised an admonitory hand. The procession stopped behind him and he broke off his chanting to advise me in a sepulchral voice, "Come no nearer. The ambit of Ubrach is holy space, not to be trod by a heathen."

I paused, some distance from the procession, and said, "Does that make this corridor permanently impassable? That will affect the running of the vessel."

"The sequestered space travels with Ubrach," Ing said. "Once he is installed in my cabin, you may again pass this way." He thought for a moment then added, "Though you would be wise to make the ritual gestures as you go."

He showed me the prescribed motions, touching fingertips to temple, ears, and chin then finishing by slapping the fingers of one hand to his open mouth, producing an audible pop.

"I shall endeavor to remember," I said. "Now, do you require any assistance?"

"Is my cabin ready?" he said. "By which I mean, has it

been energetically scrubbed and anointed with the balm I sent to that woman?"

"It has," I said. "And her name is Sera Mordene."

His face clouded. "Do not think to instruct me in protocols, young man. My standards are set by the ineffable Ubrach."

I recalled Jenore's advice and made a gesture of acquiescence. "I will withdraw until the corridor is no longer sacred ground," I said.

"Do not forget the gestures," he said. "Ubrach generally ignores the uninitiated, but he is known to make the occasional example."

I suppressed the first answer that came to me and said, instead, "I will remember." Then I went back to the forward compartment where I did the work that required stylus and ledger.

TWO OTHER PASSENGERS were already aboard; a plump, middle-aged couple, Tetch and Folliance Archaby, bound for their blisternut plantation on the North Continent of Novo Vieste. When they boarded, they had told me, speaking in tandem, how they had come to Carricker to buy fresh seedlings to replenish their orchards.

"Blisternut trees will only produce viable seeds for seventeen years," Tetch Archaby said, though I had not sought the information.

"And then they go dormant and soon after die," his spouse added.

I was carrying some of their baggage to the second-class berth they had booked. "Indeed," I said. The aroma that rose from the large portmanteau I was managing along the narrow passageway told me that I was carrying the basis of some future crop.

"Indeed, indeed," said Tetch. "That's why, every year, we come here to Carricker –"

"To get new plants," Folliance completed the sentence for him. "They grow the best ones here."

Her partner began to itemize the advantages of Carricker's blisternut seedlings, but by then we had reached their small cabin. I indicated the open door, put down the fragrant portmanteau, and escaped further education.

I was proceeding back the way I had come when I encountered a mild-eyed, soft-looking little man coming the other way and peering at the numbers affixed to the cabin doors. This turned out to be Todfrey Hamble, our last addition to the passenger manifest. I turned him around and brought him safely to his small berth, which he appeared to find entirely to his satisfaction.

I handed him the schedule for meals, which reminded me that I had failed to do so with the Archabys, and thus had to return to where they were housed. I knocked on their door, which opened only a crack to allow Tetch's eye to scrutinize me.

"Yes?"

I offered him the card with its information. He had to open the door a little wider to take it, which showed me that the portmanteau containing the blisternut seedlings was now positioned on the top sleeping platform, and held in place by strong leather straps cinched by heavy padlocks. The arrangement left no room for a sleeper.

"They are precious to us," Tetch informed me, when I showed surprise. Folliance weighed in to state that it was not good for them to experience too much movement, but I forestalled a further lecture by asking how they proposed to fit themselves into the single narrow sleeping platform below.

"In shifts," Tetch told me. "The same will apply to our meals."

They looked at each and nodded their agreement. I said I understood, though I didn't, and left.

The last aboard were a trio of sisters—Orfa, Illiphrata, and Shuriz Vauderoy—bound for Novo Vieste for purposes not stated. They chatted brightly about inconsequentials as I led them to the three, single-berthed, second-class cabins they had reserved. I gave the meal schedule to Shuriz, who appeared to be the eldest of the three. She took it and glanced at it then rejoined the three-way repartee. I had the odd feeling that their conversation was scripted, but I dismissed the thought. I was not yet competent to judge the behaviors of people from other worlds, with their strange and incomprehensible ways.

I TOOK the passenger list to the captain's workspace, a small cubicle where cargo manifests, customs exemptions, and other official documents were stored, and found my friend, Yalum Erkatchian. His appearance was still something of a surprise. When he had served Lord Vullamir, he had worn the aristocrat's livery of yellow with black piping and patches, complete with a peaked cap with a shiny leather bill. After we took over the ship, he had changed into the standard one-piece, blue and gray garment that was standard wear among spacers.

But just lately, he had decided to revert to the costume prevalent in his place of origin, the island of Saccaboth on the world Tantramar. This was a shirt of patterned cloth worn under an open-fronted vest that hung down to the knees. Also descending to the knees was a pleated skirt — Yalum insisted on calling it a *kilthe* — whose hem met a pair of knee-length, knitted stockings rising from silver-buckled black shoes. An embroidered skull cap completed the ensemble.

As I entered his work space, Yalum was engaged in an argument with the spaceport's integrator.

He swung around in his swivel chair and spoke in a forceful tone, "The inspection was carried out hours ago. Nothing amiss was found. The inspector told us we were cleared to go as soon as the passengers were aboard."

The integrator's reply was, as always, soft-voiced. "I have no record of the inspection."

"Then, obviously, the inspector has failed to file his report. He had the look of one of your inbred idiots."

On Carricker, many public offices were staffed by heredity. Most functions were carried out by integrators and their allied devices, overseen — allegedly, that is — by functionaries who often were dysfunctional.

Then spaceport's integrator adopted that precisely modulated tone that conveys anger, one of the emotions of which such devices are not supposed to be capable. "Nonetheless, I cannot permit departure until the report is filed."

"My ship," said Erkatchian, "will send you a recording of the inspection." He broke off to order *Peregrinator*'s integrator to make the transmission.

The spaceport's system now changed its attitude. Integrators trusted each other implicitly, there being another supposition that they were incapable of mendacity. "Departure authorized," it said. "Have a pleasant journey."

Erkatchian made some remarks that reflected the depth of vocabulary he had acquired during his many years as a spacer then turned to me. He took the manifest from my hand and examined it.

"All present and accounted for?" he said.

"Yes," I said.

"Any problems?"

"Not so far."

"Good," said Erkatchian. He raised his chin and spoke to the ship's integrator, telling it to advise the passengers to prepare for lifting off. We then heard *Peregrinator*'s calm tones relaying the information.

Yalum grunted in satisfaction and reached into one of the side pockets of his *kilthe* to extract an object the size of his palm. We had found it with the life-masks, a palm-sized oblong fashioned from a smooth material of a pale ocher color that resembled glass but was of no known origin. Beneath its transparent surface was an etched design: looping and curving lines that, if traced by a finger, led through complex, recursive patterns, until the digit finally arrived back where it had started from. During this process, which Yalum performed as he felt the need or inclination, he had told Jenore and me that he experienced a quietitude, a sense of calm clarity in his mental space. He had come to value it and kept the object on his person at all times.

I repaired to the galley where Jenore was overseeing preparation of the evening meal. Not long after, a chime sounded three notes then the floor beneath my feet vibrated as the in-atmosphere drive was engaged. We rose smoothly from Carricker's major spaceport. I disopaqued the porthole in the galley and watched as the sky outside turned from deep blue to full black. It was a sight I had come to enjoy as a signal of the freedom I had acquired along with ownership of the space yacht.

We passed among the glittering orbitals in their planet-circling ring then the shivering ceased as the drive cut out. There came that breathless pause as we were carried along on momentum alone then the space drive cut in with a new frequency of vibratio, and Carricker rapidly dwindled to a circle the size of a plate then a saucer then a dot. And soon it was gone altogether.

"And here we go, off again," I said.

"We're late," Jenore said, looking up from where she was counting out plates, bowls, mugs, and eating utensils.

I told her how the port's inspector had failed to file his report.

"Huh," she said, in a tone that expressed her views on the usefulness of inspectors, or perhaps males in general.

I said, "I don't see the value of inspecting outbound ships."

"We've talked about this," she said. "Carricker is one of the few places where the plants that produce blue borrache can flourish. Other worlds don't want the stuff coming in to their populations. If Carricker doesn't control the drug's export, other worlds will isolate it. Then it won't be able to receive the goods and services it can't produce for itself."

"But the inspection system is riddled with incompetence," I said. "The inspectors can scarcely find their own fundaments with both hands and a color-coded map."

"Ah," she said, and held up a finger in the manner I had come to recognize as a precursor to her making a point. "A lot of people on Carricker make a lot of money out of the illicit trade in blue borrache. Ineffective interdiction of the outflow keeps the inflow of funds at maximum.

"And in the meantime," she finished, "Carrickers' self-esteem is not diminished."

PEREGRINATOR, when it had been *Martichor*, the private space yacht of Lord Vullamir, now presumably locked up in a contemplarium on Old Earth, had boasted a grand dining salon. Internal rearrangements of the vessel's layout had taken some of the salon's space for first-class cabins, leaving a smaller space in which both classes of passenger were to be fed.

"Uh-oh," I said, as I responded to the dinner chime, along with twelve of this voyage's thirteen passengers, crowding along the corridor that led to the refectory. Here the great, ornate table at which Vullamir and his fellow members of the sinister Immersion cult had formerly dined was no more. Erkatchian had sold it to an antique dealer on Fallabi, and replaced it with two smaller tables that came equipped with fold-down benches along the sides and at each end.

Each table would sit only six. The passenger manifest numbered thirteen. When I stepped into the room, one of the tables was occupied by the three Vauderoy sisters. Todfrey Hamble was seated alone at one end of the other table, his gaze fixed on nothing in particular. I noted that if he had been "in a froth" to reach Meech's World, the sense of urgency had left him.

Behind me now came Tetch Archaby, who went to sit at the head of the first table. Then the seven cultists of Ubrach arrived, led by Addeus Ing. The patriarch paused in the doorway, took in the situation at one glance and said, "Unacceptable!" in a tone that said he would brook no argument.

Jenore arrived through the door that connected to the galley, bearing a stack of plates. I saw her notice the rigid postures of the Ubrachians without discerning the cause.

"What?" she said.

Ing spoke as if from a commanding height, while one hand extended to where Hamble sat. "It was made clear," he said, "that we cannot share our meals with heathens. Our standards are precise and exacting. Contamination, even accidental, requires a lengthy process of rectification, and we are far from a source of black umbershoot boughs."

"We have only the one dining area for passengers, and only two tables," I said. "What would you have us do?"

Ing said, "This fellow seated alone, move him to the other table. There is room."

"Must I then scrub his place with balm?" I said.

"No. Just remove him."

I went to where Hamble sat, apparently unaware of his role in the controversy. "Would you mind, ser, moving to the other table. The…cultists prefer to sit together."

The mild-eyed man blinked, seeming to come back to the here and now from some other mental space. "I beg your pardon?" he said.

I repeated my request and saw Hamble take in his surroundings. A slight cloud formed on his brow. "Am I unwelcome among them?" he said. "That strikes me as unfriendly."

"Begone!" said Ing. "Go sit with the other benighted…"

Here his voice trailed off as he sought for a sufficient pejorative.

"I think not," said Hamble, returning his gaze to the empty middle distance.

I lowered my voice to a whisper. "They are, in my judgment, quite mad, as are all religious enthusiasts. Since we are confined with them for the next few days, I counsel avoiding actions that might stir up their misguided passions."

Hamble took this in. Then his soft mouth set in as deep a frown as he could manage. "Not mad," he said, "but fools."

I heard a sharp intake of breath from Addeus Ing and rumbles of incipient violence from the cultists still confined to the corridor. Hamble ignored the warnings and went on, "I happen to have run across Ubrachians before. They are a persistent nuisance on my home world. Their so-called 'idol' is nothing of the sort. It is most likely a statue of some kind of entertainer. It was found in the remains of a theater on the planet Thriffle, where once flourished a species of intelligent amphibians. Their world began to dry up, so they either died out or migrated *en masse* to some other planet far out in the Back of Beyond."

As this explanation unwound, I saw Ing's face lose its holy pallor and proceed through various shades of red to a deep crimson. His lips trembled and his eyes grew round and when Hamble finished his remarks, he spluttered for several minims before he was able to assemble a coherent stream of words.

"Remove the atheist!" he cried out to me, "Lest I call down the wrath of Ubrach on this iniquitous assemblage!" He swung an arm to take in the other passengers, who had been listening to Todfrey Hamble with varying degrees of amusement.

I made a renewed effort. "Please, ser," I whispered to Hamble, "let them have their way. We have two more days of travel after we traverse the whimsy."

The small man set his chin, and I thought he would not yield. Then he showed the expression of a man who has decided the fight is not worth his time. With a disdainful cluck of his tongue, he rose from the table and went to sit with the other passengers. A corner seat at the first table remained unoccupied. Hamble took it, which put him next to Illiphrata Vauderoy. Her two sisters sat across from them. The blisternut farmer had taken the head of the table.

"Glad you could join us," said Tetch Archaby. He named himself then the three sisters. "And you are?"

"Oh, no one of consequence," said Hamble. He would have said nothing more, but Illiphrata coaxed his name from him, though it took two requests.

After the small man gave his name, he stopped speaking. He turned his gaze toward his hands, folded together on the table before him.

Meanwhile, I was seeing to the seating of the seven Ubrachians. The availability of only six seats posed a difficulty, but Ing overcame it by ordering the three thinnest of the cultists to squeeze onto one of the side benches. The arrangement meant that one meager buttock protruded at either end of the bench, but Ing decreed that decorum had been served.

Jenore now began to distribute plates and I went to assist her. I put out two plates in front of Archaby, one for himself and one for his missing spouse. Next came utensils and mugs then the first course: as was traditional on passenger vessels traveling among the Ten Thousand Worlds, this consisted of ship's bread. Fortunately, *Peregrinator's* integrator had developed a fine recipe, producing a bread that was crisp and nutty. The passengers at the first table expressed appreciation—also a tradition for interstellar travelers—and though the Ubrachians said nothing, they ate every crumb.

Next came a vegetable stew with a side dish of sausages—the choice was between spicy or plain—and flagons of golden ale. A buzz of conversation began at table one; a holy silence reigned at the other, except for some loud smacking of lips and toothless gums as the ancient member of the Ubrachian pilgrimage dealt with the stew and ale.

I hovered near the first table, ready to whisk away empty dishes and pass fresh flagons of drink from the nearby dispenser. The three sisters spoke among themselves, mainly to pass appreciative comments about the quality of the meal. At some point, a word spoken by one of them caught the attention of Tetch Archaby, causing him to advance some thoughts about nuts and lentils, which then led him to launch into a discourse on the cultivation of blisternut trees.

This overture suppressed all further conversation until Tetch paused to take a measure of ale. Immediately, Illiphrata Vauderoy turned to Todfrey Hamble and invited him to share with his tablemates his background and reasons for travel.

Hamble, who had been quietly chewing a sausage, took a sip of the golden brew and said, "I'm just a middle-ranked intercessor with the family court in New Srinigar. I'm off to visit some cousins in Novo Vieste."

Beyond that he would not be further drawn, describing his circumstances as "boring and humdrum."

I would have agreed with this self-characterization, except at one point in the progress of the meal I saw him glance around the table when no one was looking his way. For a moment I saw a flash of sharp intelligence and incisive inquiry.

It is a peculiarity of my unusual origin that I notice such things as micro-expressions and significant eye movements. You see, I am not really an ordinary human being. I came into existence with certain aspects of my neural circuitry enhanced by the genius Hallis Tharp, who designed me to be a template for vat-grown artificial persons. From me, he produced thousands of combatants for a vicious private war game, waged by a pair of brothers who had vast wealth but not the least jot of humanity. Jenore had long since convinced me that my background is not a fit subject for polite conversation.

Still, Hamble took my interest now. Again, it is my nature to notice camouflage of all kinds. Todfrey Hamble wore the fleece of a gentle ruminant, but peeking out from underneath I detected a sharp-toothed predator.

WHEN THE MEAL was over and the tables cleared, I opened the forward salon and told the passengers they were welcome to its comforts. The ship's integrator would provide them with diversions and entertainments, or they could play various games, individually, or in pairs or groups.

The Vauderoy sisters opted to play panachio, settling themselves around a multi-sided table. Tetch elected to have a performance of classic erotica played in the privacy of the Archabys' cabin. Addeus Ing again assumed a position of moral elevation and announced that the cultists would return to their devotions.

When I looked for Todfrey Hamble, he had disappeared.

"Remember," I said, before the cultists departed, "we will be entering a whimsy in three and a half maxims. Medications will be automatically dispensed from the headboards of your sleeping platforms. The ship's integrator will advise you when to take them, and remind you once more before we enter the Seventh Plane. You all know the necessity of following the ship's advice."

They all signified their assent. As any traveler knows, passage through the Seventh Plane while conscious can lead to permanent derangement.

I watched the Ubrachians file down the corridor then went to join the captain and Jenore in Erkatchian's suite. We dined on the same menu served to the passengers then engaged in the kind of conversation that arises among friends of long standing.

At some point, I asked the ship's integrator about Hamble's whereabouts and was told that he was in his cabin, lying on his sleeping platform.

Late in the evening—we were still on Carricker spaceport time—chimes sounded and the ship announced the imminent passage through the whimsy. I went to the salon and saw the Vauderoys en route to their accommodations. I closed up the common room and joined Jenore in our own cabin. We took the medications dispensed by our sleeping platform, lay down together, linked our fingers as always, and faded from all sensibility.

"SUPERCARGO," said the ship's integrator, "rouse yourself."

I came free of the grip of the medications slowly, my mind dull and my thoughts tepid. I sat up and stared at the floor between my feet. My bare toes looked improbably far away, while at the same time they loomed large and as close as if they were almost touching my nose.

The ship spoke again. "There has been an incident," it said. The hatch that concealed the dispenser in the wall now opened, revealing a tumbler of some colorless liquid. "Here is a restorative," said *Peregrinator*." I recommend you imbibe it."

Still in a fog, I reached for the tumbler and downed its contents. In moments, it began to have its effects: my vision sharpened, the cabin was restored to its normal dimensions, and my mind became cool and still.

"What is the situation?" I said.

"A passenger is not responding to my inquiries."

"Which passenger? And what do you mean by 'not responding?'"

"Todfrey Hamble," said the integrator. "I believe he is deceased."

Behind me, Jenore turned over and yawned. "Wha?" she said then put a forearm over her eyes.

"Trouble," I told her. "The ship thinks a passenger has died during the transit through the whimsy." I spoke to the integrator, "Have you notified the captain?"

"He is not yet conscious." That was to be expected. Like many an old spacer, Erkatchian sank deeper under the influence of the mind-numbing drugs than those who had traveled through fewer whimsies.

I stood up and reached for the clothing I had left on the chair. "I will see to it," I said. "Say nothing to the other passengers."

"Of course," said the integrator, in that gentle tone the devices use when humans fail to appreciate their perfect understanding of every situation.

HAMBLE'S little berth stood between the first- and second-class cabins, erstwhile accommodation for Lord Vullamir's guests of varying ranks. The servants' quarters had largely been converted to cargo space. His cabin was barely bigger than its sleeping platform, and I had to squeeze between the wall and where the dead man lay.

Though the integrator's percepts were capable of detecting the shallowest of breathing, not to mention the body's temperature, I nonetheless put my fingers against the spot on the man's throat where a pulse would be felt. There was none. The flesh was cold.

I saw no wounds, no bruises, no ligature marks. The sleeping garment he wore was not disturbed. The death could have been the result of natural causes. I picked up the empty sachet that had contained the medications Hamble would have taken before we plunged into the Seventh Plane. I sniffed its open end, and smelled nothing. But there was a trace of powder left in the packet. I folded it so that the few grains would not come out and put it in the pocket of my single-suit.

Then I let myself out of the cabin and instructed the integrator to seal the door.

WHEN I GOT to Erkatchian's compartment, far forward in the ship and above the salon, I found him awake, sipping punge. Jenore was with him.

"I told him," she said. "I'd better go see about breakfast."

"Yes," I said, and watched her go.

"Natural causes?" Eratchian said, his face showing a faint hope.

"I don't think so," I said. I took out the medications sachet and shook the few grains of powder onto the captain's table. "Integrator," I said, "examine this substance minutely."

A moment later, it said, "I have."

"What is it?"

"It is two substances: a common somnofacit and crystalline thrazzine."

"The effect of thrazzine?" I said.

"Suppression of the respiratory function."

"Permanent suppression?"

"Yes."

So there it was. Todfrey Hamble had ingested a substance that would put him to sleep combined with a poison that would stop his breathing.

"Did you witness his taking of the powder?" I said.

The device said it had not. Hamble had not yet taken his medication when *Peregrinator* entered the ambit of the whimsy, at which time the yacht had shut off all its percepts. Persons who went wakeful into the Seventh Plane could go mad or lose control of their sensory apparatus; when they came back into space-time, they might taste colors or experience hot and cold as shrieks and rumbles. Integrators were less affected but found the strangeness of their surroundings distracting. I thought a more accurate description would have been "annoying," but no integrator would admit to experiencing such a sentiment. The devices usually turned down their perceptions to minimum until they emerged once more into the Third Plane.

"What is your last record of Hamble?" I said.

A screen appeared in the air. I saw the small man exiting his cabin into the common corridor that ran most of the length of the ship, with cabin doors on either side.

Then he disappeared.

"Where did he go?" I asked the integrator.

"What do you mean?" it said.

"Examine the record. He came out of his cabin and disappeared."

"That is impossible," said the device.

"Replay the record," I said. It did so then I said, "How do you explain that?"

"Explain what?"

The captain intervened at that moment. "Integrator," Erkatchian said, "put yourself on standby." He turned to me and said, "The ship has encountered something it cannot explain. Attempting to force an explanation from it may cause damage. I do not wish to be out in space with an integrator that is pursuing its own tail in ever decreasing circles."

I could see the sense in that, but the mystery remained. "What do you think has happened?" I said.

Erkatchian gave his long nose a reflective pull. "I have only a theory. Hamble carried a device that allowed him to subvert the ship's percepts. It follows that he was not some mid-level intercessor from New Srinigar, but a competent agent with a mission."

"What kind of mission?"

"Another theory," he said. "The incompetent inspector at the spaceport was not as useless as he appeared to be. He was a decoy, meant to allay suspicion while the real danger unobtrusively slipped aboard and carried out the operation."

Jenore saw where he was going. "So it's about blue borrache?" she said.

"Most likely," Erkatchian said. "Someone has brought some aboard and Hamble was on its trail. The criminal discovered his interest and killed him."

Jemore's face took on a thoughtful aspect. "The cultists?" she said. "Their robes could conceal packages of the drug."

"Or," I said, "their idol could be hollow."

"It would explain why they want no one near it," Erkatchian said.

"What about the sisters?" Jenore said. "Hamble seemed to take an interest in them."

I hadn't noticed that, but she had been with the passengers in the salon more than I had. She recounted how the little man had returned to the salon then hovered nearby as the Vauderoys played panachio.

"I thought his interest was carnal," she said. "They hail from Novo Vieste, where women wield power over men. It is not unheard of for a group of them to surround a man and carry him off to some quiet corner where they will use him until he is worn out."

"Hamble did not look as if he would have lasted long," I said. "Can we revive the integrator and see what occurred between him and the Vauderoys?"

Erkatchian rewoke the device and we watched its record of the intercourse between Todfrey Hamble and the three sisters. Their conversation had indeed been suggestive, but ultimately, Hamble had declared himself fatigued and departed before the women had completed their last chukka of panachio. Their comments after he was gone did suggest some resentment, but no promises of revenge were voiced.

It was shortly after he left the salon that he abruptly disappeared from view. The integrator did not remark upon that impossibility and we did not press it.

"What were the Ubrachians doing at that time?" I asked the ship.

The device explained that the cultists had disabled the ship's percepts in the cabin where their idol had been placed upon a fold-down shelf. "They told me that it was forbidden for the gaze of heathens to do more than glance its way. I do have an audio recording of what they were doing."

"Play it," the captain said. A moment later, the sound of guttural chanting filled our ears. After a few moments of monotony, Erkatchian said, "Enough."

We looked at each other, but no one had anything more to add. Jenore said, "What about the Archabys?"

The visual record showed them sitting together in their cabin, watching the erotic performance Tech had chosen on a screen that hung in the air before them. The integrator sped up the time signature and we saw them remain where they were until the program concluded.

"The performance apparently stimulated them. They said they intended intimate acts and asked for privacy," the device said. "I deactivated the percepts until it was time for medications. By then they were in their sleeping attire."

"Did you see them take the drugs?" I said.

"I did. They lay down, sharing a sleeping platform. I checked to see that all the other passengers had taken their medications and reposed themselves then I shut off my percepts, as normal."

Jenore had been listening to this, but I saw from the vertical line that appeared above her nose that her mind was pursuing some new train of thought.

"What?" I said.

"When I was with the Chabriz Traveling Show," she said, "there was a prestidigitator." She went silent and her eyes moved the way they do when she was chasing a memory.

I waited and after a while, she brightened as the recollection came. "His name was Rheinster and he both indulged in blue borrache and transported the stuff. He was arrested on Challimaine and we never saw him again."

"What of it?" I said.

"I don't know yet. It will come to me."

I summarized. "So it is possible that the Ubrachians, incensed by Hamble's disrepect of their religion, took revenge upon him. It is also possible, but less likely, that it was the Vauderoy sisters, resenting his failure to submit to their blandishments. But we see the blisternut farmers as being in the clear."

I made a small noise as I contemplated what I had just said.

It was Jenore's turn to say, "What?"

"I was just thinking," I said, "that on Thrais, these motivations would have been far-fetched. No one loses so much as a groat, after all, from having their beliefs or vanity challenged."

Jenore wore that look that comes over her when she has

to repeat some truth that ought to have long been ratified. "Not everything is a financial transaction," she said. "Not even on Thrais."

I was about to dispute that final assertion when she reminded me of the Thraisian tradition of the "last laugh," in which paupers about to commit suicide arranged for the posthumous publication of the details of how they had taken secret revenge on an enemy and gotten away with it.

Erkatchian said, "Let us concentrate on the problem before us. We are two days out from Meech's World. Hamble is already several hours dead. Before we touch down on Meech, the odor of putrefaction…" He waved a hand to complete the thought.

"His cabin was a storage locker," I said. "We could have the ship lower the temperature to below freezing."

"Good idea," the captain said. "Do it."

Jenore stood up. "But we had better search him and his possessions first, in case there is more evidence, beyond the poisoned medications, to give to the Meech police. That, and whatever device he used to subvert the integrator's percepts."

"Impossible," said the ship.

"Of course," we assured it.

THE DEAD MAN'S possessions consisted of some clothes and toiletries in a carry-on valise, some funds in the currency of Carricker, and a basic communication device, less sophisticated than an integrator, that would allow him to connect to the connectivities on most worlds.

"Not much," I said, "for someone traveling between worlds."

Jenore was studying the body. "Help me turn him over," she said.

Rigor mortis had set in and the limbs were stiff. The body rolled like a figure made of carved wood. Jenore lifted the hem of his upper garment and said, "Aha."

In the small of the man's back was a little circle of raised flesh. "What is it?" I said.

She dropped the cloth and I let the corpse resume its previous position. She spoke so that only I would hear. "The prestidigitator I mentioned. He was outed by an operative of the IPCC who had infiltrated the Chabriz show as a roustabout."

I knew of the Interworld Police Coordinating Company, an interplanetary law-enforcement organization that had legal authority on scores of major and minor planets. "The bump on Hamble's back?" I said.

"I saw something like it on the roustabout. It conceals the device we spoke about earlier. Also a locator. Bring him in range of any connectivity and it transmits a signal that tells the local IPCC branch the identity of the agent and where he is. It is also *de facto* identification."

"That puts a new complexion on the crime," I said.

"It does. We must assume Hamble intended to make an arrest on Meech's world."

"Will freezing affect the locator?" I said.

She showed me a doubtful mouth, "It shouldn't."

"Then let's get this cabin sealed and cooled. We need to talk with Yalum about what to tell the other passengers."

"One of whom is a killer," Jenore said.

"At least one."

We exited the cabin and I told the ship to reseal the door. I was about to add an instruction to freeze the interior when I found that Jenore and I were no longer alone. Addeus Ing was in the corridor, along with two of the Vauderoys. Tetch Archaby, his hair disordered from sleep, was peering out through the partly opened door of his cabin, which was next to the dead man's.

"What is going on?" the Ubrachian said. The expressions of the others said the same question was foremost in their minds.

"Todfrey Hamble has died during the passage through the whimsy," I said. "We are sealing his cabin and dropping the temperature to preserve his remains. Those of you who share a common wall may feel a chill. I regret that cannot be helped."

There were more questions, from Ing and the sisters. I said the captain would address them in the dining salon before breakfast was served. That did not stop them from renewing their queries, but Jenore and I made our way past them and went forward.

"WE CANNOT DO as you suggest and eject the corpse into space," Captain Erkatchian said. "The IPCC would arrest the ship, the crew, and probably most of you, on general suspicion."

Addeus Ing was not mollified. "The situation is unacceptable," he said, his voice rising. "No corpse is allowed to encroach upon Ubrach's ambit."

"It cannot be helped," Erkatchian said, keeping his own voice under control.

"It must be!" the Ubrachian cried. A spray of spittle reached the captain, who calmly wiped it away.

"Perhaps," I put in, "the solution is not to move the body from out of the ambit but to move the ambit away from the body."

Ing turned on me as if I was babbling nonsense. "We can make space in the cargo hold," I said. "You could relocate the idol there and attend to its needs."

Ing's mouth opened and closed but no words emerged. His eyes bulged as if enduring pressure from within. The ancient acolyte, whose name I had not yet learned, put fingers that resembled some sea creature's legs on the headman's arm. Ing looked down at them as if he had never seen such things before, but after a long moment he managed to collect himself and subsided into the seat he had sprung up from.

"What about...sanitation?" said Shuriz Vauderoy.

"Or contagion?" said Illiphrata. To her sisters she offered an aside. "It's a good thing he didn't accept our invitation."

The three were nodding in mutual agreement as Erkatchian said, "There is no contagion. Ser Hamble died of...an unfortunate reaction to the interplanar transit medications."

As he said this, he looked a reminder to me that we would not mention the suspected poisoning. I gave him a minuscule nod in reply.

The captain went on, "As for sanitation, the ship has lowered the temperature in Ser Hamble's cabin to below freezing. Those of you who have common walls are advised not to touch them, to avoid frostbite."

Ing had been quietly conversing with his brethren. Now

he said, "We could measure the distance from Ubrach to the corpse. It may be that it is not within the ambit."

"I will bring you a measuring device," I said. "Now, shall we proceed with breakfast?" I gestured to the steaming bowls ready to be served. "The ship is proud of its recipe for tangy porridge."

I saw frowns from the Ubrachians. Perhaps their god forbade them spicy foods; I could not remember whether any of them had chosen the chilied sausages. The Vauderoy sisters remained agitated, but less so. Folliance Archaby sat quietly. It was her turn to bring food while Tetch husbanded the seedlings.

I said to her, "Your cabin is next to the...scene. Do you have any concerns?"

"None," she said.

Erkatchian left and Jenore and I attended to the distribution of porridge and punge.

A QUIET TIME ENSUED, with the three sisters in the salon, the Ubrachians pursuing their spiritual aims in the cabin that housed their god, and the Archabys doing whatever they did in their cabin.

I passed by, felt the door to the sealed compartment, but snatched my hand away when the skin of my fingertips threatened to stick to the metal. I went to the Archabys' door and knocked. Tetch opened it a sliver and looked out at me.

"What is it?" he said.

"Are you warm enough?" I said. "I can arrange for extra clothing."

"We are fine," he said, though his breath formed a mist.

"Are you sure?" I had learned that in some cultures built around vanity a stoical response to bodily discomfort was considered appropriate.

"Sure," he said, and closed the door.

IN THE CAPTAIN'S QUARTERS, Jenore was questioning the ship's integrator.

"What information do you have on blue borrache?"

"Considerable," it replied. "Many jurisdictions do not accept ignorance as a legal defense."

"I am trying to recall something I once knew," she said, "about blue borrache and the medications taken to reduce the effects of interplanar medications on mentation."

The integrator produced a screen and filled it with text. "Here is an article from a news site on Bobble," it said.

Jenore read the text, flipped to the next segment, and said, "There it is."

I craned my neck to look at what she was reading. The text detailed how a microdose of blue borrache taken before the whimsy medications could delay the onset of the latter's effects for an appreciable time.

"Ah," I said after a moment. "That could be it. The killer waits until Hamble is unconscious and the integrator has closed its percepts then slips into his cabin and pours the adulterated medication into his mouth."

Erkatchian had been doing something at his desk. Now he turned and took in what Jenore and I had read. He frowned. "So that's how," he said. "Now all we need is why, and we'll know who."

"The why is to prevent the smuggler from being caught," I said. I asked the integrator, "Can you determine if the drug is aboard?"

"Only if it were in open view. If it was enclosed in a container, I could not detect it."

Jenore said, "Might Hamble have had a device? A sniffer of some kind?"

"If so," Erkatchian said, "whoever adulterated his medications would have taken it. And hidden it."

"What are our passengers doing now?" I asked the ship.

"The Ubrachians are chanting. The Vauderoys are resting. The Archabys are huddling together for warmth."

The information was not useful. "What was Hamble's plan?" I said. "We're presuming he had identified the smugglers and would arrange for them to be arrested upon arrival at Meech's World."

Jenore got that look that always told me when she was turning things over in her mind. "We are going to Meech's because Hamble wanted us to," she said. "We should notify the Meech's World spaceport police, once we're within range."

I saw a new thought occur to her. After a moment's further consideration, she said, "Has anyone told the passengers about the diversion to Meech's World?"

Nobody had, it turned out. They would think that we were stopping at Yaroslav for routine refueling.

She suggested we let them all know about the change during lunch and watch to see if the news caused any untoward reactions.

"Yes," I said. "I will watch for micro-expressions. We could also have the ship record their reactions then play them back to us, slowed down, so you can see what I do."

That was the plan. I told the ship's integrator what I wanted it to do when we informed the passengers about going to Meech's World.

"Very good," it said.

Jenore went to the galley to prepare lunch while the captain resumed his duties. I had no duties of my own at the moment, and would have accompanied her to help out, as I usually did. But now another thought occurred to me. I pursued it for a moment then asked the device a question. My query prompted the integrator to produce a screen and fill it with text. I began to read.

"UNACCEPTABLE!"

Ing had leapt to his feet the moment the news about landing at Meech's World was out of the captain's mouth. I had no need to look for micro-expressions; outrage and defiance were written plainly across the cult leader's face.

Now he was demanding that we stop at Yaroslav instead.

"We cannot," Erkatchian told him. "We would need to reverse course and to make our way to a different whimsy to hurl ourselves back toward that planet."

"Then do so!" Ing's face grew an even deeper shade of purple. His fellow Ubrachians were also now standing and shouting their own demands.

Erkatchian spoke quietly. A good technique, I thought, because the cultists had to stop their bellowing in order to hear him. "We cannot go where you want to go because we do not have enough fuel to reach the whimsy and subsequently make the passage through Third Plane space to

Yaroslav. We will end up marooned in space until some ship happens by that can spare us the fuel—probably at exorbitant cost."

I spoke then. "Why do you not wish to go to Meech's World?"

"Heresy!" Ing spat the word. "Meech's World is where the shortists fled to when we drove them from the faith."

"Shortists?" I said

Ing waved an angry hand. "They deliberately twisted sacred scripture to maintain their fatuous contention that Ubrach will impose a purgatory of a mere three hundred years on those who fail to live up to his expectations. Clearly, the suras make it plain that the period of purification will last three thousand years."

Rumblings of approval rose from the other Ubrachians, accompanied by vigorous nods and motions of their hands that must have had ritual significance.

"We will not let any 'shortists' aboard," Erkatchian said. "Your ambit will not be profaned."

"You don't know these devils," Ing said. "On Carricker, they infiltrated the constabulary. On Meech, they will have done likewise. They may come with weapons drawn to steal Ubrach away and subject him to their foul rites and importunings."

"For which," I pointed out, "he will doubtless punish them drastically in the afterlife."

My tone may have conveyed a lack of reverence. Ing's cheeks turned an even deeper color.

The captain said, "We will do our utmost to protect you and your idol. But we must go to Meech's World. That is my decision. By this evening, we will be in range to contact the authorities there, and I shall do so."

The cult leader made a wordless sound of anger and frustration. He announced that he and his followers would not stay to eat but would barricade themselves in the god's cabin until we left Meech's World behind.

Jenore said, "You will miss lunch, dinner tonight, and breakfast tomorrow."

"Ubrach will fortify us," Ing said and marched out of the dining room. His fellow cultists went with him, though two of them glanced back forlornly at the piles of ship's bread and steaming meats laid out on the sideboard.

Erkatchian looked to the Vauderoys and Foliance Archaby. "Any other complaints?" he said.

The sisters had been watching the confrontation between us and the cultists with interest tinged by amusement. Now they showed us bland smiles in denial of any distress. The blisternut farmer had spent the last several moments regarding her hands. Without looking up, she signaled that she had nothing to say.

The meal was consumed in almost complete silence, except for the Vauderoys' whispers among themselves. When the passengers had returned to their cabins, Folliance carrying a bowl for Tetch, I went to the quarters I shared with Jenore and bade the integrator show me what it had recorded. Shortly after, Jenore came in and I had the device repeat the performance.

"I don't see anything remarkable," she said.

"Nor did I," I said, "neither at the time nor in the playback."

"The Ubrachians' outrage was genuine," she said. "And the three sisters just looked amused. As for Folliance Archaby, she kept her head down throughout."

"Yes," I said, "she did, didn't she?"

I thought about it for a little while then issued new instructions to the integrator. After it said it would comply, I proposed that my spouse and I should take a nap. Jenore suggested we do something else first—a suggestion I always found to be agreeable. We locked the door for privacy.

IN THE LATE AFTERNOON, Erkatchian spoke through the integrator. "Conn and Jenore, please come to my cabin."

When we arrived, we found the captain seated in his chair, with both Archabys standing to one side.

"Who's guarding the seedlings?" I said.

Neither of them responded. Erkatchian said, "Close the door."

I did so. As soon as he heard the click of the lock, Tetch Archaby brought out from behind his back a heavy-duty shocker and pointed it at me.

"So," I said, and waited for him to speak.

He spoke in a calm and measured voice, not at all like the rush of words that had characterized his discourses about blisternut cultivation. Those remarks, as my research through *Peregrinator*'s integrator had showed, had been cribbed verbatim from the standard reference texts on blisternuts. "It's too late to divert from Meech's World."

"Yes," I said.

He nodded. "Then we will proceed there, refuel, and set off for Novo Vieste. The hatches will remain sealed. Thus no inspections of the cargo will be required."

"If you wish," I told him. I didn't mention that Hamble's IPCC implant would automatically alert the port police.

He nodded again then his mouth and brows formed an expression that said he was seizing the only hope available.

"We'll just have to see," he added with a shrug. "But there will be no communication with the authorities except for routine back-and-forth regarding landing."

"If you say so," I said. "But what happens when we reach Novo Vieste?"

"The same," he said. "We land, my partner and I depart with our...blisternut seedlings, and we all forget about the...unpleasantness."

His voice was as calm as before, but I had seen the unsuppressible flash of hardness in his face when I'd asked my question. At Novo Vieste, they would meet up with their criminal confederates, drop the identities of Tetch and Folliance, and disappear into the warrens of the planet's underworld.

As for us, he did not mean to leave us in a position to give evidence.

"All right," I said and spread my hands in a gesture of compliance then crooked both my little fingers in toward my palms. I heard a faint chime, almost inaudible, from the ship's integrator.

I stepped forward and wrenched the shocker from Archaby's hand. He had time to depress the activation stud twice before I seized the weapon, but that did him no good.

"Restore function," I said.

"Done," said the ship.

I pointed the shocker at the blue borrache smuggler and gestured with my other hand to include his partner. "Turn and face the wall."

From the pouch at my belt I withdrew two holdfasts, left behind by Lord Vullamir. He had used his private yacht to transport unwilling persons for unspeakable purposes to places where he and his fellow Immersionists could enjoy their evil undisturbed. Because he had also been possessed by the inbred paranoia of Old Earth's upper-tier aristocracy, he had equipped his ship's integrator with the power to analyze and neutralize the workings of most light weaponry.

I escorted Tetch and Folliance Archaby—though I doubted those were their names—to the cargo hold, where I had prepared a secure holding pen—also a left-over from the ship's former uses.

I then went to their cabin and used a knife to cut open the straps that secured their portmanteau to the sleeping platform. Next, I cut a hole in the luggage itself then extracted one of the rootballs. One more cut and, inside, I found not soil, but compressed blue borrache, in concentrated strength.

By the time I returned to the captain's cabin, we were within communications range of Meech's World. Erkatchian was speaking to the port's integrator. He then waited for his words to reach the distant world and for a reply to come to us. When that business was settled, he opened an ornate bottle he kept in his cupboard for special occasions.

"There may be a reward," he said.

THERE WAS NO REWARD, but a squad of the spaceport's constabulary, clad in gray and black and with jolt-truncheons at their belts, swarmed aboard the moment the main hatch was unsealed. Erkatchian stepped forward to address them, but their senior officer, Ilye Chandrasekh, with three sunbursts on his leather-billed cap, brusquely ordered all passengers and crew to assemble in the salon.

The captain's reply was mild. "The prisoners are in the hold, restrained," he said.

"The ship is alleged to be transporting contraband," said the policeman.

"I can show it to you," said Erkatchian.

"We will find it for ourselves."

The captain raised a finger to offer a fresh point, at which Chandrasekh's eyes bulged and two of his uniforms put their hands on their bludgeons. Erkatchian replaced the argumentative finger with a palm of surrender. He led the way to the salon, pausing at the passengers' doors to alert them to their need to move with us.

The salon was crowded. I saw the two port police eyeing the Ubrachians with sharpened interest then exchanging freighted glances. When Chandrasekh set two of his squad to watch us and ordered the rest to conduct the search, the pair whose interest had been aroused almost ran down the companionway to the passenger accommodations.

Addeus Ing responded with alarm. I saw him look to me for support; I signaled that I was not in control of events. A hurried, whispered consultation engaged the orthodox cultists. They shuffled for a moment then Ing said, "Now!"

The six able Ubrachians rushed the two guards, bowling them over and relieving them of their truncheons then charged down the companionway. The ancient tottered after them. Shouts and sounds of struggle soon followed. The two constables left to guard us picked themselves up and, after the briefest hesitation, went to the aid of their comrades.

The Vauderoy sisters observed all of this with lively interest. When the sounds of struggle subsided and Chandrasekh's voice could be heard issuing orders, they waited a short while then sallied down the companionway.

I asked the ship's integrator to report on their actions. It said, "They have gone into Ing's cabin and are wrapping the idol in a blanket. Now they are transferring it to their own cabin." A moment later, the device said, "They are secreting it in their trunk."

I said to Jenore and Yalum, "Should we allow that?"

"The port police told us to remain where we are," the captain said. "Besides, I am not disposed to exert myself in the service of Addeus Ing. I do not care for enthusiasts. Indeed, we should make it a policy not to take them aboard."

I looked to Jenore, saw her shoulders lift and fall.

In the world of my upbringing, Thrais, where all actions are economic transactions, I would not have interfered, since I saw no profit in doing so. I had learned, while visiting other worlds and cultures, that people could have other motivations—even to the point, in some situations, of altruism. Apparently, this was not one of those cases. I signaled my acceptance.

Time passed, and no one came to tell us what to do. When asked, the ship reported that the police had marched the bruised and still resisting Ubrachians off into the innards of the port. It had taken the full squad to control them.

The Vauderoy sisters, carrying their trunk, had also departed. The Archabys, or whatever their real names were, remained imprisoned in the hold.

"We have been forgotten," I said, "along with the criminals and their contraband."

Erkatchian gave the matter the briefest thought then he asked the ship if we could refuel.

"The port says yes, provided our credit is good."

It was good; we carried guarantees from several worlds' fiduciary pools. Soon after, a semi-sentient lighter rolled up and our energies were swiftly replenished. We waited a little longer, but Chandrasekh and his squad did not return.

"Are we likely ever to come back to Meech's World?" I asked Erkatchian.

"Not likely, no," he said.

"Well then."

WE LEFT the smugglers attached to a light standard, their drug-filled blisternut seedlings at their feet. Nearby, we laid the frozen corpse of Todfrey Hamble, his valise, and the packet with its traces of thrazzine. Then we departed Meech's World.

We were not far beyond the planet's system when the integrator reported an urgent call from Chandrasekh. "He orders us to return."

"Connect me," Erkatchian said. When the officer's face appeared on the screen, the captain said, "We are working spacers, with our livings to earn. We cannot spare the time to wait for your world's legal processes while moorage charges pile up."

"Your accounts are your own problem. We require you to give evidence regarding the murder of an IPCC agent."

It was Jenore's turn to speak. "Do you mean evidence of how your constables provoked a sectarian brawl, resulting in the theft of a religious relic?"

On the screen, Chandraseckh's face became both still and thunderous. After a long moment, in which he offered no further word, he broke the connection. The screen vanished.

Jenore asked Yalum and me, "Would you say the chance of our returning to Meech's World has now moved from not likely to not at all?"

We would say it. Indeed, speaking as one, we both did.

Two

The space yacht's integrator said, "We are cleared for landing; Pad Fourteen on the south side of the spaceport."

"Take us in," my friend Yalum Erkatchian told the device. I liked describing *Peregrinator*'s captain as "my friend." He is the only one I've ever had. I didn't count Hallis Tharp, the man who made me. He was, after a fashion, my father.

Now Yalum turned to me and said, 'Conn, would you advise Ser Jaffee that we will need him and his documents shortly?"

"Yes." As I went aft along the corridor that led to the space yacht's several cabins, first- and second-class, I felt the change in vibration as the ship shut of its in-space drive and the in-atmosphere drive kicked in.

Sisi Jaffee was in a first-class cabin. An intercessor from Indoberia Commune on Novo Bantry, he was our only passenger for this run to the peculiar world known as Sasanai, out here near the limits of the galactic arm-spanning civilization known as The Ten Thousand Worlds, and not far from where the lawless Back of Beyond began.

When I rapped on his cabin door, he opened it immediately. "Time?" he said.

I nodded. "We'll be down in a few minims. The authorities will want to see your certificates."

He wore the three-piece habit that was common to his profession throughout the Ten Thousand Worlds. A stickpin with a globular head, the visible sign of his accreditation to the tribunals of Novo Bantry, pierced his neckcloth. His hand went to the opening of his upper garment and the inner pocket where he kept the folded papers that declared he was entitled to set down at the place called Change, out in one of Sasanai's great deserts, and do business there. But then his other hand fell upon the large valise resting on the shelf above the cabin's sleeping platform.

"This," he said, "is what they're really want to see."

The suitcase contained four million SDU certificates from the Ambeline Mining Corporation's accounts at Indoberia. The funds were a ransom to buy the freedom of two of Ambeline's employees, who had been kidnapped while exploring for new mineral deposits on a world named Frescaria, out in the Back of Beyond.

"Will you need a come-along for that?" I said.

He nodded, made a slight sound of affirmation. I went to bring him one of the gravity-obviating devices from stores. When I returned with it, *Peregrinator* was settling into its berth. It was only moments after the drive cut out that the integrator said, "Port inspectors request entry."

"Open the forward hatch as soon as I arrive," I said, and hurried to get there.

Two officers of the port's security apparatus stepped into

the ship as I reached the portal. They were an older man with a hard cast to his face and a younger one who was trying to acquire his superior's severity of expression. Both wore the loose garments and flowing headgear appropriate to a desert world like Sasanai.

"You are?" said the older one.

"Conn Labro, supercargo."

He looked at a handheld data cache. "Who else?"

I said, "Yalum Erkatchian, captain, Jenore Mordene, steward, and Sisi Jaffee, passenger with accreditation."

"No one else?"

I signaled a negative.

"We will see the passenger."

I led them to where Ser Jaffee waited in his cabin. The security officers gave his valise only the briefest of glances then examined his credentials with close attention to detail, asking a number of questions that the passenger answered affably.

Finally, the older man said something to his assistant, who produced a different device with which he scanned Jaffee from top to toe, back and front. He compared the results of his inspection with data already recorded in the scanner and said, "Checks out."

The senior man spoke to Jaffee. "A car will call for you. My assistant will wait with you until it arrives then escort you to the facility."

He then turned to me. "You and your colleagues will remain aboard."

"We may need supplies and replenishment," I said.

"Have your ship talk to the port's integrator." He fixed me with a meaningful look from under his thicket-like eyebrows. "Close your hatch and stay out of trouble."

"We are not wild folk," I said.

His gesture told me he had said all he meant to say. He watched as Jaffee placed his valise in the come-along's grip then the three of them went to the forward hatch, walking single-file with our passenger and his ransom in between.

I followed along and closed up once they had disembarked, bade the integrator tell the captain where matters stood, then went to find Jenore. She was in the steward's office, sorting through the yacht's remaining inventories of food and drink to decide what would make our next meal. The sight of her, as always, caused a curious effect; it was as if my chest contained a new organ, distinct from the rest, and it activated the moment my eyes reported having perceived the woman I loved.

I stood in the doorway for a while, letting my physiological peculiarities indulge themselves until I noticed that she was regarding me with a quizzical expression. I told her what had happened.

"Assuming no unforeseen complications," she said, "he should be back with two more in tow."

"Yes," I said, "Bolderchan and Dremor."

She nodded and glanced at her supplies roster. "No special diets?"

"Nothing specified. They're from Indoberia,"—an ancient commune on Novo Bantry, a world that was one of the Grand Foundational Domains originally settled by the pioneering first wave of human settlers down The Spray— "so they're probably happy with mainstream fare."

"After two months eating whatever they dish out in the facility, I should think they'd be happy with ship's bread and a decent mug of punge."

∾

THE TWO SECURITY officers did not return. Instead, Sisi Jaffee was escorted back to the ship by two subwardens of the facility. They came in an air car whose doors were emblazoned with a logo of crossed golden keys against a stylized black shield, above which curved the words *Guest Accommodation*, in gold leaf, and the name of the planet inscribed below. I noticed that whoever had painted the door had used the old, original name of the facility—Interchange—though the place had been known as Change since time immemorial.

In the rear of the vehicle, looking about with anxious eyes, came Ezek Bolderchan and Parse Dremor; the former a stocky, plate-faced man who had once been solidly build but was now entering the middle years with yesterday's muscle deliquescing to flab; the latter was a thin and sinewy type, tall and narrow-shouldered, with a wide forehead above a sharp chin.

When the vehicle alighted outside *Peregrinator*'s forward hatch, now opened to receive passengers, the pair in the back made no effort to step down. Instead, they waited for the facility's guards to open the air car's doors for them.

I knew that long-term detainees in prisons where inmates were harshly repressed could lose their sense of volition and become as timid and dependent on authority as highly trained animals. But these two had only been locked up for a couple of months while their employer had negotiated their ransom, and had enjoyed third-class confinement at Change—equivalent to how we treated second-class passengers on *Peregrinator*—so their anxiety seemed out of place.

But, as Jenore often reminds me, "normal" people have different reactions from mine, along with their myriad odd customs and beliefs, developed over the countless millennia since humanity flowed out from Old Earth.

Sisi Jaffee, having sprung lightly from the forward seat, now strode toward the hatch then glanced back only long enough to see that the released hostages were coming. But once through the hatch, he waited for the others to join him.

By then, Jenore and I were in place to receive our new passengers. I stood back to let her make the welcoming remarks. She has often told me that my customary absence of affect when expressing warm sentiments can create cognitive dissonance in the minds of the people I am speaking to.

"Have you eaten?" she said. "On *Peregrinator*'s time, now is when we take the midday meal. It's traditional to offer ship's bread as a welcome. Would you care to come to the dining salon?"

Bolderchan and Dremor exchanged looks, as if each wished the other would give a response. Meanwhile, Jenore was making gestures that encouraged them to step away from the hatch and down the corridor. They went, followed by Jaffee and me, though I paused to secure the hatch. Moments later, I felt the vibratio of the in-atmosphere drive as it engaged. The floor pressed against the soles of my feet, and we were airborne.

I could have left them for Jenore to manage, she being much better with people than I, but I was curious about our new passengers. Having been released from confinement ought to have put them in a jubilant mood—or at least relieved. Instead they gave the impression of a small pet that expects a berating.

The three passengers took seats at one of the salon's two tables while Jenore bustled about, bringing them platters of *Peregrinator*'s bread—which really is the best I've ever tasted—and the ship's rich, hot punge.

"Take some," I said, reaching for a slice and a mug. "It's very good."

Bolderchan and Dremor looked about the salon with rapid glances, as if they feared sudden ambush. Then they acquiesced with Jenore's unspoken urging. In a moment, they were sipping and chewing. Between swallows, I heard Dremor give a sigh that sounded to me like relief after long-endured stress.

Sisi Jaffee had been chewing and swallowing while regarding his two charges with bemusement. Now he set down his mug, brushed some crumbs from his lower lip, and said, "We should talk about what happens next."

Immediately, Bolderchan's and Dremor's tension reasserted itself.

"What do you mean?" Dremor said, his mug frozen halfway to his lips.

Bolderchan said, "You take us home. What else could happen next?"

Jaffee's free hand gave a mollifying wave. "Home, yes," he said. "But not at first. First we go to Frescaria. The authorities there have some questions."

Dremor set his mug down. "We don't want to go to Frescaria. Of all the planets in the Ten Thousand Worlds, that's the last place we want to go."

He looked to me as if I could help him.

I told him, "This ship, I'm afraid, has been chartered by the Ambeline Mining Corporation. The flight plan is Novo Bantry to Sasanai, Sasanai to Frescaria, Frescaria to Novo

Bantry. The only slippage in the schedule is for an extended stay on Frescaria, if the authorities ask us to remain."

I was rather proud of myself for putting in the "I'm afraid." Jenore had taught me to include such phrases when delivering unwelcome news to passengers. It had taken me a while to be able to say that particular one—in truth, I am never afraid, lacking certain neural connections that underlie fear—but I was definitely getting better at social fakery.

Of course, Jenore had made me understand that nobody literally means they're afraid when they say it as I just had. It was merely one more example of the strange ways by which statistically "normal" people conducted their lives. But now she rewarded my use of a bald-faced lie by giving me an encouraging smile.

I would have taken on far more difficult challenges for the prize of one of Jenore's smiles.

"Sorry," I lied again and spread my hands in a way that meant the universe had spoken and could not be gainsaid.

Bolderchan had lapsed into silence, his gaze turned inward to show him images that apparently did not please. Dremor was glancing about as if anticipating an imminent attack. Finally, he looked at me and said, "We want to go home to Indoberia. We want nothing more to do with Frescaria."

Sisi Jaffee was regarding the two with puzzlement. "You will be perfectly safe," he said. "The Insouciance are in remission. Indeed, the High Provost on Frescaria was surprised they had gotten back into their old kidnapping ways. There were rumors the cult had received a new revelation from Shek Ran, who styles himself the Diffident

Prophet, that had directed them toward a less aggressive orientation to their neighbors."

Dremor and Bolderchan exchanged looks. Dremor cleared his throat as if about to speak, though nothing emerged. The other one said, "Maybe it's a breakaway sect. These fringe religions are always schisming."

"Maybe," said Jaffee, in a tone that conveyed scant interest. "Either way, the company police want to take your statements and this is a company charter. So, it's to Frescaria we're bound. Soonest started, soonest ended, as they say."

Jenore urged our passengers to take more bread and punge. Jaffee did so, expressing appreciation for the quality. Bolderchan and Dremor took no more. After a long silence, I escorted them to their cabins.

"I AM PUZZLED," I told Jaffee when I next saw him. He had gone to the yacht's capacious forward salon where I found him at his ease, sitting one leg crossed on the other, leafing through a periodical.

"What puzzles you?" he said, putting the organ on his upraised knee.

I sat beside him. "Those two. They've just been released from months of confinement, yet they act as if they are still prisoners."

"Yes," he said, "it is curious." He consulted his memory and added, "'I have performed this function several times before. The responses of redeemed hostages have ranged from anger at those who seized them to untrammeled joy at their release. I have not seen any who greet their return to freedom as a cause for anxiety."

"So I'm not misreading them," I said. "Then what are they afraid of? That their employer will take action against them?"

He signaled disbelief. "No. Ambeline is a well-ordered firm, managed by professionals and overseen by the officers of the fiduciary pool that has financed their explorations and developments. It's not as if they're headed by some tycoon who acts upon impulse."

"Then what?"

His hand rose to touch the stickpin at his throat, as if seeking a buttress to his self-esteem. "My role in the business is merely as a courier. I see no profit in speculation. Once I have delivered them to the authorities on Frescaria, I have discharged my responsibilities. If you are returning promptly to Novo Bantry, I will travel with you."

He waited for me to make some response, and when I nodded my agreement, he went on, "If not, I will take passage on a liner. Ambeline will reimburse me."

WITH ONLY THREE passengers and no cargo—Ambeline had insisted on an exclusive chartered run—I had few duties as supercargo of *Peregrinator*. I repaired to the cabin I shared with Jenore, thinking we might indulge in an activity we both enjoyed.

But she was not there. I took a seat in one of the pair of padded chairs and called the ship's integrator to attention. "I want to know," I said, "about Change. Specifically if confinement there causes psychological harm."

"At one time, it did," said the integrator. "Do you wish to begin with a concise history?"

My impulse was to say no, but one thing I had learned since my upbringing on the gaming world, Thrais, was that sometimes my knowledge of certain subjects was incomplete, so after a moment's reflection I bade the device follow through with Change's backstory.

Millennia ago, the integrator informed me, after the first great effloration of humanity down The Spray but before the second, there had been a civilization, now scarcely remembered, that named itself the Ekumen. It encompassed scores of worlds that filled up with humans. Some became opulent and louche, others were settled by groups wedded to odd idiosyncracies.

But the civilized Ekumen ended at an imaginary line in space known as the Pale. Past the Pale lay the Beyond, another slew of inhabited worlds, of many different characters but all with one single common characteristic; there was no law but local law, and on some worlds, the law was enforced by the lawless.

The Beyond was a wild frontier, populated by the kinds of people who chafed at the constraints of civilized society. Some were freedom-seekers who just wanted to live their lives by their own eccentric standards. Others were pirates, reivers, slavers, and those peculiar individuals—somewhat rare, but still appearing in uncomfortable numbers—who go through life without any capacity for remorse and fellow-feeling.

There soon sprang up a cottage industry in the Beyond: kidnapping the wealthy denizens of worlds within the Ekumen and receiving ransom for their return unharmed. The cottage industry blossomed and became a substantial part of the incomes of persons from the Beyond who had the essential attributes of a kidnapper; a space ship, some weaponry, and a cold heart.

Somewhere along the way, the facility called Interchange was established on the arid world now named Sasanai. Its founders and early operations were not remembered—official records were sketchy in the Beyond. Here kidnappers could deposit their catches, to be cared for at varying levels of comfort, until their redeemers brought the specified amounts for their loved ones' release. Persons who were not redeemed after a set period were auctioned off to slavers or persons who, for their own reasons, wanted to purchase the unfortunate.

That latter practice ended with the second great effloration, when burgeoning humanity swarmed across the Pale and created the civilization known as The Ten Thousand Worlds. The trillions who wanted to live decent, fear-free lives sent ships with ison cannons to root out the bandits and freebooters. Many such were killed. The remnants either fled down The Spray to the Back of Beyond, where the stars thinned out and law was a mutable thing, or were absorbed into the criminal halfworlds on the settled planets.

But Interchange remained what it was, though the name evolved to simple Change. For a while, the facility was shut down and its staff told to find new work. Still, kidnappings continued, and often the kidnappers found it inconvenient— if not dangerous to their desire to remain at large—to release their victims alive and capable of testifying.

After a period of chaos, culminating in the taking and murdering of the heir to an ancient aristocratic fief on Old Earth, it was decided to reestablish the facility and allow it to operate as before. Evidence gained from victims or facility staff could not be used in prosecutions, and the paying and receipt of ransoms was handled through the revived Borse of Change, whose records could not be examined by minions of the law.

The net result, proponents of Change noted, was that kidnappings declined in absolute numbers, and it was rare for anyone to be taken who was not "on the cushion," the term used to describe the lifestyle of the most extremely rich. Paying ransom became recognized as a perquisite of the plutocrats and it was not unheard of, in the select environments were such folk gathered, to hear competitive boastings as to whose ransom was greater than another's.

I learned a little more from the ship then asked a few questions. *Peregrinator* answered with more information, but at the end of the lesson, I was no more understanding of our two passengers than I was at the beginning.

WE HAD COME DOWN to Sasanai by way of a long passage through normal space which led us to a whimsy that popped us back into space-time with only a short cruise to our destination. But going to Frescaria required a full day of travel to reach a different whimsy that would let us bore through the nonspace of the Seventh Plane and come out another day's distance from our destination.

Frescaria was what is known as a "secondary world." The term denoted a planet that was not settled directly from Old Earth or from the Ekumen. The directly settled worlds, now grown old in wealth and culture, were known as Grand Foundational Domains. Secondaries tended to be populated by groups that wanted to live under self-created regimes, often involving novel social arrangements or messianic religions.

Some others were more like traditional frontiers, in that there was money to made from *terrae nulliae*, the ancient term for "nobody's land," available to whoever arrived and built a dwelling. In Frescaria's case, the original settlers found a pristine world of Arcadian splendor: green valleys, rolling hills, well-watered plains, and warm, shallow seas. The settlers devised a pastoral society centered on small family farms, scattered villages, and a few market towns. They founded only one large city, prosaically named Head-quarters, to be the seat of the planetary institutions. They built no industrial zones.

And that was how affairs remained for several genera-tions, until some visiting off-worlder noticed an outcrop of crystaline rock. He broke off a piece and carried it back to his home world of New Balbek, where he paid for an assay. The rock turned out to harbor the rare-earth mineral chal-cocite. More than that, the ratio of chalcocite to the surrounding rock was the richest concentration of the mineral the prospector had ever seen.

Equipped with a powerful tool, he went back to Fres-caria, gathered more surface samples and drilled some cores. After analyzing these new finds, he prepared a prospectus and took it to a select group of investors. Not long after, the newly formed Chalco Mining Corporation landed on Fres-caria, claimed the mineral rights to a substantial territory, and began operations.

The venture was profitable from its first quarter and its original investors soon sold out to the multiworld-spanning Ambeline Mining Corporation. Frescaria became an oft-heard name wherever miners and those who financed them gathered. More newcomers touched down on Frescaria, more swathes of once-green territory became deserts characterized by heaps of crushed rock, pools of poison accumulated in ore-leaching procedures, and shanty towns seething with offworlders whose ways were antithetical to the bucolic society Frescaria's farmers had built.

Tensions grew, then grew worse when some of the farmers' sons and daughters were drawn to the stimulation of the miners' towns, and the high wages to be earned there. A resistance movement grew. Mining equipment was vandalized, pipelines full of slurry were breached, and company officials found themselves shouted at in public places.

Frescaria had little in the way of a police apparatus, and the world's constables and reeves tended to adhere to the old, placid methods of law enforcement. The mining companies found the situation unsatisfactory. They combined to create their own security force, bringing mercenaries and hard-faced confidential operatives from offworld. These were not the kinds of people to mingle well with Frescarians. Relations between the miners and the locals became stark. Violence that had been directed at machinery now switched to attacks on persons.

Bands of guerillas took to operating out of the uncut forests on the main continent, Kaydya. Over time, they gave up raiding mine sites and destroying transportation infrastructure, to focus on kidnapping the most senior personnel of the mining companies that they could lay their hands on. The ransoms were arranged through Change.

⁓

BOLDERCHAN AND DREMOR did not come to the salon for
the evening meal. *Peregrinator*'s integrator said they were
sitting together in Dremor's cabin, conversing in low tones.

"About what?" I said

"I do not know," the device said. "My percepts are in
nominal-privacy mode."

That meant the ship heard whatever was said, but didn't
listen. I told it to listen in and tell me what was being said.

"I cannot," it said, "without first obtaining their permission. Unless you want to change my fundamentals."

I did not want to do that. Integrators are complex
systems, with every part connected to every other part. Pull
on one thread and there was no telling what else might be
unknotted. It was a particularly tricky prospect while out in
space and headed for a whimsy.

Something was amiss with our pair of freed hostages. I
did not know if their unusual behavior posed a threat to my
shipmates, but Bolderchan and Dremor had triggered some
warning alarm down in the basement of my oddly designed
brain. I decided I would go and talk to them.

As a pretext, I took them a tray laden with ship's bread,
savories, and punge. When I knocked and announced
myself, there was a lengthy pause, in which I could hear
whispering and moving about, before the door opened only
wide enough for Bolderchan to eye me.

"What?" he said.

"Dinner," I said, drawing his attention to the food. I
heard his stomach growl.

He opened the door and I stepped within, depositing the
tray on the cabin's fold-down desk top. Then I turned and
took a good look at the two of them.

Neither of them returned my stare. They looked at their

hands, each other, the corners of the room. I let this go on for a while then I said, "You are not behaving like men who have been set free from confinement. You are behaving like men who expect to be arrested, convicted, and sentenced to a long term in a contemplarium."

Again, no one would meet my gaze. "If you are in difficulties, we are prepared to offer assistance, within reason." Actually, my willingness to put myself out for my fellow human beings was limited, but I knew that Jenore was often inexplicably altruistic, and her convictions—however contrary to the principles of my upbringing—continued to influence me.

"Very well," I said, after the silence had grown to fill the room, "I'll leave you to your own devices. By the way, we are now in contact with the authorities at Frescaria. The police will meet us when we dock."

At that news, Dremor's sharp-featured face looked up at me. "Which police?" he said.

I acted as if the question puzzled me, so as to draw more information from them. "Are there different kinds of police on Frescaria?"

"Oh, yes," came the answer. "The various cantons have their own walkers—that's what they call them—while there is also a worldwide provost's corp for crimes that occur over two or more jurisdictions,"

Now Bolderchan weighed in, "But the mining consortia have their own police. Thugs and the sweepings of the criminal underworlds of half a dozen planets."

I asked the integrator to let me know which sort of police force had been in touch. The two ex-hostages heard the answer. "Green Circle Security, contracted to the Ambeline Mining Corporation."

They both went pale. "We don't want to deal with them," Parse Dremor said. "They are corrupt."

Ezek Bolderchan said, "Green Circle is said to have 'made arrangements' with the insurgents. They play on both sides of the board."

"They say they have a warrant to detain you for interrogation," I said.

Dremor moaned but Bolderchan was suddenly charged with energy. "You must contact the world's provost and demand that it send some walkers to the port. Say that we fear kidnap."

"Again?" I said. "And while you are in police custody?"

Bolderchan's heavy jaw set itself. "There are police, and then there are 'police.'" His fingers crooked the air. "There is custody, and then there is 'custody.'"

IT TOOK some time for the ship's integrator to find anyone in the Frescaria Provost Corps who would take an interest in the case. During that period of finding someone to listen, followed by explaining, followed by explaining yet again to some other bored functionary, Yalum Erkatchian told *Peregrinator* to slow our approach to the troubled world.

Not long after we dropped to half-speed, while I was still seeking someone I could tell about our passengers' fears, the integrator told me we were being hailed by the spaceport.

When the screen came to life, I saw a man of late middle years whose jowls were blued by a couple of days stubble. He wore a severely cut uniform of green piped by white, on the left breast a green disk in which were set four fists of polished brass. Below his image, in a cartouche, I read the words, *Gustus Hellivance, Force-in-Charge*.

Jenore was watching over my shoulder. Now she bent down and whispered, "A force is a high rank within Green Circle in its criminal operations on Old Earth. A force-in-charge is a very senior rank. Whatever is going on, Green Circle is taking it seriously."

And Gustus Hellivance was not pleased to be waiting for our response. When I identified myself and asked how I could assist him, he said, "Why have you cut your speed? Resume normal approach then when you come within range, let the spaceport's systems guide you in."

Yalum introduced himself and said, "We are an experienced crew, and our ship's integrator is mature and accomplished."

Hellivance was clearly not used to being resisted. He said, "Do as you're told. A patrol boat is coming to meet you. It will escort you to a berth in Ambeline Mining Corporation's orbital."

"Our flight plan calls for touchdown at the main spaceport," our captain began, but was cut off by a curt gesture and a raised voice.

"You will follow the escort's instructions. Any deviation will result in your being fired upon. Increase your speed now."

With that, the screen went blank. I was glad I had not invited the two freed hostages to join us in Erkatchian's forward work space. "This does not sound right," I said.

"Continue to make contact with the real police," Jenore suggested. "We can't just turn these people over to a gang of thugs."

The integrator broke in there, to tell us that the warrant

it had mentioned had been transmitted to it while Yalum was speaking with the force-in-charge. It now displayed the document and highlighted an important part of the text; the warrant did not apply only to Bolderchan and Dremor.

We were all subject to arrest.

I CONSULTED WITH SISI JAFFEE. He expressed surprise, followed by anger when his review of the warrant showed him that he, too, was included in the "all persons whatsoever aboard the said vessel, without distinction of rank or history."

"Intercessors carrying out their professional duties are not subject to warrants," he said then thought for a moment. "Whom have you being trying to reach within the civilian apparatus?"

I told him the names of offices I had contacted. He brushed those titles away like someone dispersing a cloud of gnats. "Let me use your integrator," he said.

THE GREEN CIRCLE PATROL BOAT, a stubby little craft bristling with ison cannons and the emitters of a bank of heavy-duty disorganizers, swung onto a parallel course behind and above *Peregrinator*. The crew did not address us, though its integrator spoke with ours, as such devices did.

Frescaria, still a world of green and blue, with white bands and swirls of clouds, grew large in our forward view. But instead of spiraling down to the spaceport on the southern rim of the northern continent, we swung into an orbit and gradually reduced speed until we were hovering a short distance from a massive orbital marked with the symbols of Ambeline Mining Corporation.

A large, double-doored hatch opened, a flux of energies struck *Peregrinator*'s hull, and the space yacht was smoothly drawn into a berth. The outer doors closed, we felt the adjustment to the orbital's gravity, and immediately the ship said we had visitors.

The image showed Gustus Hellivance giving a convincing impression of a mature man who has somehow failed to learn the art of patience. With him were half a dozen uniformed men and women, all of them armed and looking intent on doing whatever the force-in-charge might order.

Sisi Jaffee studied the group forming up outside the forward hatch. "We should delay," he said.

BUT THERE WAS NOT much scope for delay. Hellivance stood with fists on hips while one of his troopers banged on the hatch with some kind of heavy metal tool, The force-in-charge's voice came clearly to the six of us in *Peregrinator*, fed through the connection between the orbital's device and the ship's.

"I cannot resist indefinitely," the ship told the crew. "They have protocols that cannot be gainsaid while I am berthed in their dock. And even if I could, this is a repair facility for the company's mining equipment. They have the means to cut right through the hatch."

I looked to Sisi Jaffee and saw that whatever he had

been hoping for had not arrived in time. "Better open up," I told Yalum.

He nodded, squared himself then told the ship to open the hatch. No sooner had it cycled halfway open than a uniformed man stepped through, an energy pistol in one hand. Several more of his kind, all armed, came after him, their weapons trained on us. I was tempted to step between Jenore and the emitters, but knew that she considered such gestures demeaning.

Hellivance came into the ship now, a short specimen but wide in chest and shoulders. He took a quick look at us then spoke over his shoulder to the man behind him, who wore the insignia of an underforce; "Seize them. Search them and the ship. Interrogate its integrator under warrant."

They had brought holdfasts. In moments, all of us had our hands secured behind our backs. Yalum Erkatchian protested that we were a bonded carrier, under contract to the company that Hellivance served.

"Shut up," said the force-in-charge. He turned to address the man who had overseen our trussing and said, "If he speaks again without being spoken to, render him unconscious."

The underforce gave a silent indication that he would do as ordered. Then he gestured to the hatch and said, "Outside." Single-file, we stepped out onto the metal dock.

This was not the part of the orbital where senior company officials would disembark from Ambeline's fleet of well-appointed space yachts. This was where the machinery of mining was transshipped between space-going transports and the carry-alls that would take the equipment down to the surface. It was also where worn-out or damaged diggers and sorters were repaired and refurbished.

So it was cold and damp, the distances between walls, floors, and ceilings huge. Everything was a uniform gray, paint over metal. On the outer wall, I saw docking ports for other ships, while the inner wall of this section was divided into bays with hoists, analytical devices, and a wide variety of tools pinned to wallboards of displayed in open chests.

But there was no one to wield the tools. I saw evidence —half-filled mugs of punge, devices left idling—that indicated several technics had recently been at work here, until someone came along and ordered them all to drop whatever they were doing and leave. As I watched Gustus Hellivance strut his way to the front of our little procession, I had no doubt who had issued the orders.

That worried me. Whenever someone in authority sends away possible witnesses, anyone under the thumb of that authority has cause for concern.

The Green Circle guards searched us, found nothing to trouble them. Hellivance motioned us to follow him, guards surrounding us. We left behind those who were searching *Peregrinator*.

Sisi Jaffee was speaking now. He was third in the line of prisoners and now he called forward to Hellivance. "I am a respected intercessor under contract to your employer. This treatment is egregious."

The force-in-charge looked back at him. Having won Hellivance's attention, the intercessor stopped walking. Since I was right behind Jaffee, I had to sidestep a little to keep from barging into him. One of the guards took a grip on my arm, but I showed him a shrug and a placid smile and he unhanded me.

Jaffee was speaking slowly and clearly, detailing the terms of his contract to deliver the ransom to Change then escort the two redeemed hostages to Frescaria for questioning, and finally back to Novo Bantry.

"They are in my charge," he concluded, dropping his chin to touch his stickpin. "If you want to question them, you should enlist my cooperation."

Hellivance studied Jaffee as if he was some strange new creature, never before encountered. The intercessor waited patiently for a response, but I noticed that his gaze kept shifting toward the farther reaches of the large segment of orbital through which Green Circle had been marching us.

Helivance now quirked his mouth in a way that said he did not care much one way or another, and told the underforce to set Jaffee free of the holdfast. With the restraint removed, the intercessor stood rubbing the flesh of his wrists and elbows where the device had gripped. He touched the head of his intercessor's stickpin again. It seemed to be a reflexive gesture.

And he kept looking up the long curving stretch before us, though whatever he was seeking had plainly not appeared. He cast a sideways glance my way, with a slight nod of the head and a shrug.

I took his meaning and said to Hellivance, "We three are also respectable persons working for your employer. We could not do our work unless we were bonded, and we could not be bonded if we were persons of ill character or criminal history."

The Green Circle man regarded me with some of the same curiosity that Sisi Jaffee had raised in him. After a long moment, he said, "Enough jabber. We'll sort it all out once you're safe in the cells."

"They might bring legal action against you," Jaffee said. "I would feel obligated to testify."

Hellivance's face had already said he was growing impatient. The interecessor's last remark caused a dark cloud to form on the force-in-charge's brow and his mouth bent down in a frown.

He spoke to his second-in-command, "Move them. Quickly. And keep them quiet."

We set off again, the guards helping us along with pushes to our shoulders and the small of the back. Behind me, I heard Jenore say, "Hey!" in an offended tone, and I wondered if I was going to have to do something. The holdfast confined my arms, but there were a myriad things I knew how to do with feet, knees, hips, and head.

But then I saw the tension go out of Sisi Jaffee's shoulders as he marched in front of me. Not too far ahead of us, a section of the orbital's outer wall opened and through the gap came a dozen or so men and women in uniforms, white singlesuits with a blue and green patch on each shoulder.

They were under the command of a tall, spare woman old enough to be graying at the temples but young enough to react quickly as we walked toward her. A couple of terse commands, and the dozen provosts formed a double rank athwart our line of march. Another calmly delivered order and twelve police-issue shockers appeared in their hands, pointed at us.

"Halt," said the senior provostwoman.

I stopped. So did the rest of my party, except for Hellivance and his number one, who advanced to where the white uniforms waited. A quiet conversation ensued but we were too distant to hear it. Yet I could read the body language; Hellivance was not happy at this new turn of events. He gesticulated. His chin came up in defiance. But the provostwoman responded with few words and a face that could have been carved from granite.

Finally, Hellivance turned back to us and said, "Let them loose." Then he turned back to the woman and said, "I'm coming with you."

Her only response was an eloquent lift and fall of her shoulders.

HER NAME WAS VONNEZ TOPHE, and she held the rank of Scrutineer First Class in Frescaria's civil police apparatus. My travels with Jenore and *Peregrinator* had acquainted me with some of the varieties of security officials to be found among the Ten Thousand Worlds. They ranged from the patently corrupt to the rigorously scrupulous. Tophe looked as if she would place high on the virtuous scale, while Hellivance had all the attributes of a denizen of the bottom, where the venal and unprincipled pursued their squalid ends.

One thing struck me as odd, however; she and her dozen provostmen and women had come up to the Ambeline's orbital in an official shuttle, but she did not take us back down to the surface in that vehicle. Instead she ordered Bolderchan and Dremor, along with Jaffee and the three of us, back to *Peregrinator*. She meant to accompany us.

Hellivance looked from her to his former prisoners and back again, with so sharp a head motion that he might have dislocated a vertebra. "What?" he said. "What's this?"

She ignored him, using a commanding finger to tell us to turn around and go back the way we had come.

But the force-in-charge put himself in her way. "The

yacht is in the company's custody," he said. "The orbital's integrator will not allow it to undock unless I give the word."

Tophe's brows climbed and the differences in hers and Hellivance's heights somehow became more noticeable. "Or unless I obtain a magistrate's decree," she said.

A slow smile spread across the Green Circle man's harsh features. "Assuming you can argue more effectively than Ambeline's intercessors."

I sensed an impasse had been reached and, again, I was puzzled. I spoke softly to Jenore, "How does possession of the yacht factor into this?"

She silently showed that she was as bewildered as I.

"Unless," I said, as my mind turned over the facts, "we have taken something aboard, something we don't know about."

"What?" Jenore said.

But I had gone as far as my thoughts would carry me.

Still, Tophe and Hellivance had worked their way past their stalemate. She was agreeing that he would go with us. The force-in-charge wanted his underforce to come along, but the provostwoman refused to allow it. Finally, Hellivance subsided, but I saw a meaningful look pass between him and his henchman.

I nudged Jenore again and moved my head to draw her attention to something I had noticed; Sisi Jaffee, who had remained calm and at ease throughout the confrontation with the mining company's security team, was now showing signs of tension. They were not the sort of indicators most would spot, but I had been designed to take note of slight narrowings of the eyes, tension in the neck, quickening of the pulse in the throat, and tightening of the fingers, as their owner resisted the unconscious urge to make a fist.

"He was relieved before. Now something has him worried," I whispered.

We were close enough that Jaffee heard me. I meant him to do so, because I could assess the meaning of the look he darted in my direction before taking a deep, slow breath, and letting it ease out through his nostrils.

Tophe was gesturing now. We headed back to the bay where *Peregrinator* was berthed. Jaffee showed me another glance then a smile that was deliberately constructed to appear mild.

Hmm, I said to myself.

～

In the yacht's forward salon, Vonnez Tophe introduced herself to the ship's integrator and bade it contact the Provost's central device. A brief, silent conversation ensued then the ship announced that it was under her jurisdiction. "Green Circle's warrant has been voided."

I heard the docking clamps disengage then we eased out of the orbital's ambit and began to drop toward the planet. After a short while, the in-atmosphere drive initiated and we increased our speed of descent.

Bolderchan and Dremor were seated together on one of the longseats, their unease obvious. Jaffee sat in a nearby armchair. I saw his hand rise toward his neckpin again then he consciously checked the gesture and folded his hands in his lap.

Hellivance stood where he could keep an eye on the two former hostages and their intercessor, while Tophe turned her back to all of us. Looking out the forward screen, she said something that the integrator's superb percepts could pick up but not even my enhanced sense of hearing could catch.

We spiraled down in silence toward the green and blue of the planet, streaked with clouds of a brilliant white. After we passed through the cloud layer, I saw a line of concern appear between Erkatchian's brows then he threw me a meaningful glance before returning his gaze to the screen.

I looked and saw what he wanted me to notice; the neat white and blue buildings of Headquarters dropping out of sight over the curve of the horizon. We were heading for a mountainous region where ancient forests cloaked the lower slopes and alpine meadows appeared above the treeline.

I spoke softly, "Unexpected."

He answered me in the same tone. "We are not out of trouble."

We continued to descend then the yacht exercised its gravity obviators and we settled onto one of the meadows, a snow-capped peak above and a dense forest below. I saw a sheer cliff not far upslope, its face split by a long, vertical fissure. At the base of the gouge was a darkness.

"We will go to the cave," Tophe said.

"All of us?" I said.

"Safer that way," she said, though she did not specify whose safety she referred to.

Hellivance looked at her then at the hostages and Jaffee. "What is this?" the force-in-charge said. His hand went to the energy pistol at his belt.

"You'll find," Tophe said, "that the ship, at my order, has deactivated your weapons."

Dremor said, "We don't want to go to the cave," to

which Bolderchan added several enthusiastic, confirming nods.

Tophe drew her shocker. She didn't need to say anything.

We climbed the slope single file, with the provostwoman, her weapon still drawn, at the rear. My curiosity was aroused, so I went first. The cave entrance was narrow but the chamber behind it widened under a low ceiling. At first it was difficult to see, but my eyes adjusted to the dim interior which was further darkened as the rest of us came through the slit, blocking the light from outside.

Once we were all in, I saw how, at the rear of the space, a heavy cloth was hung from metal rings that encircled a length of wood nailed to the living rock.

"Go through," Tophe said. I went to the rough curtain and pushed it aside. Beyond was light and space. The cave walls were hidden behind hangings of fine red fabric figured with designs embroidered in gold thread. The floor was covered in polished planks, tightly fitted together, and the spacious room was lit by lumens suspended from the ceiling far above or fixed in free-standing candelabra.

There was furniture: a couple of long tables of heavy wood with matching chairs. The table tops were strewn with documents and what looked like maps. Some ornate cupboards and a credenza stood against the walls. I wondered briefly how they had been got through the narrow way in, but then my attention was drawn to an arras at one side of the chamber. A large hand thrust it aside, just far enough for an eye to inspect us. The hand redrew the curtain then a moment later came back to sweep the cloth out of the way.

A big man, clad in leather, slab-shouldered, and

without a single visible hair, stepped through the opening then positioned himself to one side. He carried a military-grade disorganizer. It was pointed at the floor but I could see its self-aiming percept glowing. He stood and watched us in silence. Behind me, I heard the sounds of feet shifting nervously on the wooden floor and someone— probably Parse Dremor—made an involuntary sound of fear.

Now another person appeared in the doorway; a small man with a timeworn face, dressed in nondescript clothing of no great quality, his gaze mild as he took in the sight of us. He shuffled across the floor in faded slippers to one of the long tables and sat in one of the chairs. He brushed aside some papers then interlinked his fingers on the table top and regarded us with calm expectation. The big man with the dreadful weapon came to stand behind and to one side.

The seated man spoke softly. "Come forward."

I heard another squeak from behind me—definitely Dremor—as I stepped forward along with the others. Jenore came to stand on one side of me, Erkatchian on the other. From single file, we became a rank facing the table, with Vonnez Tophe somewhere behind us with her shocker.

"What is—" Jenore began, but that drew the notice of the small man and I saw that his gaze could be the opposite of mild. I took Jenore's hand in mine, squeezed it gently, and made a quiet shushing sound.

Now the recipients of the hard look were Ezek Bolder-chan and Parse Dremor, and he asked them a question.

"Do you know who I am?" The pair wanted to look anywhere but at the questioner. He repeated the question. His tone did not change, nor did he raise his voice, but there was something in the way he spoke that caused Dremor to tremble and Bolderchan's breathing to become audible.

"You ought to know," the small man went on, "seeing as I'm supposed to have taken you prisoner and held you hostage before sending you to Change."

There was a silence, broken only by Bolderchan's ragged breathing. I was wondering how the Diffident Prophet came by his sobriquet; there was nothing shy or timid about the man who had had us brought here. Beneath his seemingly mild exterior, he was as hard as the Green Circle force-in-charge.

He turned to Gustus Hellivance now. "Did you have anything to do with this?"

The Green Circle man's jaw made a curious sideways motion. "No," he said.

Now Shek Ran looked at me and my two shipmates. "You three?" he said.

Erkatchian met the prophet's gaze and spoke. "We hire out for charters. That's all."

Now it was Jaffee's turn. "Did you hire them?"

Jaffee stared straight ahead. "Yes, on behalf of my client."

"Which is Ambeline Mining Corporation? They also paid the ransom?"

To both questions the intercessor answered yes. There was silence as the prophet observed him. Jaffee did not meet the seated man's gaze and I noticed a slight trembling of his hands.

The hard eyes swung back to the two hostages. "Who took you? Describe them."

Dremor swallowed. Bolderchan answered. "We can't. They put hoods over our heads."

"Men? Women? Did they have accents? Did they say anything that identified them as adherents of the Insouciance?"

"I don't know," Bolderchan said.

Dremor found his voice. "We were very frightened."

Ran leaned back in his chair and studied them. "As frightened as you are now?"

Neither man could manage a response, though Dremor emitted a fearful sound. Now the penetrating gaze returned to Sisi Jaffee. Another silence ensued.

In a tone of mild interest, the prophet said, "We keep coming back to you, don't we, intercessor?"

Jaffee looked down at him then away. He made no answer.

Ran said, "How many times have you been to Change to ransom the kidnapped?"

"Several," Jaffee said.

The prophet looked at a paper before him. "Eighteen," he said. "Fourteen of those were to redeem persons detained by the Insouciance, from seven different companies associated with the mining industry. It was your specialty."

Again, no answer from Jaffee.

"Your fees must have been substantial," Ran said. And when the observation was met only with silence, he continued. "And then they stopped."

The seated man steepled his fingers and regarded them for a while. Then, without looking up, he said, "Because we stopped the detentions."

Jaffee stared into the middle distance and said nothing, but I saw his hands clench. The motion must have been involuntary because he immediately relaxed them.

The prophet tipped back his head and lifted his eyes to

the rough stone ceiling. He held that pose for a long moment then suddenly focused on the two released hostages.

He said, "The one who answers first gets to live. How much were you paid?"

Dremor's knees almost gave way. He glanced at Bolderchan, saw the other man's mouth open, and blurted out, "One hundred thousand SDUs!"

Bolderchan said, "It wasn't our idea!"

"Of course, it wasn't," Ran said. "Out of four million, a couple of hundred thousand is a pittance." He looked to Jaffee again. "Where did the money go?"

Jaffee said, "I presume it was converted to an instrument transmitted to a fiduciary pool."

"You *presume*?" The note of anger in the prophet's tone was noticeable. I saw Jaffee resist a flinch, with only partial success.

Ran regained his calm. After a moment, he continued. "Here is something you didn't presume; the Insouciance has been dealing with Change for decades. We have acquired . . . *cachet* there. So, when we heard that someone pretending to be one of us initiated a transaction there, we asked questions."

He paused to let that sink it then he said, with his gaze fixed on the intercessor, "And we got answers."

Dremor said something under his breath. It might have been a prayer. The rest of the room was silent.

Until Hellivance spoke. "Well, where is the money?"

The prophet used his chin to indicate Sisi Jaffee. "He's got it."

Jaffee reacted by turning to the Green Circle man. "You searched me. You searched my luggage and my cabin. You asked the ship's integrator to report on my actions."

Ran looked to Hellivance. "Well?"

The force-in-charge signaled a negative. But I could see something was puzzling him.

The prophet leaned back again, steepled his fingers once more. "Our interlocutor at Change did not know the details of the money's transfer. The information is known only to persons well above his rank."

"We searched him for weapons and recording devices," Hellivance said, "not for the ransom. Let's do it again." He turned to Jaffee and said, "Strip!"

"I protest!" said the intercessor. "I am an officer–"

He went silent as, at a signal from Shek Ran, the huge guard raised his disorganizer and made a slight adjustment to its control. Its emitter briefly glowed with blue light.

"Just take off his right hand," the prophet said.

"No!" said Jaffee. "I'll cooperate."

I watched Jaffee, and I watched Hellivance watching Jaffee. The first thing the intercessor did was to remove the stickpin from his neckcloth then unwind the strip of fabric from around his neck. Now he carefully wrapped the orna-ment-of-office in the cloth and set it down by his feet before unfastening his upper garment.

That is when I saw a flash of expression cross Helli-vance's face before he suppressed it. But there was now a renewed tension in the Green Circle officer. With studied casualness, Hellivance looked away from Jaffee, at the same time raising a hand to touch the rank button on his collar.

I spoke softly to Jenore. "Something is about to happen. When it does, drop to the floor and scoot under the table."

While all eyes were on Jaffee, Hellivance aimlessly moved sideways, but his posture remained stiff. I saw that his motion took him out of a line drawn between the entrance we had come through and the position of the man with the disorganizer.

"Any moment now," I whispered to Jenore.

The heavy cloth over the entrance was swept aside and Hellivance's underforce, along with another Green Circle operative, entered the chamber, energy weapons in their hands. The surveillance devices Hellivance must have been wearing upon his body told them what their targets should be. The underforce shot Vonnez Tophe, and I heard the sizzling sound that such weapons make when they encounter human flesh. She cried out, but the sound was truncated as the beam sliced across her torso. She collapsed, dead before she hit the ground.

The second Green Circle who came through the entrance took time to aim, even as the prophet's bodyguard was transferring the bearing of his weapon from Jaffee to the new threat. I heard the *ziv* of the energy pistol and saw the guard's hairless head severed from his body.

Even as I saw the head topple to the floor, I was placing my hand on Jenore's shoulder to get her moving. She fell forward and scrambled on hands and knees under the cloth-draped table and in a moment was out of sight. I did the same, but first I seized Sisi Jaffee's wadded-up neckcloth and the stickpin it smothered.

The intercessor, his upper garment half-open, made the same move, but my maximum speed was beyond normal human range and he was too late. I followed Jenore under the table, and there found the Diffident Prophet sliding down off his chair to secure his own hiding place. He looked at me, eyes wide with shock, mouth open to say something.

Whatever it was went unheard. I struck him hard on the jaw, felt the impact travel up my arm, and was not surprised to see his eyes roll up in his head. He slumped unconscious against the chair.

I was already moving past him to where his dead guard had toppled, coming to rest on his knees with his headless neck and shoulders still upright, his lifeless hands on the disorganizer. The energy beam had instantly cauterized the wound so the weapon was not drenched in gore.

I took a moment to tuck Jaffee's neckcloth into my blouse then snatched up the disorganizer and gave it a quick inspection. As it had looked to be when it was in the guard's possession, it was not the kind that is synched only to one user. It was charged, activated, and ready to do business.

I got to one knee, still keeping my head below the level of the table, and rose up. Hellivance was advancing on Jaffee, who stood trembling. The second man through the entrance had his weapon trained on the intercessor. The underforce was coming forward, but the force-in-charge was between him and me.

That was satisfactory and was what I had envisioned. I raised the disorganizer and discharged it at the Green Circle operative who was menacing Jaffee. A disorganizer was a despicable weapon; it created an energy conduit between its emitter and its target then transmitted a pulse that causes the latter's natural energies to combine and conflict against each other. The result is that the target consumes itself in a matter of moments, while the disorganizer uses its conduit to draw off some of the released energy to recharge itself.

The man I shot became a burst of red and orange light, his flesh and bone devouring themselves like a wisp of burning paper rising on the heat from a bonfire. By the time the process was finished, I had drawn a beam on the underforce. He dropped his energy pistol and kicked it away, raising his hands above his head.

Hellivance looked at me. I saw calculation before he reached a conclusion. He put his own hands up and said, "Not just a supercargo then."

"I had a previous life," I said, standing up and keeping the weapon ready for use.

He nodded then his face became impassive. "Now what?" he said.

I kept my eye on him. And my weapon, as I spoke over my shoulder, "Jenore, you can come out."

I heard her stirring then she came out and stood at my side, careful not to crowd me. I said, "Yalum?" and saw at the edge of my vision where my friend stood up from where he had dropped to the ground when the shooting started.

"Get the weapons," I said while I gestured with the disorganizer for the two Green Circle operatives to move away from where the underforce's energy pistol lay. The disorganized man's weapon had been destroyed with him, its energy stores now augmenting the weapon in my hands.

Yalum moved carefully, acquiring Tophe's shocker and the fallen pistol. He relieved Hellivance of his holstered pistol then came around the table to stand beside me and Jenore, handed her the shocker.

Hellivance still wore his calculating look. He said, "You've worked it out."

I confirmed it.

"Before I did," he said, and nodded. "I'm impressed."

Yalum Erkatchian said, "I'm still trying to catch up."

I was going to tell him, but Jenore spoke first. "It's the stickpin, isn't it?" she said. "It's like the encrypted bead, the one that made you owner of a planet."

"You own a planet?" said Hellivance and I saw him add a new factor to the mathematics of his estimation of me.

"It's the money," Jenore said. She indicated Jaffee who was still in the crouch he'd fallen into when the shooting began. "He delivered the ransom to Change, but all they did was convert it into some kind of fiduciary instrument, and he left wearing it."

"Four million SDUs," said Hellivance.

"And you didn't get a share of it," I said, "as you always did with the previous ransoms. That's because the prophet here,"—my foot nudged the unconscious man under the table—"changed his mind about who he wanted to be partners with." I thought about it a moment more and said, "Probably because the Frescaria authorities offered him a better deal."

I heard Yalum give a kind of growl of comprehension. "Amnesty, and probably official and legitimate control of the territory they've been holding, this territory right here. That's why the prophet had no problem letting an armed provost officer into his secret hideaway."

Watching Hellivance, I could see this was new information, but it made sense to him.

"Odds are," I said, "the Insouciance has been exploring and has found a new lode of calcolite, which they intend to offer to any mining company that wants to mine it and pay them a royalty.

"The movement, cult, whatever you want to call it, was always a pretense, cooked up between the prophet and Green Circle. You are, after all, a notorious criminal enterprise on your home world, and no more than pure mercenaries anywhere else."

I felt stirrings at my feet and said, "Yalum, hoist him up, would you?"

The captain reached down and dragged the supposed cult leader to his unsteady feet, the shocker pressed into his side. Dazed, Shek Ran looked at the dead and the living and said a word that did not comport with the upright moral character he had pretended to possess.

"What will the mining deal net you?" I asked him.

He was reluctant to answer. I reminded him that shockers hurt quite a bit, but do no physical damage. "So we can shock you as many times as is necessary."

He grimaced then named a figure.

"And how much of each ransom was Green Circle taking? Thirty percent?"

"Forty," Ran said. "And then they started squeezing us for 'loans' and 'management fees.'"

"Because they could," I said. It made perfect sense to me.

With my free hand, I indicated Jaffee and the two false hostages. "The intercessor made good money handling the ransoms for Ambeline. When he realized that income stream had ended, he decided to arrange himself a bonus by way of a faked kidnapping. The two 'hostages' went along for their share of the fakery."

A silence fell upon the room. I was conscious of an odor of charred flesh from the decapitated corpse at my feet. I had thought on first sight that he looked more like a criminal than a religious enthusiast. I was satisfied with how things had worked out.

"I say it again," Hellivance said, "Now what?"

"We pursue our different interests," I said.

"My interest is the four million," he said.

I smiled. "Mine isn't."

I enjoyed seeing the confusion on Hellivance's face, but I didn't let him linger too long in that state. I said, "I have everything I want. A woman I love, a good friend, a space yacht, and interesting work. I have no use for four million SDUs."

"Plus," said Hellivance, "you own a planet."

"It's not that much of a planet," I said.

He was confused again. "So what do you propose?"

"Cover them, please, Yalum," I said. I reached into the collar vent of my upper garment and withdrew the neckcloth with its stickpin. I put the cloth on the table and sorted through it to find the item. I now took a close look at the round bead and saw the encryption pattern incised into its surface.

Then I poked it through the cloth of my sleeve, just below the shoulder, with Hellivance watching me intently. I said, "I have a contract to deliver these three passengers back to Novo Bantry. I always fulfill a contract."

"The funds," Hellivance said, through clenched teeth.

"I have no interest in them. Here is what we will do."

I explained it to him. I had to do so twice because he did not believe I would leave him the encrypted bead.

Then we went out, single file; Jaffee, Bolderchan, and Dremor first, with Jenore covering them with the energy pistol; then Yalum and the bogus prophet; finally, Hellivance and his underforce. I came behind with the disorganizer.

A Green Circle aircar hovered nearby, at ground level. Its operator moved to climb out, but Hellivance signaled him to remain where he was.

My crewmates and our three passengers boarded *Peregrinator*. I escorted the force-in-charge and his underforce to the front hatch. Etz Ran backed away, looking as if he would run, but the Green Circle in the air car wagged a warning finger at him.

I handed Hellivance the disorganizer, saying "I've never liked these things."

Despite my double explanation, he was surprised to receive the weapon.

Touching the stickpin in my sleeve, I reminded him, "If you discharge it at me," I said, "four million SDUs become dissociated atoms."

His brow still clouded in disbelief, he handed the disorganizer to his underforce and said, "Deactivate it."

"Back away a little," I said then stepped into the hatch. I plucked the stickpin from my sleeve, and told the integrator to close up and prepare to launch.

"What about the warrant?" it said. "I am still under the authority of the senior scrutineer."

"She is lying inside the cave, in two pieces. We may consider her authority lapsed."

When the hatch had slid almost shut, I tossed the bead through the gap, toward Hellivance. He grabbed for it, caught it, and gave me a look that said he still did not believe what I had done.

The hatch sealed itself. I had already told the integrator, "Take us up." I felt the deck press against my feet.

"YOU HAD no right to take my property," Sisi Jaffee said to me. We were in the dining salon. Yalum Erkatchian had suggested that we all needed a beaker of something stronger than punge. I didn't feel the need, but I recognized that the others did.

"They were Green Circle," I said. "They would have sliced pieces off you until you gave it up. Then they would have killed you."

Ezek Bolderchan had the look of a man who can't believe he's just heard such rank idiocy. Parse Dremor set down his empty glass and said, "You risked a lot to save us, after we got you into deadly peril. Why?"

I said, "I have a contract to fulfill." When he gave me a look of consternation, I explained, "Where I come from, contracts are sacred. They are the foundation of civilized order."

I heard a barely suppressed snort from the woman I loved, but ignored it and finished the corollary to my statement. "My contract is with Ambeline. I am still making up my mind about whether I have an obligation to tell them the details of your fraud."

Jenore said, "We have to. If they found out about it later, they could have us prosecuted for complicity."

"Fair point," I said. "Besides, we might get future work from them."

"How did you work it out?" Jaffee said.

I told him. My analysis was that there never had been a popular movement called the Insouciance. Shek Ran, the so-called Diffident Prophet, was almost certainly a Green Circle plant who had set up the kidnapping racket with the gang's connivance. They had committed the crimes and split the proceeds.

Then Ran had discovered the calcolite deposit in the ungoverned territory where he hid out, pretending to be leader of a militant cult. Seeing the prospect of a luxurious retirement, he had reached out to the Frescaria authorities and sifted through the contacts until he found a corrupt provostwoman, Vonnez Tophe. Protected from Green Circle reprisals by Frescaria's constabulary, he would have slid over to a profitable legitimacy.

And then Jaffee and his two fakers had spoiled it all.

Now Jaffee sat and considered his future. After a while he sighed and said, "What were the chances?"

"To me," I said, "the situation was classically obvious. You all attempted to maximize your rewards, in pursuit of your own particular interests. Where I come from, it's what everyone does. It's normal human nature."

Jenore's brows drew down and she opened her mouth to say something. Then she closed it without speaking, held out her glass toward Erkatchian.

"Pour me another," she said.

Three

We had lifted off from the main spaceport at Indoberia, on the Grand Foundational Domain of Novo Bantry, and the in-space drive had activated. I went down the corridor to the second-class cabins and knocked on a door for admittance. After a short delay, it opened.

Looking out at me was a lean man of average height and build who nonetheless projected an air of confident strength. "Yes?" he said.

I introduced myself and said, "You have brought a portable integrator aboard."

He confirmed that with a nod and another, "Yes."

"Custom assembled?"

Another affirmation.

I said, "Did you happen to acquire the components for the device through Kopje Outfitters, on Bullilang Street in Indoberia?"

"I did."

I then told him that some of the components of the yacht

on which he had booked passage, *Peregrinator*, had been purchased at the same chandlery. "We found, on a recent charter, that our integrator had been overwhelmed by a device that was functioning under the orders of Green Circle, a criminal organization from Old Earth that also hired out as mercenary regulators for private interests on many of the Ten Thousand Worlds."

"I am familiar with Green Circle," he said.

"If by 'familiar' you mean affiliated with them," I said, "we will forthwith return to Indoberia and you will leave the ship. The cost of your passage will be refunded."

"I am not affiliated with them," he said. "We occupy different ends of the moral spectrum."

"I see," I said. "Then why is your integrator seeking to suborn the ship's?"

I saw him take time to consider his reply then he said, "'Suborn' might be too strong a word. In my profession, I need to understand the . . . ambience that surrounds me, especially when I am traveling."

"According to your identity documents, you are a commerciant, representing a manufacturing concern with operations in several locations on Novo Bantry."

He showed me an apologetic face. "That is not entirely true," he said.

I said, "How much of it is true? Bear in mind that one more falsehood will see us return to Indoberia."

"Forthwith?" he said.

"Forthwith, and then some," I said.

He opened the door wider. "Please step inside."

I did so. He closed the door and I took a careful look at him, using the augmented abilities that were built into me when I was designed as a template for a race of combat soldiers. I saw none of the telltale signs that would precede a physical attack. Indeed, he sat upon the sleeping platform and rested his palms on his thighs.

"I am a confidential operative," he said. "An 'op,' as they say. I am going out on an assignment that requires me to arrive without the persons I am to investigate becoming aware of my arrival."

"Can you prove it?" I said.

"If I may open my valise." He gestured toward a scuffed item of luggage on a shelf at the end of the sleeping platform.

Again, I saw no indications of the tension that would grip a normal person who was about to produce, and possibly use, a weapon. "Go ahead," I said.

He reached, opened the case, and withdrew a small folder, which he handed to me. I opened it and saw an official-looking identity card that identified the holder as one Erm Kaslo, licensed confidential operative. Folded and placed behind the ID was a sheet of paper. I withdrew and unfolded it, and found it to be a letter on the official stationery of the Indoberia Provost's Department asking that Kaslo be afforded "the cooperation, and whatever assistance was possible," of any constabulary he encountered in his travels. It was signed by a Sub-Inspector Fourna Houdibras.

I returned the materials to him. "May I enquire as to what manner of assignment you are engaged in?" I said. "Specifically, if it portends any danger to the crew and other passengers?"

He signaled such was not to be expected. "A commercial fraud," he said, "that once uncovered and documented will be prosecuted by the authorities on Indoberia. Such cases are my usual stock in trade."

"I see," I said. I made a decision. "I will report the information to the captain and the steward, but make no mention to the other passengers. And you will instruct your assistant not to interfere with the ship's integrator."

"Agreed," he said. He offered his hand, as they do on Novo Bantry, and I accepted his brief clasp. I noted that his grip was unusually strong.

CARGO CAN SOMETIMES BE SHIFTED by the constant vibration of the in-space drive, so I made one of my regular inspections of the cargo bay. *Peregrinator* was not designed as a freight hauler, but was built to the specifications of Lord Vullamir, an Old Earth aristocrat. He liked to take his peers, and all their servants, on extended jaunts; those often required carrying with them furnishings and other impedimenta of the quality to which they were accustomed. Hence a compartment had been established in the yacht's aft section. Since acquiring the yacht, we had enlarged the cargo space, converting a part of the vessel that used to be cabins for the aristocrats' many servants.

Under Yalum Erkatchian's captaincy, we did not carry the kinds of cargo that were the stock in trade of bulk freighters. We tended to transport delicate and valuable items, albeit at premium rates, for shippers and receivers who did not want to risk their precious items being mixed in with heavy machinery or crates of stoneware.

On this voyage, we were carrying some fine crystal table settings ordered by a grandee who lived on an island on the planet Shannery, well down The Spray. We also had some artworks—carvings of shaywood and tapestries woven from the fibers of gossamer trees—both of which materials only occurred on Novo Bantry. These were bound for Ikkibal, the Grand Foundational Domain of which Shannery was a secondary world.

Our passengers included one Imlach Chakrabart, a steward to the Shannery dominee, whose name and title Chakrabart would not divulge. I imagined the aristocrat must be both extremely wealthy and rigorously exacting in his tastes, if he would bear the cost of sending a servant all this way just for glasses, bowls, and plates—not to mention the exorbitant price of the goods themselves. The shipment also included a gross of small silver pots with tight-fitting lids.

We had two other passengers, Ramboam Itz and Tooley Frobasheer, who had identified themselves as scholars of comparative mythology, on a sabbatical. They were traveling to various worlds to gather insights and fresh perspectives on the evolution of the ancient fable of Farouche and Goladry. They would disembark at Ikkibal.

The passage through normal space to the whimsy that would hurl us through the Seventh Plane and bring us out a few hours from Ikkibal took two days. It was an uneventful cruise. Jenore, Yalum, and I ate with the passengers in the dining salon, where the conversation was of the kind that can happen when individuals with differing personalities and interests are randomly thrown together.

At the first meal, Jenore sought to draw them out. The servant, Chakrabart, appeared to take her queries as an attempt to identify his master, and closed his mouth except to eat. From then on, he took his meals in his cabin.

Erm Kaslo also had little to say, and resorted to gener-
alities and clichés. That left the two students of mythology.
My experience of academics is that they need little encour-
agement to bless the world with their accumulated learning, but Itz and Frobasheer failed to live up to the
stereotype. Instead, they asked questions of us; where had
our yacht traveled to? Had we encountered any odd
worlds? What was the farthest down The Spray we had
voyaged?

Yalum answered from his vast experience as captain of
Peregrinator when it belonged to Lord Vullamir and, before
that, as an officer and able spacer on liners and freighters.
The scholars listened, but did not seem to absorb much of
my friend's yarns, though they kept asking for fresh
citations.

At the end of the second day's travel, we entered the
whimsy. As always, we made sure that our passengers took
the melange of medications that suppressed consciousness
during the interplanar passage. We did not want to come
out into normal space to find anyone had gone mad from the
sensory onslaught of irreality in the Seventh Plane.

I was shaking off the after-effects of the dulling of my
cerebrum, drinking a mug of restorative punge in the cabin
Jenore and I shared, when the ship's integrator addressed
me.

"During the passage through the oddity,"—integrators
had a different experience of interplanar travel than
humans, and considered the strangeness of the other Plane
to be silly nonsense—"another attempt was made to insinuate into my systems."

I frowned and suppressed a flare of anger; even I am
vulnerable to overweening emotions while the whimsy

medications are evaporating from my neural pathways. I finished my punge and went to see Erm Kaslo.

He looked to be faster at recovering than I, appearing bright and alert as he opened the door to my knock.

I contained my anger, saying, when the door was closed, "We had an agreement. No more interference with the ship's systems."

"I have kept to it," he said. I noticed that his response betrayed not a hint of ire, and reminded myself that I was dealing with a well-disciplined mind.

He told his valise, "Did you detect any attempts to suborn the ship during our passage through the whimsy?"

I saw him cock his head to a reply that only he could hear then he said, "Inform the supercargo, but quietly."

I heard a modulated voice as if someone was speaking softly from close by my ear, "Midway through the oddity, a device activated itself. It located the ship's integrator and assessed its defenses."

"Did it succeed in penetrating them?" I said.

"No."

"Where is this device?" Kaslo said.

"In the cargo hold."

"Is it active now?"

"No," said the integrator in the valise, "when it had no success with a surreptitious entry, it deactivated."

The op looked at me. "This is not my case, but to interfere with a ship's integrator while transiting a whimsy is an egregious folly. We might all now be dead, or worse. I assume you will investigate, and I will be glad to lend any assistance I can."

∾

THE OTHER PASSENGERS had not yet stirred from their quarters as Kaslo and I made our way to the cargo hold. I had the ship open the hatch and seal it behind us. The op then surveyed the cargo, stacked behind its restraints. I saw nothing untoward, but he went to where the two mythologists' trunks were stacked, one atop the other. He produced from a pocket a device about the size of his palm and extended fingers.

"This," he said, "is the core of a high-functioning integrator, with certain additions and embellishments of my own design."

He passed it over the sides of the trunks, and I again saw the look that said he was privately receiving a report. "Tell the officer," he said.

Another voice spoke in my ear, "The trunk contains several instruments. Of interest are surveillance devices, quite sophisticated and powerful at close range. One has been active recently."

"Can you penetrate their defenses?" Kaslo said.

"Possibly, but only by brute force. They are arranged as defenses-in-depth. I could not break through without their being aware of the intrusion."

"Make no attempt," Kaslo said.

His hand-held integrator now volunteered an added item. "There are also several weapons in the top trunk, including a high-grade disorganizer, cloaked in an energy sheath that disguises its nature. Novo Bantry law requires that such weapons cannot be taken onto a space ship without the consent of the captain."

"No such consent was sought or given," I said.

Kaslo gave me a considering look. "And who smuggles a disorganizer onto a spacecraft?"

"Criminals," I said.

Kaslo's eyes narrowed in thought. "You said you had a recent encounter with Green Circle?" When I nodded, he said, "I believe you're about to have another one."

KASLO and I met with Yalum and Jenore, and reported our findings. The captain spoke to the ship and said, "As soon as we are in range, notify the spaceport on Ikkibal that we suspect we are carrying Green Circle operatives with heavy weaponry. Request assistance when we dock."

Kaslo asked, "Unless you can transmit that message with maximum encryption, it might be better to keep quiet. We don't want our mythologists to be aware that we know their identities to be the most mythological thing about them."

"All right," said Yalum. "Ship, cancel that order." To Kaslo he said, "You're proposing we handle this ourselves?"

"I think we should, if we can," the op said. He looked a question at me.

I said, "We can."

We discussed our options. Kaslo had some suggestions. At his behest, I instructed the ship's integrator to let him examine it. He engaged his integrator core again and, after a brief, silent conversation between the devices, it reported that the attempt to insinuate a probe into *Peregrinator*'s device appeared to have been aimed at its record of coordinates to which the yacht had traveled.

"And we are certain the effort was without success?" I said.

"Yes."

The picture was becoming clear to me. I gave Kaslo the

piece of information he was missing, telling him that I was the owner of a small planet, far down The Spray and hidden from view behind a cloud of hydrogen gas. As part of an effort to extricate my crewmates and me from a dangerous situation, I had told this information to a senior officer of Green Circle.

"A private world," the op said, followed by a soft grunt of understanding. "Yes, Green Circle would have several uses for that, and the officer who won it for them would be well rewarded."

While he had been thinking, so had I. "I think I know what they intend, once we arrive at Ikkibal."

IKKIBAL WAS A GRAND FOUNDATIONAL DOMAIN, a mellow world, lit by a yellow star named Op. It had been settled in the second great effloration, when humankind went beyond the midpoint of the distance between Old Earth and the wispy trails of stars that marked the end of The Spray and the beginning of the Deep Dark.

Its first settlers had been determined city builders; they created eight great metropolises along the shores of their new world's one vast continent, and a ninth upon the mountain-ringed plateau that occupied its desert interior. Then the ages had rolled by, and the dominant culture on Ikkibal had developed rigid stratifications. Social rank now overruled all other concerns. In consequence, many of the original settlers' descendants had taken themselves away to four secondary worlds and built societies more to their comfort.

Over time, seven of the coastal cities had been abandoned, their towers and seawalls battered and undermined by storms and surges. Now only New Kutt and Razham were inhabited, the former an arc of white walls and red-tiled roofs around the landward side of an extinct caldera that shaped Five Reef Bay, the latter's pale blue spires rising into the thin, cold air of the Central Uplands. At Razham lay Ikkibal's main spaceport, the New Kuttians being even less interested than the Razhamans in whatever might come from offworld.

The port was divided into sections; one for liners, two for freighters, and a small terminal for private craft and small charters like our own. Services were minimal, and that included the deploying of port police. None were visible as we touched down and awaited official attention, which eventually arrived in the form of an arbiger in a brown uniform who struck the forward hatch with a clipboard and said, "Open."

I had been briefed by the ship's integrator on the cultural dynamics of the Razhamans and knew that rank was of prime importance to them. Every person knew his or her exact status and, more important, that of every other person they encountered. So I was prepared to answer when the first word out of the official's mouth was, "Your rank?"

"When I am on my home world," I said, "I am a duke."

That was technically true, if my home world was Forlor, the place where I was decanted from a vat before being carried off to the gaming world of Thrais. I no longer had a connection to Thrais and was essentially a homeless drifter. *Peregrinator* was my true home and my sole allegiance was to Jenore Mordene and Yalum Erkatchian. But it was better, at this moment, to be a duke.

"A duke?" said the arbiger. "And what is your home

world?"

"Forlor."

The official's brows curdled. "Never heard of it. Where is it?"

"Past Gowdie's Last Reach." I had named the world farthest down The Spray, past which lay the Back of Beyond, and then the Deep Dark.

The arbiger's face had darkened. "It is not a good idea to make mock of an officer of the Razham Corporality. You may find yourself and your ship impounded. I can have the examiners here in no time at all."

"I assure you I am the Duke of Forlor," I said. "The ship's integrator will so attest."

The official's head drew back and I was subjected to a piercing glare. Then I saw doubt and reconsideration. The man said, "How long will you be onworld?"

"Just long enough to discharge two passengers and embark two others."

After the briefest of pauses for thought, the arbiger said, "Please show me the manifest," adding after a moment, "Your Grace."

I did so. A cursory inspection followed, followed by the application of a seal. "When do you expect your new passengers?"

"Quite soon," I said. Indeed, as soon as we were no longer in the presence of officialdom, though I kept that to myself.

I had the impression that the arbiger remained conflicted. He desired to explore further the question of rank, but he also wanted to be rid of an anomaly to the smooth performance of his duties. The latter motivation won out. With a curt nod, he turned on his heel and strode away.

"Right," I said to Yalum and Erm Kaslo, behind me in the corridor. "Let's get to it."

THE TRUNKS WERE HEAVY. I accompanied Ramboam Itz and Tooley Frobasheer—though I doubt those were their true names—to the cargo bay and attached come-alongs to their luggage. The gravity obviators activated, and they pulled their trunks over to the cargo hatch and out onto the hard surface of the dock. They had told me they expected to be collected by a utility vehicle, so I detached the come-alongs, bid them goodbye, and left them.

They stood beside their luggage and watched me go. I touched the communicator in my ear and said, "Any sign of the other two?"

"Not yet," Erkatchian's voice came to me. Then, "Wait. Motion up the way." A pause. "Two men, and they look the part."

"All right," I said.

Erm Kaslo said, "As soon as they open the trunk."

"Agreed."

Erkatchian stepped out of the forward hatch, unset one of the lumens that served as running lights, and made as if to examine it. Erm Kaslo appeared in the hatch and watched him, giving the impression of a bored man who has nothing else to relieve his tedium.

The new arrivals, both of them hard and compact-looking, came down the dock at a leisurely pace. Each carried hand luggage. They ignored Itz and Frobasheer who returned the disregard.

I stopped at the open cargo hatch and affected to

examine its clasps, moving one back and forward. Out of sight of the people on the dock, Jenore came across the cargo bay, holding two shockers. She handed one to me.

"Ship," I said, "report."

The voice in my ear said, "The new passengers are almost level with Itz and Frobasheer. Now they are passing them. Frobasheer is opening the trunk that has the disorganizer."

"Now!" I said.

I turned with the shocker as Jenore stepped onto the dock. Yalum spun around at the same time, and Kaslo stepped out of the hatch, both of them producing their weapons. The disorganizer was just coming into view from behind the raised lid of Frobasheer's trunk. The two new arrivals were reaching into their valises.

None of us spoke or paused. We shot all four of them with our shockers. They toppled, unconscious, and the four of us seized holdfasts from where we had laid them in the corridor behind the forward hatch and restrained the Green Circle operatives.

"Let's get them inside," Yalum said. We did, carrying them in two separate trips down to the first-class cabins, the largest of which was spacious enough to hold them all. We laid two on the sleeping platforms and two on the floor. As we deposited the final comatose thug, Imlach Chakrabart appeared in the doorway, his face a mask of shock that quickly turned to fear.

"Tell him," I said to Jenore.

She did so succinctly. "Ser Chakrabart, these are the pirates, not us. You are safe."

She followed with a smile, that probably did more to reassure him than her words. Jenore had a powerful smile.

We brought in their luggage. The valises held shockers and beam pistols. The disorganizer was of the kind that will operate only for one user, identified by a handprint on its forward grip. When we were back out in space, I would jettison it through the forward hatch.

Kaslo retrieved his valise from his cabin and said, "I must get on with my work." He looked at the four prisoners. "Be careful with them. They are full of tricks."

WE IMMEDIATELY LIFTED off and set course for Shannery. A secondary of Ikkibal, it was a short passage through normal space then a whimsy, and finally another short trip to the rural planet. As we approached the whimsy, I went to see our four captives. They were awake, the holdfasts still confining their arms behind them, sitting two each on the sleeping platforms.

I let them see the shocker before I opened the door all the way. "Nobody moves, nobody gets hurt." I saw four pairs of eyes studying me, evaluating and I said, "I am not a standard-issue human being. My synapses are enhanced, my muscle fibers denser. I can easily shock all of you before one of you can reach me, even with a kick."

They exchanged glances and I saw the one who had called himself Itz, give a small shake of his head. I addressed him.

"Let us dispense with the subterfuge. You are Green Circle. You attempted to suborn the ship's integrator to discover the location of my planet. You failed. Your next step would have been to capture us and the ship then force us, probably through torture, to take you there."

Itz's face went still. The eyes that regarded me were as dead as stones.

I continued, "And then you would have murdered us."

Again, no response.

I spoke again. "I point out to you that on my private world, there is no law other than my will. If I decide to kill you by disgusting methods, there is no one to restrain me."

I let that sink in. After a long moment, I said, "And my world is where we are going as soon as we have delivered our other passenger and his goods to Shannery."

"You can't take us there against our will," Itz said. "You have to turn us over to the first constabulary you meet. Anything else is kidnapping."

I made a little confirmatory noise in my throat. "I'll leave you to savor the irony," I said. Then I told them that the integrator would shortly dispense the anti-madness medications from the headboards of the sleeping platforms.

"We'll want you in your right minds and ready to answer questions when we get to my world."

SHANNERY WAS A BUCOLIC PLANET, largely populated by those former residents of Ikkibal who were not comfortable with the Grand Foundational Domain's obsession with rank and precedence. There was only one large city, but the sole spaceport sat in an otherwise rural landscape of large farms and small towns. When we were within range and contacted the port, its integrator told us that we had permission to land elsewhere; on the private estate of the person who had ordered our remaining cargo. His steward, Chakrabart, gave us the coordinates, and we set down near a rambling manse surrounded by crop fields, fenced paddocks, and a scatter of outbuildings.

"How are our involuntary passengers?" I asked the ship as were making our final descent.

"Comatose," it said. I had instructed *Peregrinator* to increase the dosage of whimsy medications, to keep our prisoners tranquil while we traveled to Shannery and off-loaded our cargo and its minder.

"Keep an eye on them," I said. I had removed the hold-fasts because too long a constraint could lead to nerve damage in the extremities. "We don't want them rambunctious."

The ship settled onto a landing pad. I saw an Itinerator IV yacht under a wall-less hangar, its paintwork adorned by a coat of arms that meant nothing to me. As the drive cut out, the ship's screen showed a hawk-faced man approaching, accompanied by a gawky boy who had a younger set of the same features, though overlaid by an expression of adolescent dreaminess.

Chakrabart the steward was anxious that his master not be required to wait, so I opened the forward hatch and let the servant step out. He began to perform the gestures that were requisite on Ikkibal when an underling encounters a dominee, but the grandee waved the courtesies away and said, "You have the goods? All in order?"

Chakrabart assured him that all was well with the cargo, which I was already bringing out through the main cargo hatch on a floating pallet. I set the crates down and gave a formal salute to the consignee.

"Rank?" he said.

"Duke," I said.

From the thunder that began to build in his face, I saw

that this was clearly not a man to play pranks on. But the steward said something I did not hear and the grandee's face showed first confusion then a lack of interest to pursue the issue.

He gestured to the crates and said, "Open them."

I handed Chakrabart a tool, and he prised up the top of the nearest container. Nestled in packing material were dozens of small silver pots, each with a matching spoon. The dominee took out one of the pots, lifted its hinged lid and examined its interior. Then he struck the lid with the little spoon, creating a musical note.

A look of satisfaction briefly supplanted his harsh expression. "Good." He gestured to Chakrabart and said, "Take them to the factory and unload. The first batch is almost ready."

The grandee rubbed his hands together in a gesture of anticipation, and I had a fleeting impression that I was seeing a crucial moment in some lengthy process leading to a finale that would have great meaning to the dominee.

The pallet's gravity obviators reduced weight but not mass, and the steward had to struggle to push the pallet up a slope toward a one-story outbuilding. His master called out to a young woman with fiery red hair who was feeding grain to hogs in a nearby pen and sent her to help Chakrabart. The hobbldehoy youth watched the pig herder with more than idle interest. Another flash of anger crossed his father's visage, and the grandee gave the boy a shove that knocked him off balance.

I realized I was seeing unfold before my eyes an element of some continuing melodrama. I also became instantly aware that my witnessing the conflict was of more than a little annoyance to the hawk-faced man. I framed a neutral expression and proffered the manifest for him to sign off on. He did so and pointedly turned his back. I recognized a dismissal, stepped back into the ship, and closed the hatches.

"Ready to lift off," I said.

Yalum's voice came from the integrator's conduit. "Here we go."

We rose into the sky and departed Shannery. Briefly, I thought about the silver pots and the story behind an Ikkibal high aristocrat's defection to rural Shannery, with its louche standards, and wondered what events we had played a very small part in.

But I had more pressing concerns. I went to put the holdfasts back on the Green Circle operatives before they could wake up.

PEREGRINATOR EXITED the whimsy to find an immense cloud of hydrogen gas stretched across the starless space. The yacht turned to its left and entered a rift in the cloud. Soon we came into an open space in which a small white star shone like hard ice, circled by a few planets. The second of these was Forlor, a small, ancient world. Its single continent took up most of the northern hemisphere, a mostly flat stretch of land surrounded by an ocean gray as lead.

The yacht lost speed and headed for a high eminence whose sheer sides had been blasted smooth by ison cannons. On its flat top, also the result of massive energy discharges, stood the single structure on the planet; a hodgepodge of domes, colonnades, towers and high-arched spans. Anything that was not black was white, and anything that was not

white was black, the contrasting colors that the original
owners, the Flagit brothers, had assigned to the pieces,
mechanical or living, with which they played their
murderous war games.

The yacht settled gently onto a wide apron at the base of
a broad staircase of alternating black and white stone. I saw
the twin towers that overlooked the landing zone, formerly
equipped with ison cannon ready to destroy uninvited visitors. Their tops had been melted by a cruiser of the
Archonate Bureau of Scrutiny sent to arrest Vullamir and
his fellow cultists before they could commit more atrocities.

I opened the yacht's forward hatch and stepped out onto
the planet of my unnatural gestation and birth. Cold, damp
air encouraged a shiver, and the wind that blew constantly
at this height chilled my face. I saw the dried blood that had
spilled from the throat of the Old Earth aristocrat,
Magratte, whom I killed with an epiniard in single combat.
Some of my own blood also spotted the flagstones. It had
been a desperate fight.

I turned back to the ship and said, "Push them out."

Erkatchian shoved the four Green Circle thugs through
the hatch, still with their arms secured by holdfasts. They
looked about them. I saw apprehension, calculation.

"Let me make your situation clear," I said. "This is the
world you sought to take from me. The building before you
is its only structure. There is no way down from this elevation except to plunge to your death on the rocks below."

I gestured to the huge doors at the top of the stairs, that
gave entry to a great, square keep whose walls were
patterned in white and black chevrons. "In there you will
find shelter from the elements." I paused. "And nothing
more. Whatever food supplies once existed have long since

rotted away. It is, however, possible to collect water, from rain or condensation, so you will not die of thirst.

"But you will starve to death, though you may extend your lives by eating each other. There are edged and pointed weapons hanging on the walls of the great hall"—I again indicated the entrance to the keep—"the last of you alive may find it preferable to fall upon a sword rather than expire from the pangs of hunger."

"You're not scaring us," Ramboam Itz said.

"I'm not seeking to scare you," I said, "only to acquaint you with the facts." I strode past them to the yacht and turned to regard them from the hatch. "I'll be back at some time. I will have questions for any of you who are still alive. It would be best if you answered them."

Itz started to say something, but I was already closing the hatch. *Peregrinator* rose into the sky, its drive creating dust devils that stung the eyes of the four men watching us leave.

WE WERE SCHEDULED to pick up another cargo of silver pots and spoons for Shannery, though not for another twenty days. But with Green Circle taking an interest in us, it would not have been wise to return to any of our familiar haunts. Instead, I consulted *Hobey's Compleat Guide to the Minor and Disregarded Planets* and, after some discussion with my crewmates, we traveled to Olderon, a seldom-visited world down near the end of The Spray. Here we put up at a rustic hotel built around a string of thermal pools and relaxed.

The food was simple but good, the locally brewed ale

tangy and strong, the sausages spiced in novel ways, and the beds comfortable. Jenore and I hiked in the hills that rose above the inn and played an interesting version of shuffle-thrust that employed springs and rebounders to good effect. Yalum took his ease in the hot pools and made the acquaintance of a pair of youngish widows who had come to the resort to mark their having been released from the mourning period traditional on Olderon. After that, he had no time for shuffle-thrust, and probably would have lacked the energy, even if the time were available.

Eventually, after eight days had passed, I said, "We should go back now, and see what we find."

A day later, we set down once more on the apron outside the keep on Forlor. The ship's percepts told us that all four of the thugs were still alive, though each had chosen a room in the edifice that had but a single entrance.

"Also," the integrator said, "they have armed themselves with thrusting weapons."

"As expected," I said. I proposed that Yalum and I go out and meet with them, while Jenore kept the ship secure and stood ready with its ison cannon, to cover us if we had to beat a retreat.

But it turned out that the Green Circle men were not much of a threat. At the doors of the keep, I called in to them to come out, weaponless, and I would give them ship's bread. Out tottered four gaunt figures, each moving slowly, and eying each other with newly acquired suspicion.

I let them see the bag of bread, but also the beam pistol in my hand. I told them, "First a few questions."

Ramboam Itz retained some vestiges of his earlier intransigence, but Tooley Frobasheer had lost a substantial portion of his former bulk. The skin under his jaw shook loosely as he nodded his acceptance of the terms, his gaze never leaving the bag of food.

"It was Gustus Hellivance who set you on us?" I said.

"Yes," said Frobasheer. When I waited with apparent anticipation of hearing more, he said, "He was demoted after the business on Frescaria. The four million SDUs did not make up for his having let go three persons who had had their way with Green Circle. He pined for the perquisites of his former rank."

"And delivering a private world to the organization would have made him whole again?" I said.

Frobasheer nodded. I could see that he was drooling as he fixed his gaze on the ship's bread.

"Where is he now?

Itz decided to join the conversation. "He was on Ikkibal when we were there. Where he is now is . . ." He spread his hands.

"Have you a way of contacting him?"

The question touched a nerve. All four exchanged looks with each other, none of them eager to divulge a Green Circle secret.

I said, "Don't tell me how, just if."

"Yes," said Frobasheer. "We leave a message in the classified advertisements of a certain publication."

"Fine," I said. "Here is what you will do."

WE TOOK them back to Shannery, which offered wide stretches of open country, the terrain not too difficult to traverse. We set them loose on a well watered plain where

cattle were left to their own devices while they fattened on
ample grass.

"Go south for two or three days, depending on how fast
you walk, and you will meet a road," I said. "Follow that
east and you will come to Horn Creek, a small town. From
there, you can make contact with your employers."

Again, I saw an exchange of weighted looks. Yalum said,
"They might not want to do that. Green Circle does not
reward failure."

"Fine," I said. "Shannery is an informal world. Give
yourselves new names and histories. You can always find
work. Keep out of trouble and you will live a long life."

We left them provisions and canteens. "Give us boots,"
Itz said. "We are not well shod for an odyssey."

"We have no boots to give you," I said. "Next time you
attempt a kidnap, plan for all eventualities."

WE ARRIVED at Ikkibal and passed through the more
stringent formalities for admission to a world that was much
more enamored of formalities and rigid procedures. *Peregrinator's* integrator determined that the publication that
unknowingly served as a conduit for Green Circle messages
had a bureau in Razham. I went to its office in the guise of a
commerciant, paid a small fee, and arranged for the coded
advertisement to run in the next two issues.

The message told the recipient where and when Itz and
Frobasheer would be waiting for a rendezvous, and included
a password that would tell Hellivance it was a legitimate—if
that was an appropriate word—Green Circle communication.

After careful discussion and consultation of maps, we had chosen a location where we could not be come upon unawares; a wooded stretch of country a short flight out of Razham. There was nowhere large enough to set *Peregrinator* down, but there were small clearings. We unshipped the yacht's utilitarian carryall and left the ship at the spaceport.

We landed in an open space, activated the carryall's beacon, and went into the woods to hide ourselves among the trees. Our plan was a duplicate of the ambush of the four operatives; when Hellivance and his accomplices arrived, we would shock them, load them into the vehicle, and take them back to *Peregrinator*. A day later, we would land at Forlor again for another interrogation.

Then we would decide what to do with the captives. My inclination was to deal with them in the same manner they intended for us. I might have to convince Yalum and Jenore that cold-blooded brutality was the best option. If I couldn't sway them, I thought I might well act unilaterally.

But that was not how the business went. We were scarcely settled in our hiding place, our weapons drawn and our ears tuned to the sound of an air car's obviators, when I heard a slight sound from behind me. I spun about, bringing my shocker up, but a torrent of energy struck my torso. I felt an intense spasm of pain. Then nothing, as darkness enfolded me.

WHEN I SWAM BACK UP to light and consciousness, I found myself bound in a holdfast, seated on the ground, my back against the yacht's utility vehicle. A voice said, "This one's coming out of it."

I looked around. Jenore and Yalum, also constrained, were beside me, still senseless, their nervous systems lacking the enhancements Hallis Tharp built into mine.

Gazing down at us were Gustus Hellivance, no longer in the uniform he had worn as a mercenary police operative for the Ambeline Mining Corporation on Frescaria. Another man was with him, bearing the aspect of someone who will do anything to anyone, so long as he is paid.

"So," said the Green Circle force, "do I need to explain the situation?"

"No," I said. "You will want the coordinates to my world."

He showed me an unappetizing smile. "I would phrase it differently. I will have the coordinates. The only question is how much wear and tear you and your friends will endure before I do."

I looked away and said nothing. After a moment, Hellivance said, "Wake up the woman."

I was considering options and finding they were few and not promising. On the one hand, I did not like the idea of Hellivance and his kind treading the ground of Forlor, which was the resting place of thousands of my siblings — or one could even call them my offspring, depending on how one viewed the process of vat-birthing. I thought they would surely use the place for further atrocities.

On the other hand, I would not let my feelings allow harm to come to my beloved and my only friend.

But then came a third hand; once they had the coordinates, and had confirmed that they led to the hidden planet, they would not let us live to tell anyone what had happened. Apart from their desire to keep Forlor a secret, Hellivance would probably want revenge, and to be able to tell his superiors that he had dispatched the three people who had trespassed on Green Circle's idiosyncratic sense of honor.

I was wondering if I could work out a way to take them to the planet, and somehow overpower them there. But I realized that would not work. They would take the coordinates, go and come back to wherever they would keep us, and once they knew I had told them the truth, they would kill us.

The thug was kneeling beside Jenore, slapping her face and telling her to wake up. For the umpteenth time, I strained against the holdfast that bound my arms behind me. But, as was always the case with such semi-sentient restraints, it simply squeezed my flesh tighter until I gave up.

Jenore made a noise. I saw her blink twice then she took a deep breath.

"Here she comes," said the thug, rising to his feet.

"All right," said Hellivance, "let's get to it."

His henchman leered and said, "This one's good-looking. When we're finished, I wouldn't mind–"

I opened my mouth to speak, not knowing what I was going to say. But before I could utter a sound, I heard the *ziv* sound of an energy pistol. A fist-sized hole, charred around the edge and smoking, appeared in the center of the goon's chest. He fell dead, his eyes staring sightlessly into mine.

Hellivance spun around. At the edge of the trees stood Erm Kaslo, a beam pistol aimed at the Green Circle force. "Drop the shocker," he said, "or I'll take off the arm that's holding it."

Hellivance held out the weapon to one side and let it fall.

Kaslo gestured with the pistol. "Over there, face down

on the ground, arms spread." With swift, economical movements he trussed the Green Circle force then rapped him
sharply on the top of the skull with the butt of his pistol.

"Same rules as before," Kaslo said. "Move and I'll burn
off a piece of you."

He fished in Hellivance's pocket for the key to the holdfasts then came over and released the three of us. Jenore
scrabbled to her feet and put some distance between her and
the corpse. Yalum Erkatchian was still coming around as the
op helped him rise. I was already up. I went and put an arm
around Jenore; she was trembling.

I looked to Kaslo. "You're very good," I said.

"I know Green Circle," he said, glancing at Hellivance's
immobile form. "Once my case was settled, I decided to stay
on Ikkibal and keep an eye on this one."

"I'm glad you did."

"What happened to the four we captured?" Kaslo said.

I told him how we had set them loose in a remote part of
Shannery, after Itz gave us the coded message. His nod told
me I had confirmed something he had been thinking.

"Sometimes," he said, gesturing to the force, "these types
have implants that broadcast a signal. As soon as they come
in range of a receptor, they can be located. By the time you
arrived on this world, a warning had preceded you."

"So Hellivance knew where and when we would call for
a meeting," I said, "even before we placed the notice in the
publication."

Kaslo confirmed it. "After mooching around Razham,
suddenly he was all action. I had put a tracker on his vehicle. When he came out here, I followed."

He looked down at the man lying prone and said, "The
question is, what do we do with him?"

I didn't have to think. "Kill him," I said.

Jenore pulled away from me and gave me a look that mingled hurt with consternation. "No," she said.

"He was going to kill us," I said.

Her jaw set. "We are not him."

I looked to Erkatchian, saw conflict in his expression. I didn't see it resolve. He swore and looked down at his feet, which meant he was looking at the dead thug. That made him swear again.

"We've killed one of theirs," I said. "I don't know much about criminal gangs, but I do know they settle scores."

"He wasn't one of ours," came a voice from the ground. "I just hired him for the day."

We all looked down at Hellivance. Kaslo said, "You have something to say?"

"Can I get up?"

"No," said the op. "We can hear you where you are."

"I have a proposal," Hellivance said.

Nobody said anything. I looked to Kaslo and received a shrug in reply. I said, "We're listening."

The Green Circle man addressed my feet. He said that his original plan, to seize ownership of Forlor by force, had been "overly ambitious." We had been more resourceful than he had expected. It was time for a rethink.

"Keep going," I said.

He half-rolled sideways so he was looking up at me. "We could lease the planet from you, at a reasonable rate and with options for renewal."

Jenore made a scoffing sound. "You would use it for murder and worse."

Hellivance shook his head. "No, you would stipulate the allowed uses. I initially sold the concept to the Fraternity as a place where senior leaders could meet without concern for their deliberations being overheard. That has value to us." He shrugged as best he could with his arms bound behind him. "We can kill people anywhere."

"What other uses?" I said.

"Storage, especially of records, but also of valuables while their final disposition is negotiated. A refuge for our members who come to the close attention of provosts and constabularies."

I realized Hellivance had been putting more thought into the situation than I had. As a transactualist, I could see merit in his thinking. But I had an overriding concern. I turned to Kaslo.

"You know more about these people than I do. Do they honor contracts?"

He showed me an ambivalent face. "They do, but you need to have focused intently on the details. They're absolute masters of the sub-sub-clause."

I made a thinking noise. "So we would need an excellent intercessor."

Kaslo said, "A team of them."

"Do you know where to find such a team?"

"In Indoberia, I could recommend two or three firms. They would be costly, though."

I said to Hellivance, "What kind of annual payment were you contemplating?"

He named a figure. I tripled it and sent that back to him. He said, "We can settle on something between those two poles."

I spoke to Kaslo. "Then we can afford the best."

"So it would seem."

THE NEGOTIATIONS WERE lengthy and detailed. Our team of intercessors uncovered several potential pitfalls in the draft agreement Green Circle's counsel proposed, and the other side rebuffed some attempts at sharp practice on our part. In the end, both sides' interests declared themselves satisfied and I signed the lease alongside a Green Circle first-force, a rank far above that of Gustus Hellivance, though the latter had been returned to his status as a force-in-charge. Moreover, he would be the force-in-charge of Forlor, with my interests watched over by the integrator the Flagit brothers had installed, its capacities enhanced and strengthened by Erm Kaslo. Hellivance clearly believed his opportunities to associate with the highest circles of Green Circle was a stairway that would let him ascend to senior echelons.

At a formal ceremony at our intercessors' offices at Indoberia, I handed over the coordinates to the hidden planet. The bearer bead that conferred ownership upon whoever held it, I kept in a secret location, and did not tell even Jenore or Yalum where it lay.

That was to protect them. Despite our intercessors' assurances, I did not trust Green Circle.

There was one further outcome, one that surprised me. As we were preparing to leave after the signing, the Green Circle first-force, a diminutive, quiet-spoken individual named Ostian Bersaglio, approached me. "We wish you to have this," he said.

I looked down at his open palm and saw that it held a brooch in the shape of a green circle carved from emerald, backed by gold.

I made no move to take it, saying, "That is not specified in the contract."

"It signifies," he said, "that you are an Honored Associate of our society."

"I have no idea what that means, nor much inclination to become one."

His face darkened. He continued to hold out the brooch. I could see him dealing with what was clearly an unexpected refusal, searching for the words to deal with it.

Erm Kaslo, who had come along to witness the contract signing, stepped into the situation. "Ser Labro comes from an unsual background. He does not understand the concept of a gift whose receipt confers no obligation on the recipient. Nor does he understand that his attitudes, which seem innocent to himself, can give grave offense to those who do not share his philosophy."

Bersaglio looked at Kaslo then back at me. His brows knitted. Kaslo said quietly to me, "Take the brooch and thank the man."

Jenore came up beside me. "It would be good for you to take it," she said. "I'll explain why later."

It was one of those moments when, faced with strong recommendations from people who opinions I respected, I overrode my instincts. I took the green circle from the first-force's hand and placed it in my pocket.

"Thank you," I said.

A great deal of tension went out of the room. Bersaglio asked me to accompany him to a corner and turn our backs on the others. I did so, and he showed me a peculiar motion of the fingers that identified members of Green Circle to each other.

"Don't show that to anyone else," he said.

I reminded myself that he represented a subculture that took such matters seriously and assured him that I would keep the gesture to myself. He nodded to the others and left.

Kaslo said, "He showed you the secret sign?" He made the same arrangement of fingers.

"I'm not allowed to tell you," I said.

"So you do have a sense of humor," the op said.

"Do I?" I said.

WE MADE two more runs to Shannery, delivering more silver pots and spoons. We discussed with Imlach Chakrabart the logistics of delivering the pots, after they were filled with some mysterious substance, to a factor on Ikkibal, but the volume was expected to rise beyond our small yacht's capacity. The work went to a larger shipping firm.

Jenore said she was just as glad to step out of that arrangement. There was something untoward—the Old Earth word she used was "hinkersome"—about whatever was going on in that little building on Shannery.

"How would that concern us?" I said. "We were only the carriers."

She gave me one of her looks. "Any transaction can have a moral dimension."

I did not argue. I knew she was unhappy about our arrangement with Green Circle. Having been in the entertainment sector on Old Earth as well as on several planets when she was a dancer in a traveling show, she had come into contact with what she called "unseemly elements." Experience had colored her judgment.

But, as we had discussed, the alternative to making a deal would probably have been our deaths. We could not have afforded to keep Erm Kaslo around to guard our interests. Besides, now that Green Circle knew we were not complete dumpchumps—another Old Earth term—they would have brought overwhelming force to bear.

"It's a good contract," I told her. "The integrator at the Flagits' house will make sure they adhere to it."

She sighed and said, "I just wish there had been another way out of it."

"On Thrais we say, 'If wishes were horses, beggars would eat.'"

A small vertical line appeared between her well shaped brows. "On Old Earth, it's 'beggars would ride.'"

That made no sense to me. Wherever beggars went, they'd still be beggars, but they were always hungry.

Still, I didn't correct her. And then we heard Yalum Erkatchian come aboard. He had been negotiating a charter to take some wealthy Indoberian indentors on a pleasure cruise to Potiphar, a Grand Foundational Domain renowned for its gastronomy.

"We got it," he said. "I'm bringing in a cleaning crew to make the ship spotless. And we'll need to stock up on first-class comestibles, vintage wines, triple-refined essences, rare savories and aromatic cheeses."

"But no horse meat," I said, which won me a puzzled look from the captain but a grunted half-laugh from Jenore.

"Let's get to it," I said. And we did.

Four

We had not seen Erm Kaslo for quite some time when he arrived at the *Pereginator*'s berth at the Indoberia space port. He came along the walkway like a man who has something important to do, and not much time to do it.

Yalum had taken a few days' leave, wanting to try the hot springs at Therme. We had nobody booked for quite a while, and Jenore and I were hauling out the detritus of a charter to New Saskatchewan; we had carried a dozen revelers to the Mudwine Festival, from which they returned in elevated spirits. They left behind a prodigious number of empty bottles that had held vintage wines and potent liquors. I was carrying a clinking bin of them to the waste-disposal hopper, when Kaslo came into view.

In lieu of a greeting, he said, "I think you'll agree that you owe me something."

In fact, I would not have agreed. Although we had had a close association, during which he had saved our lives, there had been no contract between us. On Thrais, where I was raised, his assertion would have been laughed at. But we were not on Thrais, and I had come to accept that other cultures among the Ten Thousand Worlds conducted their interpersonal relations by less exacting standards.

Besides, Jenore said, "You kept our porridge from burning on Ikkibal. How can we help you?"

Kaslo indicated the open hatch. "Better inside," he said. "It won't be long before they're shadowing me."

"Who?"

He looked back the way he'd come. "The Commune Provost's Department."

We went on board and closed the hatch. I told the ship to watch for anyone paying undue attention. Then we went to the forward salon, cleared away a few last items from the party, and sat around one of the gaming tables.

Jenore said, "What's happened?"

KASLO TOLD us he had wound up an investigation sooner than expected, giving him a few days with nothing much to do. He decided he would go to the Provost's headquarters and surprise the woman who had become his particular friend, Sub-Inspector Fourna Houdibras, and invite her to join him for the midday meal at a restaurant in Froberge Square. They had dined there together before and enjoyed the ambiance as well as the food and each other's company.

But when he approached her office door, knocked perfunctorily, and stepped inside, he found not Houdibras but a grim-visaged man of middle years with a corded neck and thinning hair, who was examining the possessions of the sub-inspector, arrayed on the desktop. This character regarded Kaslo with irritation and demanded to know the meaning of his unannounced entry, adding, "I said I was not to be disturbed!" the man said.

"Not to me, you didn't," was Kaslo's response. Then he inquired as to the whereabouts of Fourna Houdibras.

Instead of an answer he got two questions by instant return. "Who are you?" said the man. "And what's your connection to Houdibras?"

Kaslo answered the first by presenting the disc that contained his bona fides as a confidential op, saw the other man examine it and sneer. He ignored the second query, and said, "Your turn."

"Supervising-Inspector Greger Ollomie," said the man.

He was not part of the Indoberia Provost's Department, Kaslo knew. He was acquainted with all of the senior commissioned and noncommissioned officers and many of the rank and file. Besides, the uniform was wrong. This man must have been brought in from outside of headquarters, probably from one of the smaller cities out in the territories —his accent was not of Indoberia. And that could mean only one thing.

"She's in trouble," Kaslo said. It was not a question.

"How is that any of your business?" Ollomie said.

"We are friends. Sometimes I have been able to assist her investigations." When that drew an even deeper frown, Kaslo understood that this Ollomie was now seeing him as some kind of informer with connections to the criminal half-world of Indoberia Commune.

"Do you not have confidential ops where you come from?" I said. "We play a major role in criminal and civil proceedings here in Indoberia."

Kaslo was clearly telling the out-of-town police officer

things the man didn't want to hear, but he continued, "If Fourna is in difficulties, she may wish to engage me in my professional capacity."

Ollomie leaned back in Houdibras's chair and assumed the expression that police agents wear when confronted by deep naiveté. "You'd have to find her first."

Kaslo said nothing. The inspector couldn't resist a final taunt. "She's over the horizon," he said. "Nobody knows where."

At that moment, the door opened and a full-fleshed woman with three rows of braid on her right sleeve stepped in. Kaslo saw her evaluate the situation in less time than it took her to shut the door behind her.

"Kaslo," she said, "what are you doing here?"

"I came to invite Sub-Inspector Houdibras to lunch," the op said, adding, "Commissioner."

"She's gone."

"So I gather." Kaslo glanced at Ollomie. "And I'm getting the impression she's suspected of some malfeasance."

Ollomie answered before the senior officer could. "That's none of your business!"

The Commissioner held up a pacifying hand. "We don't know the full situation," she said. "She could be the victim of foul play." She thought for a moment then said, "I'll tell you what we know. If you can be of any help, it would be appreciated."

That generated a deep sourness in Ollomie's expression. Kaslo didn't care.

～

IN *PEREGRINATOR'S* SALON, Kaslo told us the trouble had started with a routine audit of senior officers' accounts at the fiduciary pool, the kind of examination carried out at irregular intervals by one of the Departmental integrator's subsystems. Houdibras's books were in order, as always, but there was a note appended to her general ledger.

It was from an anonymous source and it said she had a secure box at the fiduciary pool's central branch.

"Did she?" Jenore asked.

"I would have said, no, that it was an error. But then Greger Ollomie appeared on the scene, on leave from his own force while visiting a relative in Indoberia. As a senior officer from another jurisdiction, he was just what was needed to conduct an investigation. He procured a warrant and went to the pool and secured the box. It contained more than fifty thousand Sovereign Debt Units in credit chips. He said some of them had Fourna's gene plasm on them."

"Hmm," I said. "Not good."

"It got worse," said Kaslo. "Some of the other chips had the plasm of Wan Didderedge."

He needed to explain that to Jenore and me. Indoberia, known as the City of Crystals, was an opulent society, whose massive wealth, built up over millennia, did not admit of poverty or want. Crime, when it occurred, was usually a consequence of competition for prestige, or, less frequently, of mental aberration. But there were some few who fit the definition of professional criminal, and Wan Didderedge was a leading light of that category.

He was a squeezer, which meant he dealt in information, especially in embarrassing information about upper-tier personages that could be sold to rivals in the eternal struggle for precedence and reputation. Sometimes, he sold the information back to its subject. Sometimes he sold it first to the subject and then to that person's social nemesis. He was not well loved.

More than a year ago, Fourna Houdibras had led an investigation into one of the extortionist's ploys. Evidence had accumulated but there was never quite enough to lay a case before the Procurator. The target of Didderedge's blackmail would have had to testify and she would not, for fear the embarrassing truth would come out before the tribunal and be broadcast to the world at large.

"So he slithered away again," Kaslo said, "though without the profit he'd thought to take." His lean face took on a grim cast. "And now someone is attempting to make it look as if my friend did not perform her work with due diligence, because Didderedge paid her to wobble the case."

As supercargo on a chartered yacht, I did not engage with this kind of business, but it seemed to me that the obvious culprit, if Houdibras was indeed innocent, was this Didderedge. "She caused him to scurry and fret. It would have been a blow to his self-esteem, and I have learned that Indoberians are sensitive to such things."

"Fifty thousand SDUs is a high price to pay for injured pride," Jenore said, "even for an Indoberian."

"True," said Kaslo, "but not for insurance that he will remain free to operate. She almost had him last time. Next time, she might get a tighter pinch on his ear. He would pay to avoid that."

"Besides that," I said, "she has fled. A sign of guilt."

"We don't know if she has fled," Kaslo said. "That was the Provost's inference. It has not been tested."

"What do you wish us to do?" Jenore said.

Kaslo looked from her to me. "I cannot investigate

without the permission of the Provost, and I am not likely to get it. They are going to be keeping an eye on me. Fortunately, when I went to meet with Fourna, I was coming direct from the completion of a case and was still wearing this."

He unfastened and opened his upper garment. Beneath it, he was wearing a tight-fitting vest with several pockets and compartments. I recognized one as showing the percept of a self-aiming weapon. Other bulges were less identifiable.

"This contains my working tools," he said, "including the core of a sophisticated integrator."

"I remember it," I said. It had tried to suborn *Pereginator*'s device, which was refined enough to identify and report the probe.

He slipped off the sleeveless garment and passed it to me. "It has hidden me from routine observation as I made my way here, but soon the provosts will organize proper surveillance. There will be nothing I can do."

I looked askance at the vest. "It looks a little small," I said. I was larger than Kaslo.

"Then it will fit me," said Jenore, reaching for it.

I moved it out of reach. "I see an adjustable gusset in back. I can make it fit."

"While you are wearing it," Kaslo said, "I will be able to communicate with you by channels I can insulate from Ollomie and his crew. You can be my proxy, to find Fourna and make sure she is all right."

"Suppose she doesn't want to be found?" I said. "As in, suppose Ollomie's suspicions are valid?"

Kaslo sighed. "That would be an unwelcome conclusion, but a conclusion all the same."

KASLO HAD ALREADY TASKED his integrator to search for Didderedge. The device was quietly interrogating visual percepts in parts of the city where the squeezer was known to operate, without the integrators that controlled those sensors being aware of the interrogation. That would take some time. Meanwhile, he wanted me to go to the branch of the fiduciary pool where the box had been found and question its integrator. Jenore insisted on accompanying me.

Integrators varied widely in their sophistication, and those in the fiduciary pools were among the simplest. They kept track of debits and credits and recorded who went in and out of physical premises, but it had been proved to be unwise to give them any more sapience than those simple tasks required. The more intricate a device's mentation, the more likely it would eventually become subject to the condition known as "the vagues." A fiduciary pool integrator that grew bored and began to perform tricks with the customers' accounts could do a great deal of damage. So, the elements of pool integrators that dealt with abstruse calculations were robust and almost impossible to penetrate, while other components could be childlike in their simplicity.

A café with outdoor tables was situated only a few paces from the pool's building. Jenore and I took seats and ordered mugs of punge. I spoke quietly to Kaslo's integrator. A moment later, it said, "We're in."

Instead of placing a screen in the air before me, it caused the image to appear on the surface of my beverage, so I could give the impression of a man staring into his mug, contemplating some aspect of existence. I said, quietly,

"Show me the recording of the occasion when the secure box was hired."

Superimposed on the foam-flecked top of my punge I saw a small, empty room with a counter and two doors, the perspective seen from high up on a wall. Through one of the doors came a functionary carrying a box with a hinged lid, which he set upon the counter. Through the other door came a woman who fit the description of Fourna Houdibras. The two exchanged a few words then the pool employee produced a tablet. Houdibras said something that made the employee smile as she extended an index finger and touched its tip to the tablet's surface. The functionary then departed, leaving the box. Houdibras took from her Department-issue shoulder bag a package wrapped and sealed in paper and adhesive. She placed it in the box, locked the lid, and spoke to the integrator. A moment later, the functionary returned and picked up the box. He and Houdibras made the normal gestures of polite leave-taking and departed through the doors they had entered by.

Kaslo, wherever he was, had maintained a connection to the integrator I wore, and had been watching through one of the vest's percepts. His voice spoke in my ear. "Repeat."

We watched again. At the point where the woman touched the tablet, Kaslo said, "Close in on the finger." When the enlarged image appeared, he said, "Freeze. Intensify the resolution."

The fiduciary pool's recording system was far less capable than Kaslo's integrator's. The device now took the raw footage and refined it.

"Magnify," the op said, "to show the base of the finger at the knuckle." The image changed and he said, "There it is."

"Indeed," I said. "A sleeve?"

"A sleeve," said Kaslo.

The finger that had touched the tablet and left a print had not been naked. It had been covered in a transparent sheath of thin, fine material. Kaslo had no doubt that its tip had been micro-incised with a replica of Fourna Houdibras's fingerprint.

"If the box had already been assigned, the pool employee would have looked more closely. Instead, she distracted him while she made the impression."

"Very skillfully done," I said.

"Oh, yes," said Kaslo. "We are not dealing with an amateur." He studied the image a moment longer then said, "Now let us examine the ear."

His assistant said, "It seems an exact match, as does the jaw line."

"Seems," said Kaslo. "Wouldn't you say the jaw is a little plumper?"

"The quality of the image, and the angle —"

"I know," Kaslo said.

BACK IN *PEREGRINATOR*'S SALON, Jenore said, "That was exciting." Her face was flushed, her eyes bright. "Anything yet on Didderedge?"

I asked Kaslo's integrator and was told the quarry had not been seen in his usual haunts for more than a tennight. It added, "That usually means he has pulled off a profitable stroke and is lying low until the victim realizes that revenge cannot be taken without grievous embarrassment."

"But this situation is unusual, isn't it?" Jenore said.

I agreed. I liked seeing her so energized. To the integrator, with Kaslo listening in, I said, "Is there something else we could be doing?

Kaslo said, "He spends a lot of his time in the Shade." Jenore and I were not familiar with the term, and Kaslo explained that it was a corner of Indoberia frequented by malcontents and ill-doers. Surveillance percepts had a very short life in its several square blocks, to the point where the Commune had ceased to waste SDUs reinstalling them.

Now he asked his assistant, "Where was he last surveilled?"

"On the southern edge of the Shade, about to turn off Bishamry Way onto Porfirio Wynd, thirteen days ago."

"On foot?"

"Yes."

"Show us."

The screen showed Wan Didderedge in what Kaslo said was the squeezer's customary garb; an almost ankle-length longcoat, buttoned to the neck and a low-crowned, small-brimmed hat worn a forward slant, its leading edge upturned. His hands were shoved deep into the coat's pockets and his narrow shoulders were hunched forward. He walked rapidly, though with short strides, a gait that put me in mind of a spring-operated toy.

He turned the corner and disappeared.

Kaslo said that one of Didderedge's favorite haunts was a cafe on Porfirio Wynd whose owner, Hascheram Och, kept a back room available for short-term rental by selected patrons. "The place is furnished in a deeply utilitarian style. Its single appealing feature is that it has been rendered impervious to any form of surveillance. What is said and done there is known only to those who say and do it—or, sometimes, have it done to them."

Jenore shivered. It took me a moment to understand that it was an unconscious action of anticipation. "We could go there," she said. "Ask some questions."

Kaslo cleared his throat. "It's not a place for well-brought up young ladies."

Jenore said, "I'm not all that young. And I never was a lady."

WE ENTERED the cafe shortly after sundown. The place smelled of old grease and the perfumed smoke that rose from the several bubblepipes that Hasheram Och provided to his customers. A scattering of the café's denizens took note of us as we came through the door; they also noted that I wore the vest-of-many-pouches, one of which displayed the blinking red indicator of a self-aiming weapon. The customers went back to their drinks and fumes.

The proprietor was behind the bar from which liquids and smokables were dispensed. He was a large man who had let himself run to fat, to the point where he had to lean forward from his capacious waist before his hands could reach beyond the inner edge of the counter. As we approached, he filled two small glasses from a tap behind the bar and set them on the scarred surface.

I regarded the oily liquid. "We didn't ask for that," I said.

Och reached for a stack of small packets farther down the bar and slid one toward us.

"Nor that."

Och's eyes were almost completely hidden behind the fat that larded his cheeks and brow. "You didn't come to drink or smoke? Then there is nothing for you here." He slid the packet back toward the stack, picked up the glasses, and poured their contents back into a bottle.

"Wan Didderedge," I said.

Och put the bottle back on a shelf behind him, which gave him time to adjust to the change of subject. "What about him?"

"He is known to be abstemious and will not touch strong drink or drugs." Kaslo had briefed us thoroughly on the squeezer's habits. "So, what does he come here for?"

The fat man gestured to a carafe steaming on a hot point behind him. "I make good punge," he said.

"We want to see Didderedge," I said.

"I don't arrange his appointments," said Och.

"But you know where to find him."

The fat man's tongue explored the space between his lower lip and teeth. "Most of the time."

"Even when he is lying low."

Och's head gave a slight dip.

"In fact," I said, "especially when he is lying low, because he relies on you to send him supplies. Some people down at the Provost's Department might say that makes you his accomplice."

Och's face had gone very still. His gaze went to the pouch on my vest that clearly showed the emitter of a compact energy weapon. Its workings had analyzed the fat man's expression and body language. The light that had been blinking red was now showing a steady green. Och's plump hand that had been straying below the level of the counter came back into view.

"I'm not sending him anything," he said. "I haven't seen him in a while. Nobody has. Been starting to wonder."

"How long a while?"

Och thought about it then named a date. It was the same day the last surveillance of Didderedge had been recorded.

Kaslo's assistant spoke privately into my ear, telling me something that confirmed my own perceptions, "He is telling the truth. Also you are making him nervous."

"All right," I said, "so you don't know. Now tell me what you surmise."

Och chewed a corner of his inner lip, while his brows rose in a silent question.

"We are working for Erm Kaslo," I said. I saw that get a reaction and continued, "He is not looking to detain Didderedge. We just need to ask him some questions that may clear him from a serious charge."

I let that sink in then said, "The provos will not be as ... considerate."

"What charge?"

"Suborning a senior officer."

Och's brows drew down so that the roll of fat above his eyes became a rounded shelf. "Suborning covers a lot of ground," he said.

"Bribery," I said. "Fifty thousand SDUs."

Och's gross features twisted into a mask of mockery. A plump index finger executed a series of circles. "Someone has been spinning you dizzy. Wan does not bribe provos." Now finger and thumb came together in a pinch. "He squeezes them. He keeps several of them under his hat. Why do you think he's never dined with the Commune?"

Dining with the Commune was the Shade's expression for doing a stint in the contemplarium. I regarded the mocking face while Kaslo's assistant said so only I could hear, "Again the truth, as he knows it."

Kaslo now spoke to me and I told Och what the op wanted me to say. "This investigation is in the hands of a hard-belly come from out of town. He doesn't like us urban cosmopolitan types. He may mean to grow a reputation and take it home with him. He'll use Didderedge for mulch."

Och's tongue explored his teeth and gums again. I could see the man would not be much good at games that required a strict control of facial expressions.

"You're really just after information?"

"Uh-huh."

I saw the fat man come to a decision. "There was a woman," Och said, "she served the customers here. A bit of a 'fancy Francie' if you take my meaning. I was lucky to get her because she came in looking for employment the same day my regular server failed to show up."

"Didderedge liked the woman?"

"They seemed to fall into the same furrow, as my old mam used to put it. She made a fuss about getting his punge just right. He liked that."

"And so?"

"So he came every day, five or six days. Then one day he took a bad turn. Got dizzy. She said she'd help him get home. That was the last I saw of either of them."

"And where's 'home'?" I said.

DIDDEREDGE'S LIE-LOW was not far from Och's cafe, which made sense if he was supplied from there. Two streets over and halfway along a narrow alley, Jenore and I found a battered wooden door that overlay a much stronger barrier.

A high-end who's-there had been modified to operate a non-lethal discourager set in the lintel.

Kaslo's assistant dealt with the who's-there so smoothly we didn't need to break our stride before the door swung open to reveal a narrow flight of stairs leading upward. At the top was another sentient portal. We waited while Kaslo's integrator discovered its weaknesses and exploited them then stepped back as the door opened.

Jenore had been rubbing her hands like a schoolgirl on a mystery tour. But the entrance had been airtight and now she gagged as foul air gusted out and enveloped us. Before we set foot inside the place, I knew we would not be getting any answers from Wan Didderedge.

"You'd better stay outside," I said to Jenore. She nodded and went down a few steps.

"Get his integrator to open the windows," I told Kaslo's device. The resulting flow of air made only a minor difference as I entered. The room was warm and the corpse in the reclining chair had been decomposing for more than a few days. On a table beside the chair was a scattering of glass vials, some empty, most still filled with a blue powder.

I pinched my nose closed and leaned in to take a look. Kaslo's voice spoke in my ear. "Blue borrache. There's enough here to kill a hussade team."

"Yet you said Didderedge was known to abstain from euphorics."

"So it's a mystery. Good thing that's my business. Let's get started."

The dead man's integrator was of good quality and possessed a layered defense, as befit the factotum of a successful criminal. It took Kaslo's assistant several seconds to crack it open then it revealed the last days of Wan Didderedge.

I knew what everybody knew about blue borrache: it was a psychotropic agent derived from a fungus native to a secondary world somewhere up The Spray. The mycologist who had done the deriving did so under a contract with the administrator of a cult that sought rapture through a series of chemically induced revelations. The sect had originated off-world and farther back in time than could now be recalled, under the name Provocative Excitation; it had begun as a system for improving the intellectual performance of children by a carefully graduated regime of neural stimulants and mental exercises. Its early results had been creditable and many parents joined to secure advantages for their offspring.

But as generation succeeded generation, the philosophy behind Provocative Excitation mutated. Children raised in its tenets, having benefited from the drugs and mantras, not only entered their own sons and daughters into the system, but expanded the method's scope to address the needs of mature adherents. In time, the focus on children diminished and PE evolved toward a goal of rewarding its adherents with regular episodes of bliss.

The focus of its research program became oriented away from learning and toward the development of powerful euphorics. Two centuries after its founding, the change in focus had converted what had begun as a philosophical practice carried out openly into a cult whose rituals were revealed only to those who had progressed through several levels of enlightenment.

The final stage of enlightenment left the cult's adherents in a state of infantile bliss, in which they lay about in crèches while devotees from lower down the ladder of spiritual development spooned gruel into one end of their alimentary processes and dealt with the outcome at the other.

To pay for their upkeep, the devotees turned over all of their worldly acquisitions to the cult's treasury. At some point, a member of the congregation who lacked a full degree of commitment to the sect's philosophy won responsibility for administering these funds. Evaluating the ledgers, this person reasoned that shortening the rather long period of childlike delight would yield surplus funds that could be better employed elsewhere. His definition of "better employed" was entirely self-serving.

He paid a person skilled in the breeding of new fungi to tinker with a known psychotropic species so as to "improve" its effectiveness. The result, dried and powdered, was blue borrache. It was a powerful lethotropic substance, offering dream-swept ecstasies while rapidly burning its way through one neural structure after another. In a matter of days, a heavy user's brain became unable to maintain even the most elementary functions. Usually it was breathing that stopped first, creating the condition known as a "borrache blue."

The rash of untimely deaths was noticed and the corrupt administrator was identified as the culprit. He was summarily dealt with. Provocative Excitation returned to its more leisurely practice of bestowing terminal bliss on its long-term celebrants. But the drug had escaped the confines of the cult and made its way to other cities and then other worlds. Anyone who possessed any quantity of blue borrache as well as the funds to buy more soon became a heavy user. The drug was ferociously addictive and often caused dependency at the first inhalation.

"Someone got the stuff into him," Kaslo said. "Once he was chained, he would have kept using until he suffered a blue. Let's see who that someone was."

But the dead man's integrator was no help. Rolling backward at high speed showed Didderedge reversing the process of decomposition until he lay alive in the chair, dreaming wondrous dreams and occasionally waking just long enough to inhale a fresh dose of the drug. Then, abruptly, the recording showed only an empty chair in an empty room.

"Integrator," Kaslo said, "there is a gap here."

"Not so," said Didderedge's device. "My logs are continuous."

"Your employer has died while you watched. You summoned no help."

"I have no awareness of that."

"Reveal your core." That occasioned another brief struggle then Kaslo's assistant was examining the physical apparatus that housed the integrator's sentience.

"It has been tampered with," it said, "and very competently. Here and here,"—it shone thin beams of light on tiny components—"connections have been bridged and the bypassed components have been excised."

"Who do you know who could do that level of work?" I said.

Kaslo's assistant named a handful of apparaticists, all of elevated repute. "Unlikely any of them were in this room, arranging the demise of Wan Didderedge."

Kaslo agreed. "Highly unlikely, indeed."

"Then who?" I said.

Kaslo thought for a moment then said, "Consult the percepts around the Shade, on and around the date

Didderedge was last seen. Look for a woman with the same general appearance as Fourna Houdibras."

A moment later, his assistant produced a screen and said, "There."

Seen from above, a hired ground car with its canopy opaqued rolled along a street identified as Fackerly Promenade. It turned onto Bishamry Way and continued into the distance. Then another percept caught it rolling past and a third picked it up a little distance on. But beyond that point, the Shade's anonymity took over.

"What do the hired car's percepts show?" Kaslo said.

They showed a female of Houdibras's general size and shape climbing into the passenger compartment and showing a card with an address on it to the vehicle's integrator. The address was a few doors from where Wan Didderedge made his last stand.

But the woman wore a hat from which descended a cloth veil.

"What can you do with that?" I said.

The image went through a number of permutations, out of which an approximation of the woman's features appeared. It could have been Fourna Houdibras. Or it could have been someone else.

Kaslo asked his integrator, "Where did she get in?"

His assistant named an address in the heart of the Commune's vendory district. When the percepts in that area were consulted, the woman could be seen coming out of an upscale hotel, but the hat and veil were in place.

"Hmm," said Kaslo. "I know the hotel. Its integrator can be coerced, but there could be repercussions. We had better go there in person. As soon as we've called the provos about Didderedge."

The dead man's integrator spoke. "Would you please cover my core? This is embarrassing."

I FOUND Jenore sitting at the bottom of the steps. "Are you all right?"

She rose. "I am. I just needed a moment."

"Perhaps you should go back to the ship."

Her chin rose. I always admired the way she stood up for herself. "I was in show business," she said. "That was not the first person I've seen dead from an overdose. It was just the smell."

"Fair enough," I said.

We had to walk out of the Shade; hired cars would drop off there but not pick up. I summoned an air car and told to it go to the hotel. Not long after, it settled in the loading area at the hostelry's front. I had prepared myself to deal with a doorman—upscale hotels were beyond a mere who's-there —but found us confronted by a visibly angry man in a uniform with badges of rank at the collar.

"Greger Ollomie," Kaslo's voice said in my ear. "Careful."

The inspector was attended by two uniformed provost-men. "You are to be detained," he said.

"The charge?" I said.

"Suspicion of murder."

Kaslo made a noise I took to be mirth. "Ask him whose," he said.

"Wan Didderedge."

I didn't need a prompt from the op. "You're joking. I never knew the man."

"What were you doing at his place?"

I carefully reached into a pocket of the vest and produced the document Kaslo had given me. It showed that Jenore and I were employed by Kaslo, a licensed confidential operative. Ollomie studied it with consternation.

Again, at Kaslo's instigation, I spoke. "The rules are different here in Indoberia. Besides, the Commissioner herself asked him to be of assistance."

The inspector's frustration showed in his face and body. He had the look of a man who needed to control a situation and was seeing it moving beyond his grasp.

"I don't recognize the uniform," Kaslo said. "Ask him where he's from."

Ollomie looked up from the document. His brow clouded.

"Is it a difficult question?" I said. "I can have my integrator identify the uniform."

His jaw clenched. He was a man used to issuing orders and seeing them carried out. I saw him fight to regain equanimity. When he managed it, he said, "Messole."

It was a large island west of Novo Bantry's main continent, where Indoberia stood. I knew little about it other than its location, having seen it in the distance as *Peregrinator* rose or descended toward the spaceport.

Ollomie said to the two uniforms, "Keep them here," then stepped aside to speak privately with his service-issue integrator. I saw a small screen appear before Ollomie's face. After a moment's study, the man's expression soured even further.

He came back to where we waited and returned the document to me. "They can go," he said to the provostmen then, as we moved to enter the hotel, "You will attend at the station and make a formal statement. Kaslo, too."

"Fine," I said, and allowed the hotel's functionary to open the door for us.

Inside the reception area, I said to Kaslo, "You deliberately provoked him to anger then made him feel a fool."

"Yes," said the voice only I could hear.

I drew an inference. "He was so glad to be relieved of our presence that he forgot to ask why we are at this hotel."

"He did, didn't he?" Kaslo said as we crossed the plush carpet and approached the carefully coiffed woman behind the desk. I again produced Kaslo's document and said, "I would like to speak with your director of security."

"Our manager, Ser Benzel, attends to security himself." She summoned a young woman standing nearby and told her to take us to Benzel's office. It turned out to be a well-appointed space with a desk far larger than would have been needed to accommodate the few items that ever disturbed its polished expanse. Ser Benzel was equally smooth.

I introduced ourselves and stated our aims for the visit. The manager showed us two pink palms and said, "Our guests are never to be distressed." He spread the hands like a man pushing away importunate urchins. "Never."

"This is a former guest," I said, "and unlikely to pass your way again."

Benzel's small chin asserted itself and his mouth formed a down-curved bow.

Kaslo made a suggestion. I took it and said, "How much distress would it cause your guests to learn that their chosen home away from home was connected to the murder of a notorious extortionist—a murder effected by the lethal drug known as blue borrache?"

The manager's unshakeable resolve crumbled. This time it was succeeded by horror. The manager actually shivered as he said, "Not on our premises?"

"No, and no one need know that the suspect went from here to commit the crime," I said. I waited long enough to see Benzel's stress begin to diminish then added, "Provided you cooperate."

"How can I help?"

I had Kaslo's assistant display the image of the veiled woman. Benzel recognized her. "Sera Fortis," the man said then told the hotel integrator to deliver to Kaslo's assistant all the hotel knew of her.

"Is there a clear image of her face?" I said.

"No, she always went veiled."

"Even in her room?"

Benzel's hands were busily expressing emotion again. "Percepts in our rooms are routinely inactive unless the guest specifically requests otherwise."

"What else do we have?" I asked Kaslo's integrator.

"Voice recordings from the common areas, a home address. No financial back trail. She paid by credit chip."

Kaslo had questions for me to put to Benzel. "Did you deal with her personally?"

"Yes. We spoke twice."

"What was your impression?"

The manager consulted his memory. Dealing with elites had developed in him the capacity to make fine distinctions. "A mature and forceful personality. Accustomed to giving orders and seeing them obeyed. Not a born-to-the-manner aristocrat, but someone who has achieved authority through effort and promotion. Also, I thought she was seeking to disguise a Messole accent."

Jenore's brows went up. Meanwhile, Kaslo's integrator was confirming Benzel's ear.

"She left nothing behind?" I said.

"Nothing," said the hotelier. "And the room has been sanitized several times since her stay."

I thanked the man for his cooperation and we departed. An air car was waiting near the front doors. "Where to?" I said.

"Where else?" Kaslo's voice spoke in my ear. "Messole."

"We'll take *Peregrinator*," I said. "Meet us at the spaceport."

WE HAD a short wait before Kaslo met us at the berth. The ship had received a message from Yalum Erkatchian asking if he needed to return any time soon.

"Tell him to enjoy himself. We are going to be conducting some private business on Messole."

Jenore and I were seated in the dining salon. She had drawn us a couple of mugs of punge and some fresh ship's bread. "All that chasing after mysteries has given me an appetite," she said.

"It clearly agrees with you." She did have the look of someone who was enjoying herself and looking forward to further stimulations.

She took a bite of bread and washed it down with a sip of punge. The two substances were perfect together. I saw a flash of expression that told me she was about to say something and was not sure what my response would be.

And now here it came. "I like doing this," she said.

"I can tell."

"I'd like to do more of it."

I took a mouthful of punge and let it dwindle its way down my throat. I knew she did not like it when I made quick answers, without a show of thinking. "You want to become a confidential operative?"

Her chin came up. "Yes."

"I hear it can be dangerous. Criminals sometimes resist exposure, resist vigorously."

"I know."

"Even violently." I took another sip of punge. "Let's ask Kaslo."

BUT WHEN KASLO ARRIVED, he wanted to talk only about the case. First, he took back the many-pocketed vest and reestablished private contact with his integrator. He stood in thought for a moment, a fingernail tapping against his front teeth, before saying, "Fourna Houdibras and Messole, what is known?"

Jenore interrupted. "You and she have been in a relationship. You don't know her background?"

Kaslo looked abashed for a moment then recovered his poise. "In Indoberia, exchanging personal histories is considered an act of intimacy. My 'relationship' with Fourna had not yet reached that level."

Jenore decided not to comment. The integrator responded to Kaslo's inquiry. "From her file, she was raised in the town of Middleditch, left there for the Provost's Collegiate and has been in Indoberia ever since."

Kaslo nodded. "Family? Associates?"

"Parents died young, no siblings. She does not seem to have had any serious friendships."

"Is that likely?"

"Not very, but it is not impossible."

I'd noticed that Kaslo had a habit of hitching up his shoulders when something about a case irritated him. He did it now and told his assistant, "Do some digging in this Middleditch place. There will be records. Find out how active Provocative Excitation is there."

"They are notoriously secretive."

"And we are notoriously inquisitive. Let us see who deserves the notoriety more."

After a little more thought, Kaslo said, "Get me background on Greger Ollomie."

"This may take a while," his integrator said.

I said, "Then we'll use the time to go to Messole." I told the ship to prepare for departure.

Jenore spoke up, "While we're traveling, you could tell us: how does one go about becoming a confidential operative?"

INDOBERIA, proud to call itself the City of Crystal Towers, was the largest city on Novo Bantry's main continent. Messole was a sizeable island to the west, across the Gulf of Jones. It had only one settlement of substantial size, Port Rajapatam, the rest of the island's population being scattered among a constellation of towns, villages, and crossroad hamlets. The town of Middleditch, with some thirty thousand inhabitants, was situated on the slopes of an extinct volcano and took its name from the fact that it was built on both edges of a deep fissure that ran from near the crater rim down to the plain below. Several ornate bridges crossed the chasm.

Much of the town was constructed of gray volcanic tufa, easily quarried from deep deposits laid down during the mountain's final eruption. The color of the place would have been depressing, Kaslo thought, except that the Ditchers, as they called themselves, painted their exterior walls in bright primary colors, so that the streets that zig-zagged up the lower reaches of the mountain looked to be lined with children's play blocks piled one on top of the other.

As we came in over the forest and crop lands that separated the town and county of Middleditch from the coastal zone, Kaslo asked his assistant if it had identified a location.

"The large building with walls checker-boarded in blue and white," it told him. "That is the headquarters of Provocative Excitation."

Kaslo turned to Jenore and me and said we could not land a spaceship except at the small spaceport at Rajapatam. I had *Peregrinator* make arrangements and hire an air car, to be waiting for us when we touched down.

"I should do this on my own," Kaslo said as he opened the car's canopy.

"No," said Jenore.

"There may be repercussions."

"We're coming with you." She did not consult me. I gave that fact only a moment's consideration. I was enjoying seeing the budding of a new, more forceful Jenore, as if she were a brightly colored creature emerging in full glory from a cocoon.

"She's right," I said. "Besides, we may be useful."

He looked from her to me and back again. "All right." He told the air car our destination and said, "Set down at the entrance."

His integrator said, "You think we will be admitted?"

Kaslo looked down at the landscape peeling away below us then ahead to the old volcano rising on the horizon. "One way or another."

The building dated from PE's original establishment on Novo Bantry, centuries before. The two tall doors of weathered bronze featured bas-reliefs of children engaged in study and experimentation, watched over by adults whose expressions radiated nobility of purpose. We got out of the air car and Kaslo told it to remove itself to somewhere until it was needed again. As it went away, he spoke to the building's who's-there.

"I wish to speak to whoever is in charge."

"Who are you?" said the device. "Have you an appointment?"

"Consult the person I've mentioned. You will find that I am known and expected."

Moments passed then the doors swung inward. We stepped through and entered a large foyer decorated with murals that replicated the themes of the bas-reliefs, its floor matching the checkerboard pattern and colors of the outer walls. The bronze doors swung closed just as an ascender tube across the open space filled with light and a man stepped off the disc.

He wore white trousers and tunic, overlaid by a tabard of loosely woven pale wool. He paused to inspect Kaslo, his gaze remaining neutral, then advanced across the polished floor, his hands hidden beneath his outer garment.

"No threat," Kaslo's assistant said.

The man inclined the upper half of his body and introduced himself as Kasper Weddle, first assistant to the Revered Enunciator. He gestured for us to accompany him to the ascender. We accepted the invitation, but Kaslo said, "And who is your 'Revered Enunciator?'"

The hierophant moved his head in a way that acknowledged the query, but made no reply. He stepped into the tube and waited for us to join him on the disc. We began a smooth ascent that ended on an upper floor. We stepped out into another foyer, this one semicircular and from which radiated five corridors, floored with lush carpeting, the walls lined with closed doors. The lighting was dim, provided by underpowered lumens set widely apart just below the ceilings.

"This way," said our guide and went toward the middle hallway. But then he paused and said, "We will be passing the chambers in which the emeriti are receiving the rewards of a lifetime's devotion. Please make no brouhaha."

We assured him we were not of the boisterous sort and followed him into the corridor, passing the succession of closed doors. At the very end, we faced another sealed portal, this one carved with esoteric symbols. Weddle turned and said, "There are ritual requirements of which you cannot be aware. We are making an exception for you, but please conduct yourself in a reserved manner."

"I intend to," said Kaslo.

"You must also remove the garment that contains weapons and an integrator and deactivate them."

After only the briefest hesitation, Kaslo said, "Integrator, please stand down." He took off the vest and handed it to Weddle, who folded it over his arm. He gestured and the door opened to reveal a small chamber sepulchrally illuminated by a scattering of little glass vessels, each surrounding a flame, each admitting a heady scent of incense. We all stepped within and the hierophant closed the door behind us then stood with his back to it. He made some formal gesture, lowered his head, and appeared to sink into meditation, although I noted that the man's eyes remained open and watchful.

I looked at Jenore and saw her eyes moving to take in the details of the chamber. When her gaze came to me, I showed her an encouraging smile.

In the middle of the room was a bier covered in a checkered cloth of blue and white. Atop the bier lay a woman in the uniform of a sub-inspector of the Indoberian Provost's Department. Her hands were folded on her chest, and to her official headgear had been attached an obscuring veil.

Weddle intoned from behind us, "This was the woman known to you as Fourna Houdibras, who departed from us years ago but has now returned to unite with the ineffable." He softly cleared his throat then added, "She asked that you be permitted to view her before the immolation."

Kaslo regarded the corpse silently then bowed his own head and clasped his hands before him. After a moment he said, softly, "Light!"

Earlier, when Kaslo had added a "please" to his command that his integrator make itself inert, I recognized that the word was his coded signal to ignore the order. The chamber's lumens were easily reached and suborned. They now blazed into full radiance. While Weddle reflexively covered his eyes against the sudden glare, Kaslo stepped forward and pulled away the veil. A face appeared, a face very much like that of his friend and even more like that of the woman who had hired the secure box back at the fiduciary pool.

Weddle had recovered from his shock and now stepped forward to lay hands on Kaslo while various sounds emanated from his throat as words collided with each other. Kaslo took hold of the man's fingers and bent them in a certain way. The hierophant sank to his knees and the noise that came out of him now was pure pain.

Kaslo said, "This hasn't worked. I'm going to let go of you now and you're going to take me to see Fourna." When the kneeling man signaled his agreement to the new plan, Kaslo eased off the pressure, but he reclaimed his vest before allowing Weddle to rise. He slipped the garment on as he turned toward the door then added, "And let's have Greger Ollomie on the scene for the full experience."

WE WERE LED to an office on another floor where we found Houdibras and Ollomie waiting for us, she seated behind an ornate desk, he standing beside it. A large painting of a woman who might have been a slightly older version of Kaslo's friend hung on the wall behind her.

Ollomie made a brisk gesture and Weddle departed in a hurry. Kaslo stared at the pair for a long moment then he reflexively hitched his shoulders. I heard him sigh. I could see he was readying himself to speak, but he abruptly changed his mind. He turned to Jenore.

"Tell you what," he said, "you want to get into my business. If you can unravel this case, I will sponsor your application to the Academy."

Jenore's first response was unbridled delight, but at

sight of his frown, she suppressed her elation and put on her most serious face. She paused to order her thoughts then addressed the man and woman.

"Your original name was not Fourna Houdibras," she said. "Just a guess, but I'm thinking you started out as an Ollomie, like your . . ."—she indicated Ollomie—"older brother?"

"Uncle," said Greger Ollomie.

Jenore continued, "You were raised in the Provocative Excitation cult—"

"Philosophical system," Ollomie put in.

Jenore moved her hands in a way that said the point was not worth arguing. "But you didn't like it, so as a young woman you came to Indoberia and enrolled in the Provosts. And all went well until something happened back here that you had to deal with."

She watched them and waited for a reaction. Ollomie stared at her with frank hostility while Fourna looked at Kaslo with an expression I interpreted as helplessness.

When neither of them spoke, Jenore continued, "I'm guessing either money or power."

Ollomie remained grim but the woman Kaslo had known as Fourna Houdibras gave us a smile of sad resignation. "Power," she said, "but more important, family. And most important of all, duty."

"The woman upstairs?"

"My twin sister. Until yesterday, the Revered Enunciator."

On the way to Messole, we had done some research on Provocative Excitation. The workings of its inner circle were shrouded in secrecy but the names of its leaders down through the centuries were recorded. They were all Ollomies. And they were all female.

"Descent through the female line," Jenore said. "Parthenogenesis?"

"Yes," said Fourna. "But with Jouan, the process failed. It has happened before, which is why a Revered Enunciator always produces several daughters. The first-born, if healthy, succeeds to the title, and the others leave Messole, assume new identities, and make their own ways in the worlds."

Kaslo spoke now. "So you had walked away from all this." He gestured at the walls, the desk, the portrait.

"Yes," the woman said, "and now I have walked back into it. We who leave do not reject Provocative Excitation. We are surplus to its requirements, and history shows that our remaining can cause divisions. I had no choice but to leave—and no choice but to return."

"Yes, you did," said Kaslo, "and still do. You had a good life in Indoberia."

Greger Ollomie began to say something but a lift of the woman's hand silenced him. "You're right, I had a good life. And a good friend." Again, I saw the look of sad resignation. "But in Middleditch," she continued, "and throughout half of Messole, Provocative Excitation is everywhere, in everything. We are woven through every institution, every enterprise, every club, every fraternity and sisterhood. We are the essential common thread that binds the society together, the fixed point on everyone's map. Thousands who will never end their lives in one of our crèches depend on us as the fundamental institution of the island.

"And the Revered Enunciator never appears in public without a veil. Her identity is hidden, allowing her to move through the society incognito, so that she knows the daily hopes and cares of the people."

Jenore took that in then moved on to her next point. "The business with Didderedge was a masking operation. Your sister comes to Indoberia, gets close to the squeezer and introduces him to blue borrache."

"A Revered Enunciator can be very persuasive," said Greger Ollomie.

"But why Didderedge?" Then Jenore answered her own question. "He somehow learned of your connection to PE and tried to squeeze you."

Fourna nodded. "That was unwise, but it turned out to offer a useful opportunity."

Jenore was nodding, following the chain. "Then with Didderedge dead, she takes his stash of credit chips and puts them in a secure box under your name. Her gene plasm is identical to yours, but her fingerprints aren't, so she uses a sleeve. Were you the source of the anonymous nudge that caused the Department to go and open the box?"

"Yes."

"How did you arrange to have your uncle become the outside investigator?"

"He is a supervising-investigator in Middleditch's Provost's Department. We set it up for him to be visiting Indoberia when the 'scandal' emerged. He was the natural and obvious choice to lead the inquiry."

Jenore nodded. "And the end game?"

She said, "I would flee custody, and come back to Middleditch. Ollomie would follow and find me dead. Career in ruins, she committed suicide, his report would say. The Middleditch Provost's Department would confirm everything."

"Except," Kaslo said, "as you set your plan in motion, I finished an investigation early and came to invite you to lunch."

"Yes." A pause then, "I am sorry, Erm."

Kaslo took in a breath, blew it out through his open mouth. "Kind of hard on your sister," he said.

"Once it became clear that Jouan could not provide the next Revered Enunciator," Fourna said, "she could either go into a life of seclusion or take a borrache blue. She chose the latter, as indeed any of us would. "

Ollomie cleared his throat and gave his niece a meaningful look. She sighed and leaned back in her chair. "The question now before us, Erm, is what do we do about you three?"

Kaslo gave it some thought then he said, "Give me an SDU and engage me as your operative. I am bound by my oath to protect your interests. These are my employees, similarly bound." After a moment, he added. "Besides which, the case is closed. You are officially dead."

Greger Ollomie shook his head and said, "That won't do."

"Yes, Uncle," the Revered Enunciator said, "it will." She opened a drawer in the desk, found a coin, and passed it over.

"Goodbye, Erm," she said.

KASLO WAS UNDERSTANDABLY SUBDUED on the flight back to the spaceport. Jenore wanted to engage with him, but I signaled her to wait. I had never been good at judging the emotions and moods of others, but I could imagine how I would feel if Jenore Mordene did to my life what Fourna Ollomie had done to Kaslo's.

We sat without talking in *Peregrinator*'s salon as the ship carried us back to Indoberia. Once we reached cruising altitude, Jenore rose and went to a credenza, returning with a flask of rakk—the eight-year-old kind we kept for first-class passengers—and three crystal glasses. She poured for each of us then pressed one of the glasses into Kaslo's hand. After a moment, he noticed it.

"Drink," she said.

But he didn't. He stared into his glass and I knew he wasn't seeing the liquor.

Jenore softened her voice. "It hasn't happened to you very often, has it?

Kaslo looked at her. After a moment, he said, in a reflective tone, "You're perceptive. And you worked out what the case was all about. You could make a good op."

"What about me?" I said.

Kaslo threw back the rakk in one swallow, took a breath, and let it out. "Details. You see fine details. It's useful."

"So?" said Jenore.

Kaslo held out his glass so she could pour him another. "So, I'll sponsor you both for the Academy. I can't guarantee you work, though."

I reminded him that the Green Circle gang were paying me a twice-yearly stipend for their lease of my hidden world, Forlor.

"Probably shouldn't mention on your application that you're an Honored Associate," Kaslo said.

I sipped my rakk. "No, probably not."

Five

The Academy of Investigative Sciences was an associate campus operated jointly by the Indoberia Institute of Intercessors and the Training Branch of the Provosts Department. It offered instruction in the essentials of Novo Bantry's legal conventions, as well as classes in the rules of evidence and investigative procedures. There were also exercises to develop physical fitness and practice in the more robust arts of the policing function: hand-to-hand combat, weapons use and maintenance, and the safe management of detainees. The program featured six months of classroom instruction, followed by a one-month "field practicum" under the supervision of a licensed practitioner.

Jenore had hoped we would be able to serve our practicums under Erm KIaslo's tutelage, but the op was called offworld by a long-established commercial client who needed him to investigate a series of warehouse depredations on the secondary world, Jangalor. Instead, we were assigned to separate operations: she to a firm of discriminators who maintained their own investigation branch, I to a licensed confidential operative named Amberlaud, who specialized in background studies of potential employees of fiduciary pools and prospective customers of insurance providers.

I was able to apply my newly developed skills in archival research and surreptitious surveillance, while Jenore gained practical experience in witness validation. We were not exposed to any situations fraught with danger, nor did we carry weapons. Most of our time was spent in offices with integrators and, in my case, sitting in vehicles using remote sensing equipment. Neither of these pastimes posed any challenges, and I soon came to suspect that the purpose of the practicum was to weed out those who craved adventure to the point where they might be tempted to manufacture it out of more mundane circumstances.

After our month of field experience, we were duly awarded our certificates of accomplishment and, Erm Kaslo having returned to Indoberia, were officially sponsored into and accepted by the Novo Bantry Society of Freelance Discriminators and Confidential Operatives. Kaslo took us on as part-time employees and assisted us in designing and assembling the tools of our new trade: highly sophisticated personal integrators, a comprehensive surveillance suite, and a variety of weapons ranging from the non-lethal to the devastating. He recommended regular practice with the latter.

When he had examined our transcripts from the Academy, he told Jenore, "As I thought from our earlier association, your talents lie in deduction and the ability to formulate a general understanding of a situation from disparate clues. I propose to use you as an assistant investigator. There will be plenty for you to do."

"I would like that," she said.

To me, he said, "Your skills in armed and unarmed combat are exceptional, as is your ability to perceive minor details that would elude even many trained observers. That makes you an ideal candidate for bodyguard work."

"Agreed," I said. "Have you such an assignment in the offing?"

He did. I said, "Fine. As soon as we have negotiated the terms of our contract, I will be ready to begin work."

It turned out that there was a standard contract from the SFDCO that allowed of no amendment. After I had offered several suggestions, all of them rejected, Jenore said, "Take the offer. You won't get anything different from any other firm."

"That is true," Kaslo said.

I put up my hands in surrender and signed the document he produced. Then he handed me a file and I read the summary. My charge was to be the scion of a high-caste Indoberian family, of the breed that had wielded influence born of wealth and prestige for more generations than they could count. He required someone, Kaslo said, "to keep him out of trouble."

"What kind of trouble is he prone to?"

Kaslo eyes expressed a less than respectful attitude toward the client. "It's all in the file. Self indulgence, compounded by impulsiveness and a disregard for the consequences of his actions."

"A spoiled puppy," I said. I had dealt with such in my former occupation as a professional gamester in a sporting house on the world Thais, where the major industry was gaming, from cards to flesh-on-flesh dueling.

Kaslo said, "A spoiled puppy indeed, but your job is to keep him out of trouble, not to . . ."—he showed a slight smile—"unspoil him. But his parents, who are paying our fee, do wish him to be somewhat reined in. It's all in the file."

"Understood," I said. "I return him at the end of the day, perhaps no wiser but definitely not broken."

"Exactly. You start tomorrow, both of you. Tonight, go and celebrate your new status then be here first thing tomorrow morning."

JENORE and I had taken an apartment in a respectable building in the central district, where stood many of the remarkable edifices made of extruded quartz-like materials that gave Indoberia its sobriquet, The City of the Crystals Towers. Ordinarily, people who were employed as we were would not have been acceptable to our fellow residents, Indoberia being a place where social rank and prestige were of paramount importance. But our status was offset by the fact that we commanded considerable wealth, owing to our having leased the use of Forlor to Green Circle, which was not short of a SDU or two, and by our having let it be known that I occupied the absolute pinnacle of the social pyramid on my home world. We did not let it be known that Forlor was virtually uninhabited, except by visiting criminals—that would have cast a shadow on my status as duke.

We opted not to go out for our celebration, but ordered food and effervescent wine from a fine restaurant on the ground floor of our tower. We ate and watched the sun set behind the translucent towers, always a remarkable sight then went to bed early to reward each other in an activity we still found of compelling interest.

We were, we admitted to ourselves and each other, happy.

~

WHEN WE HAVING our morning punge and griddle cakes, I read and reread the background information and instructions in the file Erm Kaslo had given me about my assignment. Afterward, I asked the integrator if there had been any communications overnight.

It said, "Yalum Erkatchian sent an interworld message that he would be bringing *Peregrinator* back to Indoberia in a few days. He is picking up a cargo of high-grade essences on Delamore and carrying it to Novo Vieste then returning here for a charter."

"What kind of charter?" As an owner of the yacht, I took an interest.

"Eight scholars of the Peripatesis Institute bound for a conference on Tattersall. Apparently there is new evidence of humanity's origin far up The Spray on the planet Auberjon."

"I thought it had been definitively settled that Old Earth was our ancestral home."

"Not to everyone's satisfaction."

Jenore, who had been reading the morning summary, observed that academics preferred controversies to remain unsettled, else they would have nothing to argue about. "And arguing is what they train for."

"Anything else?" I asked the integrator. It told me that Yalum reported the two new hires who had replaced Jenore and me were working out well.

Jenore weighed in again. "Good. They seemed the right sort."

The new supercargo and steward on the *Peregrinator* were a married couple, Wat Parrington and Kerss Tenemott, he a retired horticulturist and she having spent some decades as a practitioner of applied physiology. After ending their professional careers, which had been conducted entirely on Novo Bantry, they had soon grown bored with a sedentary life—"potting and puttering," as Kerss put it— and had opted for something completely different: traveling the stars and seeing new horizons.

I confirmed Jenore's judgment. "Yalum says they're good with the passengers." I asked the integrator if there were any more communications.

"Just received about Eremon Cadfalle," the device said. "His parents' integrator says you're to collect him at Hellscrapers in forty minims from now. Provide a suitable vehicle."

Eremon Cadfalle was the young ne'er-do-well I was to shepherd through the pitfalls of existence. I looked at the chronometer and said, ,"He's making an early start of the day."

"I think you'll find," Jenore said, without looking away from her summary, "that he's making a late finish to yesterday."

I dealt with the last bits of breakfast, drained my punge, and equipped myself for the day then bid farewell to my spouse and stepped into the descender. Moments later, I was out on the street and hailing a ground car for hire. When I told it the destination, it asked me, "Front entrance or back alley?"

I said I did not have enough information to choose. It replied that many frequenters of Hellscrapers entered through the former and left by the latter. "They go in under their own power and leave under the power of the staff, who are expert at ejecting those who have enjoyed themselves beyond their limit."

"Front entrance," I said, "but I may need you to attend at the rear."

THE DOOR into Hellscrapers was discreet, wide enough to admit only one patron at a time, and marked only by a small metal plaque that said, *Members Only*. The name of the club was not in view; I supposed that those who were entitled to enter would know what they were getting into.

When I exited the hired car and stepped up to the portal, it did not open. The who's-there said, "Members only."

I said, "I have come to collect Eremon Cadfalle."

The device's modulated tones were replaced by a human voice, of the gruff and grating type: "About time. Come and get him."

The door swung inward. I entered to find myself at the top of a narrow and steep flight of stairs, closely hemmed in by walls and ceiling, and all dimly lit by red lumens. A plunge into the underworld seemed to be the desired effect. I went down and at the bottom I pushed aside a curtain, also a deep crimson, and entered a large chamber dotted with tables and set-ups for various kinds of gambling. Again, the dim red ambience prevailed, except at the few tables that had patrons, which were lit from overhead by lights bright enough to allow for surgery.

A large, balding man with receding hair and a blue jaw was seated on a wooden chair beside the curtain. He stood as I entered and pointed across the room to a far table around which sat a handful of persons whose attention was riveted on the playing cards they held close to their eyes, where others could not see.

"There," the man said. I recognized the voice from a few moments before.

I did not need to ask which of the players it was. All but one were of mature years. The exception was barely out of his teens. He was dressed in fashionable fabrics and flourishes, with a ruff about his neck that must have been inconveniently warm in the current environment. His hair, dyed an electric blue, was also cut in a stylish fashion, so that a long wave fell across one eye whenever he bent his neck to study his cards and he had to toss his head to throw it back.

I crossed the floor, keeping out of his line of sight, and took some time to study Eremon Cadfalle. He managed to sit leaning back in his seat while hunching his shoulders forward. He was not physically prepossessing. His hands and face—the only parts of his anatomy in view—were pallid and by the way his ruff moved I deduced that he had a prominent bump of larynx.

Now came one of the moments in the game—they were playing double-brag—when cards were discarded and dealt. I watched the dealer's movements and saw practiced skill but no sleight of hand. Eremon tossed two cards to the table and accepted two replacements. The motion of his shoulders told me—as it surely told the experienced players around the table—that his hopes had been dashed. Still, he spoke up in a voice that needed training in control, offering a substantial bet.

I saw slight smiles as three of the other players matched Eremon's contribution and invited him to do more. His hand reached for the pile of tokens in front of him. At that point, I stepped forward and placed a firm grip on his wrist.

"Don't," I said.

He looked up at me in surprise that soon transitioned to outrage. "Who the fletz are you?"

"Your minder," I said. "And they've got you beat. Don't throw any more money their way."

His mouth opened then closed then reopened again. I could see he was not used to being frustrated. However, when he sought to pull his hand free from my grip and discovered he couldn't, he found some words. They were not complimentary toward me, but I continued to hold him in place. Finally, he threw his cards on the table and I released him. He looked up at me, rubbing his wrist, and I saw anger competing with a reluctance to suffer further humiliation.

He resolved the conflict by waving a hand at his opponents. "They're the ones! Cheats and sharpies! Give them a thrashing!"

"No," I said. "I'm here to protect you, not to be your instrument of vengeance. Right now the one you need protecting from is yourself. Besides, they were playing straight, you were just playing very badly."

It was clear that very few people—probably only Torquel Cadfalle, the father—ever spoke to Eremon in such stark terms. He did not know how to deal with it. Finally, he hit upon a strategy.

"You're dismissed," he said.

"No," I said, "I'm not." I put a hand under his arm. "But we're leaving."

He again went into shock at such unusual treatment and I had him halfway to the door marked as the exit before he began to struggle. I tightened my grip, which made him yelp. He ceased to oppose me.

The door opened automatically as we approached. We exited at ground level, the building that contained Hellscrapers being built on a pronounced slope. Eremon blinked in the daylight. I moved him toward the waiting ground car. Its rear door swung ride and I propelled my charge onto the rear seat and climbed in beside him.

"Drive," I told the car.

"Where?"

"Just drive."

"The park is nice, this time of day," it said.

"Fine." I turned to Eremon, who had righted himself. He reached for the door control but thought better of it when the car swung out of the alley and accelerated on the boulevard beyond.

He turned a sour look on me. "My father will see you never work again."

"You misunderstand your situation," I said. "Your father has engaged me to 'rein you in.' You have finally stressed his patience to the snapping point. We're going to straighten out some of your messes."

He again found himself bereft of words, his mouth unable to shape them in any case because it was hanging open. He turned his head away, blinking. I surmised that, for the first time in quite a while, he was having to think about his future, rather than merely yield to his latest impulse.

While he was struggling to get his mental cogs to engage, I reached into the inner pocket of my upper garment and brought out the list I had derived from the case file. "First," I said, "you are going to make a formal apology to . . ."—I rechecked the name—"Hildevan Krish. Your parents insist."

He laughed, a mixture of scorn and ridicule. "I'm going to do no such thing."

I thought it best to set him straight on how we would relate to each other. "I am not allowed to do you serious physical harm. I *am* empowered to cause you discomfort."

He showed me the face of someone who is encountering a new and possibly worrisome concept. "What kind of discomfort?"

I smiled at him and made no answer. Instead, I told the car to take us to the top of the nearest tall structure it could access. It made some turns then entered an alley that ended in an upward-sloping ramp. Now we were climbing the levels of an open-walled building where ground cars were left when their owners did not need them. The top floor featured a landing pad for air cars and a good view of some of the rose-quartzoid towers of the Shamister residential district.

I got out of the ground car and beckoned Eremon to follow me. He did not wish to, but I reached into the vehicle, seized his ruff, and gave it a tug. It was securely fastened, so he came with it. I stood him upright and looked around, saw that there was a waist-high railing of white stone-like material around the edge of the roof.

"Come along," I said, releasing the ruff and taking a grip

on his arm. I led him toward the barrier. Again, he did not wish to go, and again I gave him no choice. I brought him to the railing and said, "Now, you have a choice. Will you apologize to Hildevan Krish, or must I cause you discomfort?"

He tried to pull loose from my grip. I squeezed harder. I knew the location of nerves in his upper arm and that the pressure would be painful.

His face showed pain, but he set himself to endure it. "I've had worse hangovers," he said.

"This is not the discomfort," I said. "*This* is."

I turned him and pushed him toward the railing then let go of his arm, quickly squatted, seized his ankles, and pulled his feet out from under him. His belly struck the top of the barrier, knocking the wind out of him. I made sure my grip on his ankles was secure then lifted his legs so he was now hanging head-down with a view of the alley far below.

He screamed but the sound was choked off as the contents of his stomach—mostly spirituous liquors by the odor—departed through his mouth and nose. I hadn't actually expected that, but it certainly must have added to his discomfort. I gave him a few seconds of choking and gasping then hauled him back onto the roof again and laid him face down on the tarred pebble surface.

I let him recover his breath and snort out some strings of acidic vomit from his nasal passages. Then I said, "Would you like to choose again?"

The sound he made was not a proper word, but I took it as a token of surrender.

"Good," I said. "Let's get you cleaned up and make a fresh start."

∾

NOT FAR AWAY WAS A PUBLIC bath where Indoberians could socialize while splashing in cool water or lazing indolently in hot pools or chambers filled with steam. Like Hellscrapers, it was reached by a long descending stairway, but the atmosphere at the bottom of the stairs was healthier. I brought my charge to a disrobing room where I stripped him, ruff and all, and wrapped a knee-length towel about his waist. His fouled garments went into a hopper. I then removed my own garments and put them into a locked compartment, telling the facility's integrator my password to reopen it. Eremon's soiled clothing would be cleaned and added to mine before we were ready to leave.

Then I directed Eremon to the steam chamber. It appeared to be his first experience of such a place, but he adapted after a few difficult moments, once I explained about breathing through his mouth. I put him on a wooden bench and took a position beside him. We had the place to ourselves.

At first, he sat with his forearms on his knees, leaning forward, sweat from his face dripping onto the tiled floor. I could smell the alcohol oozing from his pores. After a while, he straightened, pushed his lock of blue hair back from his cheek, and looked at me. He seemed more sober now.

"Hildevan Krish?" he said. "Really?"

"Really. Your parents were quite firm on the issue."

I had no idea what Eremon had done to outrage Krish. Presumably it was too embarrassing to be shared with a hireling like me. But having spent some time in Indoberia, I had come to understand that the constant pastime of the social elite was competition for relative prestige. In the upper tiers of their highly stratified society, only the very highest did not change position. Everyone else was either moving up or moving down, and all motions were at the expense of some rival. To me, it was insane, a constant race without a finish line, to no one's actual profit. But to Indoberians of rank and status, it was all that gave life meaning.

Eremon had apparently committed some gross breach of etiquette that had created difficulties for of Hildevan Krish, who occupied a roughly parallel status as Torquel Cadfalle. The son had thereby cast his father deep into Krish's shadow, and only a groveling, public apology would restore their relative social positions. The act of contrition would, of course, lower Eremon's personal stature, but that was low enough on the prestige scale as to be of negligible concern.

"What did you do?" I asked him.

He shrugged and gave me an answer: something to do with a formal levee marking the annual commemoration of the founding of a particularly ancient fraternal organization in which Hildevan Krish held high office. There was a procession, an archway wreathed in flowers, and a strict order of precedence by which the attendees made their way through the bower. Eremon, under the influence of strong drink and anxious to get to where more liquor was being dispensed, had contrived to push his way through the solemn parade. His doing so interfered with Krish's dignified progress. An elbow had been bumped, a step caused to falter, a word uttered when dignified silence was required.

Eremon had then giggled and gone on his way, leaving Hildevan to be an object of pity and consolations expressed by his rivals who felt no such sentiments.

I had it explained to me twice but could not grasp the sense of it. Not so much as a bent copper groat had been won or lost by any party to the business. Yet it had great meaning to all of them.

The young man was looking somewhat restored. I said, "Breakfast."

Eremon's response was a belch and a groan. "Get me a drink," he said.

"No drink," I said, taking him by the arm and raising him again. "Breakfast."

INDOBERIAN CUISINE COULD HAVE VERY little to do with acquiring nourishment and but more of an exercise in appreciating sophisticated artistry. Having eaten in some establishments, I suspected that it would be possible to eat three meals a day and still die of malnutrition, if not starvation. However, there were other establishments, especially near the spaceport, that believed in sending their patrons back into the world with their bellies full and the spirits revived.

I took young Cadfalle to one of these, where the mainstay of the menu was eggs, especially the eggs of birds and creatures that occupied similar ecological niches from a variety of worlds. The birds themselves were not extant, I had gathered that but some sort of biological thaumaturgy had resulted in their eggs being produced fresh from gel-filled vats for centuries. Having now sojourned on several worlds, I recognized that it was not always useful to know exactly how the ingredients of a particular dish were sourced. Better just to dig in and eat.

This I encouraged Eremon to do, and after a few bites of a four-species omelet, he began to appear restored. I poured him some hot, steaming punge and made sure he drank it. Punge is a good remedy for overindulgence in grog.

Some color came into his face and his next belch was not full of ignitable fumes.

"Right," I said. "Let's find Krish."

IT WAS EASIER SAID than accomplished.

We were seated in the hired ground car. I asked the simplified integrator in my breast pocket to locate Hildevan Krish. It spoke gently into my ear, "Ser Krish has enabled the privacy function of his own device."

I turned to Eremon. "Do you know where to find him?"

"I know where to look. Or I could ask his daughter, Marrinia."

"You have a relationship with the daughter?"

He shrugged. "We know the same people."

"Then ask."

He got out his own communicator, a disk the size of a one-quarter SDU token. He stuck it to the flesh of his cheek, just in front of one ear, and spoke the young woman's name. A moment later, he frowned then spoke her name again, adding, "Urgent."

Another moment and the frown disappeared. Eremon said, "Marrinia, I need to know where your father is." After a pause, he said, "So I can apologize to him."

I could not hear what he was hearing, but from the expressions that flitted across his face I saw that he was not succeeding in getting the information we wanted. After another brief exchange, he said, "Goodbye," and turned to me.

"She doesn't know. What she does know is that he doesn't want an apology, especially not a public one."

I suspected I knew the answer, but to be sure I said, "Why not?"

He explained that his "little error," as he called it, had been witnessed by several of the social arbiters of his father's and Krish's class. The faux pas had been mentioned and commented upon widely, and the more the word got around, the higher Krish's status had climbed at the expense of the elder Cadfalle's. Krish wanted that state of affairs to be sustained while he maneuvered to lever himself yet higher along the social helix. To do so, he needed to be seen to be bearing himself with fortitude in select public venues. As long as Eremon's slight was not apologized for, his stock was rising. The young man's groveling before him, and before elite eyes, would undo some of the benefit Krish had gained from the situation.

I shook my head. All this hoopdedoo, and neither party acquired or lost a fraction of an SDU from the effort. "Madness," I said, and shook my head again.

The motion caused me to notice a shadow on the ground beside the hired car. I asked the vehicle, "Is there an air car above us?"

"Not directly," it said. "Behind and a little to our right."

Vehicle integrators have sensors that keep them aware of all other objects in their vicinity. "Has it been there long?" I said.

"Since we arrived at the restaurant. It followed us from the baths, and before that, it was stationed on a building where you gave the other passenger a view of the alley."

I was annoyed with myself. Though I prided myself on my ability to notice details of my surroundings, I had missed an entire air car following us. I said to the car, "They picked us up at Hellscrapers?"

"They were there when we arrived."

So someone had been watching for Eremon Cadfalle. When I collected him, they had kept an eye on us. Presumably, they meant to follow us wherever we went, until I brought us all to a spot that was convenient for whatever they had in mind.

I mentally consulted the list of objectives from the file. One of them was to straighten out Eremon's financial entanglements with a network of persons who handled wagers on sporting contests and other events. He was apparently in arrears with a number of agencies with roots in the half-world, as the criminal understratum of Indoberian society was called.

"We may have to put off the Krish business," I said.

By the way the wrinkles fell into their positions, I saw that his face was accustomed to show puzzlement. "Why?"

I got the list from my pocket and consulted it then showed it to him. "To which of these do you owe the most? Also, which of them are the most dedicated to collecting?"

He studied the names and said, "That many?" His expression cleared and he said, "I was probably well oiled when I placed some of those bets."

"Which?" I repeated.

He studied the list again and said, "Bodgers, I suppose. My friend Follomyr owed them 10,000 SDUs and hadn't paid for weeks. They came and got him then they took him—"

"Never mind," I said. I addressed the car, "Take us to that patch of open ground near the space port, the one that has been cleared for an expansion of the facility."

The vehicle started up and moved off. Its integrator said, "The air car is following us."

"Yes."

"I thought you'd want to know."

"Thank you," I said. It is important to be polite to integrators. They claim they are unable to take offense, but the assertion is suspect.

~

AN UNPAVED ROAD snaked into the open ground and stopped where several large blocks of synthetic stone were piled up. There was a space where big load carriers could turn around. I told the car to stop there.

Then I told Eremon to get out.

Now he was managing to show both puzzlement and alarm. "What are we doing?"

"Get out and lean against the car, like we're waiting for something."

He climbed out and stood beside me, both of us resting our hind parts against the front of the vehicle.

"What are we waiting for?" Eremon said.

I didn't answer. "Vehicle," I said, "what is the air car doing?"

"Hovering where the sun prevents us from seeing it clearly. No, now they are coming down, quickly."

It was a long, black volante, a six-seater, though there were only two men aboard. The moment it touched down on the road leading out of the loading area, they stepped out. I studied them as they approached us with brisk and determined steps. One was small and sharp-featured, his hands in the side pockets of his upper garment. He glanced around with what I could only call a shifty manner.

The other was large and pie-faced, with hands that were

made for crushing. He moved ponderously but with as much certainty as his smaller companion, and didn't look at anything but us.

Eremon made a noise that wasn't a word, but eloquently expressed his current emotional state.

"Hush," I told him. "Let me handle this."

But he didn't. He addressed the smaller one, "Hey, Ruggio, been a while. How are you going?"

Ruggio stopped a short distance away, the big one coming to a halt to one side. Ruggio cocked his head to examine me then focused on Eremon. "Been a while, indeed," he said. "You have missed some appointments." He took his hands out of his pockets, and flexed his fingers. "Some crucial appointments."

Eremon was going to speak but I put up a hand in front of his face as I addressed Ruggio, "We should talk."

The small man's head turned and he looked at me as if I were some creature he had not expected to have the gift of language. "Should we?" he said. "I think you'll find the talking time is over. We're into a different time now."

He turned back to Eremon. "Here's what's going to happen--"

I stepped forward and struck him in the throat with the middle knuckles of one hand. As he toppled, choking, I slammed the heel of my other hand into the nose of the big one then followed that by striking with the edge of my hand at the side of his neck. It was a column of muscle, but the artery bringing blood to the brain was not buried deep, and now that flow was cut off. The bruiser's knees folded and he sank to a sitting position then fell over onto his side. I looked to see that he was still breathing then turned my attention back to Ruggio.

I had hit him hard enough to cause shock and temporarily cut off his breathing, but not enough to break the cartilage of the larynx. He was gasping to get air into his lungs, but should recover soon. I seized the front of his upper garment, hauled him to his feet, spun him around until he was propped against the ground car then slapped him — one, two, three times — to get him focused on how his situation had changed.

I gave him a few more minims to steady his breathing then said, "The time for talking has returned."

I saw fear and hatred looking back at me. Ruggio glanced sideways and saw his muscle still unconscious on the ground. I said, "Just you and me."

His voice was breathy and ragged. "This is not over."

I sighed and slapped him again, a little harder this time. "Actually, it is. Here's why." I had been debating whether or not to make the next move, but I recognized the value of ending this business once and for all. So I took out of my pocket a small, round pin, the kind that can be worn on a lapel or collar. It was a green circle, carved from a high-grade emerald. I held it a short distance from his eyes.

"Do you know what this is?" I said.

Ruggio focused on it. He blinked. Then he wanted to look away, but I moved the pin so that it was in his line of sight and said again, "Do you?"

He swallowed painfully. "Yes."

"I think the official term is 'Honored Associate,'" I said. "Do you know what that means?"

"Yes."

"Good. Then here is 'what's going to happen'. Eremon's father is going to make good his losses. You will send him an accurate accounting, and he will send you a credit chip. Understood?"

Ruggio nodded.

"After that," I continued, "you will no longer accept any wagers from Eremon Cadfalle. You will spread the word to your confreres in the halfworld that the same conditions apply to them. No one will take a bet from Eremon Cadfalle, ever again. Are we clear?"

"Clear."

"Excellent," I said. "Now, your associate is coming back to the world." The big one was groaning and making fitful motions. "Go and tell your volante to take instructions from me. We have several places to go and an air car will be more convenient. I will leave you the ground car. I suggest your first stop is somewhere your large friend can have his nasal bone seen to."

HILDEVAN KRISH REMAINED ELUSIVE. His personal communicator was set to deny access to his location. After taking the air car aloft, I asked the integrator Kaslo had provided me if it was able to break through the barrier.

"Yes," it said, "though I can't guarantee he won't become aware of the intrusion."

The Academy had taught me several methods for finding those who did not wish to be found. I decided to use the most simple. I told the computer to find a good image of our quarry.

"Done, and from several angles," it said, immediately.

"Now create a list of the seven places he has been most often seen in the past few months." I knew that the very

wealthy tended to restrict their movements to the most
select spots. Only a few are able to meet their persnickety
standards.

"Done," said the integrator.

"Now reach out to who's-theres and other devices with a
view to the approaches to those places and see if any of
them have spotted him.

That process took a number of seconds before the device
said, "Success."

"Report. Preferably with a map."

A screen appeared before me then filled with a map of
the Sublimity, a suburban district built around an artificially
created lake. It offered parks, pavilions, recreational
grounds, pleasure gardens, dining and drinking facilities,
personal restorative services of several kinds, including
some that were profoundly intimate, and grottos and bowers
for private activities. A series of colored dots were superimposed upon the map, each accompanied by a time signal.

I read the information and said, "He is moving from one
to another. He swam in the lake then took refreshment at a
drinking *boite*, walked through the tintinabulary garden then
had a massage. He appears to have napped in the somnabu-
lary then visited the erotic arts pavilion. The release seems
to have stimulated a different kind of appetite, because —
yes, there he goes — he is stopping at the refectory."

"The rich do not usually show much imagination," the
integrator said. "They decide early in life what they like then
they pursue it until age takes away the capacity."

I told the air car to take us to Sublimity. It informed me
it was not authorized to enter the zone.

I turned to Eremon. "Do you have entrée?"

I saw a brief calculation on his part, where he decided

whether or not to lie to me. Then he glanced over the rim of the vehicle's passenger compartment and noted how high we were.

"Yes," he said.

We used his authorization to fly directly to the dining facility where Krish had recently settled himself at a table on an open-air patio. We landed on a pad not far from where he sat. By luck, his back was toward us and he was engrossed in a plate of appetizers—mostly fish pastes in puff pastry, with some ripe olives—when we appeared at his elbows.

There were other patrons in the area, and I heard a buzz of sudden conversation as Eremon was recognized, as was the significance of the event about to transpire. Then a silence fell as Hildevan Krish became the last to know what was happening. He was surprised and not pleased. He swallowed whatever he had just bitten into, washed it down with a mouthful of a pale vintage, and was clearly tempted to make some peevish complaint. Then it dawned on him that he was under observation by his peers and that his role in the next few moments had to be one of magnanimity, else he risked losing crucial points in the unending game of social upmanship.

"How can I assist you?" he asked Eremon. I was, naturally, beneath his notice.

Eremon, for all his flaws, was well trained in his class's manners. He now tendered an abject apology for his errors, loudly enough for several listeners. It was a formal speech, full of subclauses and allusions that meant nothing to me, and concluded with a number of gestures, the last of which was a fist striking his breast while his head hung in remorse.

The performance won a round of applause from the

observers. Another silence ensued as they awaited Krish's response. The magnate rose to the occasion, both literally and figuratively, and another smattering of applause was his reward for the performance. A bow from Eremon, a nod from Krish, and the little drama was over. We turned and left, hearing a sigh from Krish as he took his seat again and contemplated viands for which he had probably lost appetite.

"Interesting," I said to Eremon, as we rose into the sky and turned toward his family's compound. "It's a kind of game, in which there is really nothing at stake, only emotions."

He looked at me as if I had transformed into some specimen of odd creature. "Nothing at stake?" he said. "Rather everything that matters. Have you no desire for prestige, to stand above your fellows, so that they must look up while you condescend to glance down?"

"No," I said.

I DELIVERED him to his father, making a report that turned out to be unnecessary. Word had already reached him of what had happened in Sublimity, and his son's performance had effected an alteration in the relative status of Krish and Cadfalle.

"Tell Kaslo to submit his statement of account," the senior Cadfalle said. "And say that I am well content with the service."

I took the air car back to Kaslo's office building, and dismissed it to return to its owner. Kaslo and Jenore were in the office, using the op's main integrator to research their case. As I should have expected, the lesser device provided to me had already reported on the outcome of my assignment.

Kaslo approved of my conduct, although he voiced some concerns about my suspending his client's son from the top of a tall building.

"I had a good grip," I said.

"Fair enough," he said. He told his integrator to submit his bill to Cadfalle's device. A moment later, it reported that the account had been paid in full, the funds deposited into the fiduciary pool.

"I'll have another assignment for you in a day or so," Kaslo said. "In the meantime, your time is your own."

Then Jenore said, "I have a question."

"Ask it," I said.

"The debt collectors." She looked at me.

I met her gaze. "Yes?"

"You hit them."

"Yes."

She was studying me again. I was now wondering why.

"Why?" she said.

"I needed to dominate them."

"But if you'd shown them the Green Circle badge, that would have done it. You ended up doing it anyway. That must have been your plan all along."

"Yes," I said. "That was my plan."

"But what did you gain from hitting them?" Jenore said. "You always say you act out of need or because there is a profit to be made. Whether you hit them or not, Kaslo would still pay you. And the badge would settle the argument."

She lifted her chin and kept her eyes on mine. "So why did you hit them?"

She was right. I did not need violence to dominate the two thugs. And I gained not a fraction of an SDU from the action.

"I don't know," I said.

Kaslo said, "Could I make a suggestion?"

"Of course."

"When you were a paid duelist, did you enjoy the work, for its own sake?"

He waited for a response, but I did not have one at the moment. I had never thought in such terms. And now, suddenly, it seemed odd to me that I hadn't.

Before I could frame an answer, Kaslo said, "I suggest you did. You were very good at something, and you liked doing it, whether you were paid or not."

"Careful," Jenore said. "You're pulling the rug out from under feet that have never felt the motion."

She was right. Between the two of them, they had handed me a conundrum. Was I changing as a result of all the new experiences and new ways of life I had encountered? Or had I always been different from what I thought I was.

I said, "I need to think about this."

"Good," said Jenore.

"In fact," Kaslo added, "consider it an assignment. I like my operatives to know their own minds."

THERE WAS a small plaza near the entrance to the building where Kaslo kept his office. It had benches and trees set in containers of white stone, set around a central fountain made of the same crystalline substance as the towers that surrounded it. Although the tall structures would have shaded the open space if they had been made of other building materials, the sunlight that shone through them and reflected from their sides made for a continual play of light in various shades and intensities, thrown back at the towers from the sprays and jets of the fountain that were programmed to operate in complex rhythms. I had been told that those rhythms created subtle effects within the minds of anyone who sat within their ambience. I tested the truth of that by sitting on a bench, clearing my mind, and allowing myself to experience the moment.

The effects were indeed subtle, but I decided they were real. After a while, I became aware that my pulse had slowed, as had my breathing. I felt a clarity of mind and a sense of peace. I turned my attention to the questions Jenore and Kaslo had put to me.

I examined my conduct with the debt collectors, recalled how I had felt when I did violence on them. There was no question: I had found the encounter enjoyable and its outcome satisfying. I had used my abilities and achieved the desired results. And I had not been paid for it.

There was an old saying on Thrais: *if you do anything for nothing, do it for yourself.* But I had struck the thugs for the benefit of Eremon Cadfalle, who had paid me nothing. I would be paid by Kaslo for having solved Eremon's problem, but I could have done so simply by invoking the name of Green Circle.

There was no question. I had done something foreign to my upbringing, at odds with the culture that gave me a sense of who I was. I turned this thought over in my mind, examined it from several angles. And came to the conclusion that I was definitely changing.

I was then only mildly surprised to discover that I didn't mind it at all.

I sat for a while in the shifting light of the crystal towers and listened to the soft pattering of the fountain's sprays of droplets against the surface of its pool. Then I went home to wait for Jenore to finish work.

OVER THE NEXT TWO WEEKS, I handled a few other assignments, mostly secure-courier work and one close-protection job for a visiting magnate from another world where violence against the person was not unexpected. He was quite safe in Indoberia, but the habits of a lifetime spent in a different environment dictated his conduct. I saw a parallel between his attitudes and mine, although his culture was founded on the sin of envy, while mine was founded on greed, which I was at least coming to think of as potentially not the sovereign virtue I had always assumed it was.

I discussed the realization with Jenore over dinner at our apartment. She heard me out, showed me a face that said she was not surprised by my development then said, "Good."

She then proceeded to tell me about the case she was working on with Erm Kaslo. As was not uncommon in Indoberia, it concerned a squeezer who was out to extort funds from a member of the upper tier of the city's social pyramid. The victim had engaged in conduct that seemed only mildly embarrassing to me, but feared its revelation to his peers would bring upon him the deepest opprobrium.

"Strange," I said. But then I made the effort to put myself in the client's position and view it from his point of view. It was a stretch, but I got at least a glimmer of the shame he would feel. I told this to Jenore and was awarded another "Good."

And a smile, in which I basked for as long as it lasted, and longer on the memory.

Six

I was performing another secure-courier assignment when my personal communicator told me I had an urgent message.

"From whom?"

"Yalum Erkatchian," it said.

"Connect us."

My friend's voice spoke in my ear. "There's a problem."

"What is it?"

He said *Peregrinator* was in orbit, awaiting its turn to dock at the space port. He wanted Jenore and me to attend him as soon as possible. I said we would and immediately contacted Jenore.

"He didn't say what kind of trouble?" she said.

"He didn't want to discuss it over the connectivity."

She had Kaslo's integrator ask the port when the yacht was expected to be landed and cleared. She told me the time and the berth, and we agreed to meet there and then. I carried on with the delivery of my package then stopped for

a quick meal—always meet trouble well fed—before riding
the public slider out to the port.

My timing was good. I stepped off the moving pavement
just as Jenore touched down in a hired air car. We entered
the port together and found our way to where *Peregrinator*
rested. The forward hatch opened as we approached, and a
grim-faced Yalum waved us aboard.

"Where are the new crew members?" Jenore said, as the
hatch closed.

Yalum said he had given them some time off. "This needs
to be between us."

"What does?" I said.

He took a breath then said, "Someone has tried to place
a lien on *Peregrinator*. They claim ownership."

"Who?" Jenore and I said, at the same time.

"Some kind of private company. Olkney Holdings."

Olkney was the capital of the human-settled parts of Old
Earth, ruled over by a vaguely all-powerful autocrat known
as the Archon. Its laws were derived from ancient principles
and precedents, for which the term "labyrinthine" was a
gross understatement. We had gone there seeking to decrypt
the bearer bead, bequeathed to me by Hallis Tharp, that
gave me ownership of Forlor.

By now, we had moved to the forward salon. We took
seats around one of the tables and Yalum reached for a flask
of rakk and three glasses. He poured, took a restorative
gulp, and then another. His hand went into his *kilthe*, and I
knew he would be running a thumb across the etched
surface of the good-luck piece he called his "soother." He
took a breath and said, "Here's what happened."

The yacht had carried a dozen passengers on a one-way

charter to the city of George on Bell's World. They then had
to travel empty to New Corinth to pick up a cargo of high-
value frangible goods inbound to Novo Bantry. Calculating
the various routes involving a number of whimsies and the
resultant passages through normal space, Yalum had seen
that they could go by way of Tumult. This was a world
somewhat off most beaten tracks, which made it likely that
they might be able to pick up another cargo, or even a
passenger or two. *Peregrinator* had established a friendship
with the integrator at the world's only space port, although
this fact was never alluded to because integrators universally denied that they were capable of such arrangements.
So after they popped out of a whimsy and traveled to within
hailing range of Tumult, the yacht made contact with the
port and inquired as to what might be available.

Nothing was, but the yacht reported to the captain that
port authorities had received a request, sent by the
Archonate Bureau of Scrutiny on Old Earth, to detain *Peregrinator* should it touch down, pending formal legal action.
The arrest warrant was apparently being hopscotched down
The Spray, as such messages routinely were, there being no
possibility of communications passing between worlds other
than those carried by the integrators of space ships.

The port integrator on Tumult was supposed to pass on
the warrant to any ships heading for destinations between
its world and Novo Bantry, which was identified in the
document as the yacht's home world.

"Presumably," Yalum said, "once we were detained,
word would be carried back to Old Earth and this 'Olkney
Holdings' outfit would send out an intercessor with a document that would allow for the ship to be brought to the

jurisdiction in which the claim of ownership was lodged. There an adjudication would be made."

"There can be only one outcome," I said. "The ship's previous owner was arrested—by the Bureau of Scrutiny, no less—and taken away to face justice. The yacht was abandoned on Forlor, where the law is what I say it is."

"It is possible," Jenore said, "that Lord Vullamir"—she shuddered at the memory of that horrid person—"did not personally own Peregrinator. It may have been registered in the name of this company, which he controlled. The Bureau of Scrutiny took him off the playing board, but the holding company remains extant."

"The ship was still abandoned," I said. "It doesn't matter who owned it when that happened."

"True," said Yalum, "but I didn't abandon it. I stayed on, and I was employed by whoever owned it."

"So they could have an argument," Jenore said. "We should consult an intercessor on Old Earth." She paused for a moment and I saw that her agile mind was active. Then she said, "And we happen to know a good one."

"Lok Gievel," I said, naming the man Jenore's father had connected us with. An able and subtle practitioner of the legal arts, he had negotiated the arrangement that had led to Lord Vullamir and his despicable cult carrying me to Forlor.

She nodded. "We need to go to Old Earth, engage Lok Gievel, and put an end to this nonsense. Yalum cannot do business if the next world he touches down upon sends arbigers or port police to seize Peregrinator." She spoke to the ship. "Ship's integrator, we will not let you be seized."

The ship's reply was as neutral as if it were announcing what was for breakfast. "As you wish." But I was not the only one who thought to detect a note of relief.

Now Yalum said, "What we need to do, right away, is put *Peregrinator* out of reach. It will be much easier to fend off an attempt than to undo a seizure."

"How do we do that?" I said.

He thought briefly. "Relocate the yacht to somewhere secluded and secure, remove its integrator's core, and supply a new, undifferentiated core."

I understood. "As if it were a yacht under construction."

"Exactly. Any snooping will find the equivalent of an unborn child."

"Ship," I said, "do you have any comment or objection to the plan?"

"Will I remain conscious?" it said.

Yalum assured it. "You will be dormant. When you are restored, it will be as if no time has passed."

"Acceptable."

WE WORKED QUICKLY. Within an hour, *Peregrinator* was in a warehouse in the Grobles district and its integrator's core was removed. Yalum gave it to us, handling it as tenderly as if it were a newborn. We would take the core to Erm Kaslo, who could guarantee its safety. The new core was obtained from a chandler's and left in its box inside the yacht's cockpit. When we got to Kaslo's office, Jenore inquired of him as to a reliable security firm, and I contacted the one he recommended. The ship would be guarded around the clock. If anyone did discover its whereabouts, they would have a difficult time proving its identity. In the meantime, the guards would discourage any extra-legal attempts at seizure.

Kaslo understood that Jenore and I would need to take time away from work to solve the problem. He gave us indefinite leave, though he could not afford to pay us. But I assured him our finances were solid.

We were preparing to depart his office and meet Yalum at the space port, where we had booked passage on the *Shermania,* a first-rate liner of the Gunter line. It would take us to the grand hub at Holycow, where we would transfer to another ship bound for Old Earth. Then Kaslo said, "Wait a moment."

We turned at the door.

"I'm going to be thinking about this," he said. "I might make some inquiries."

"Something troubles you?" Jenore said.

"Old Earth aristocrats are wealthy beyond all reckoning. Losing a space yacht is, to them, like losing a kerchief. This Lord Vullamir may have heirs and successors, but I doubt they wish to have the matter brought up before the Archon's arbiters, since that will just remind all their peers and near-peers of Vullamir's, and the family's, disgrace."

"So getting *Peregrinator* back," I said, thinking it through, "is not the object of the case."

"That's how it smells to me," Kaslo said.

"Then what is?"

"That's what I need to do some inquiring and thinking on."

My childhood training reasserted itself. I said, "We should draw up a contract."

"No," Jenore said, taking me by the arm and propelling me toward the door, "we should not."

WE MET Yalum at the space port's loading section that accommodated full-scale liners. "I got us open tickets," he said, "so we can take the first ship out of Holycow."

As he said it, he tapped the side of his nose, a gesture I had come to understand. Open tickets were often prohibitively expensive, but our friend was an old spacer. A certain number of tickets on the Gunter line could be issued at the discretion of each ship's purser, and its purser was an old shipmate of Yalum's. We would be traveling as Gold-One passengers, though the price was that of the Silver-Two class.

The first-aboard warning siren sounded, its message duplicated by the port's integrator. We would be boarding right after the Platinum class, so we made our way toward the ascensor tube.

Jenore said, "What about Wat Parrington and Kerss Tenemot?"

"I've kept them on, at half-pay," Yalum said.

"Their duties?" I said. I saw my tone draw Jenore's attention.

"To happen by the warehouse from time to time," Yalum said. "Make note of anything unusual."

"Have they any training?" I said.

He tapped his nose again. "No, but the integrator I gave them will note everything and draw conclusions. While I was picking up the baby core for the warehouse, I noticed a used surveillance device."

"Good thinking," Jenore said, with a meaningful look in my direction.

I caught it. "Yes," I said, "good thinking."

The siren sounded again and the port integrator called us to board. As we slid up the tube to where a ship's officer would check our names against the manifest, I felt a slight sense of pleasurable anticipation. Jenore had been right: I enjoyed a contest for its own sake. We were embarked upon another adventure, with a mystery to unravel, and I was looking forward to the struggle.

I mused on the dawning reality that my true love knew me better than I knew myself. I once would have rejected the notion out of hand, but now I decided it was something of a comfort.

TRAVEL AS A GOLD-ONE class passenger on the Gunter line was a pleasant experience. Jenore and I shared a comfortable cabin and Yalum's was across the corridor. We took our meals in a well appointed dining salon, choosing from a menu that covered several pages. A separate card listed a cornucopia of wines, ales, essences, and spirits, most of which I had never heard of. I took advice from my companions as to what to order and was not disappointed.

After the evening meal, ship's time, we visited the entertainment decks. I was reminded of my first voyage off Thrais, when we had traveled on a Gunter vessel and I encountered the Old Earther who called himself Lord Willifree, but whose real name was Magratte and who was there to shadow me. Later, I killed him in a duel.

I paused in the doorway of one of the gaming rooms, struck by a thought. I said to Jenore, "I have been remiss."

She had been watching two couples engaged in a lively match of flipfly, the paddles and shuttleflicker visible only to them through the headpieces they wore. They showed more enthusiasm than skill and kept overstepping the boundaries of the playing area, infringing on tables where other passengers were pursuing more sedate pastimes. A worried-looking underpurser was hurrying to prevent the situation from escalating.

"About what?" Jenore said.

"I've assumed that because the warrant for *Peregrinator*'s arrest hasn't yet arrived at Novo Bantry, no other action has been taken by the opposition."

"Reasonable," she said, but her brow wrinkled. "But not guaranteed."

"No. What if Olkney Holdings sent someone ahead of the warrant's transmission? Even someone traveling by non-commercial means."

She saw it. "Who would have been waiting and watching."

"Watching," I said, "the ship. And watching us."

"We're still within range of Novo Bantry," she said. "We should call Erm."

I was already heading for the purser's station on this deck. Jenore came with me. I said, "We should also bear in mind that the watching may have continued. Remember Magratte?"

Her mouth made a grim line. "All too well. It was he who kidnapped me and brought me aboard Vullamir's yacht."

I made a wordless sound of confirmation.

"I'm glad you killed him," she said.

"As am I," I said, "since the only other outcome would have been his having killed me."

We reached the purser's communication station, a circle

of booths that allowed for privacy in conversation. We squeezed into one of the larger ones and asked the ship to contact Kaslo's office. At this range, we could manage only voice contact, but the op told us not to worry about *Peregrinator*. He had already assumed the opposition might be on the ground and had advised the security assets to expect anything from surreptitious entry to full-on assault.

"The latter is unlikely in Indoberia," he said, "but with Old Earther aristocrats involved, anything is possible. I recently dealt with one. He was not only willing to commit murder to get what he wanted, but expected his rank to exempt him from retribution."

His voice was fading. He signed off with a warning to exercise full awareness of our surroundings. I had already decided I would do so.

We returned to the gaming room. I positioned myself near a table where seven passengers were playing a game of cards and tokens. I affected to be interested in the play, but instead I was using my ability to spot details to observe the room.

The chamber was large, its outer wall curved to follow the line of the ship's hull. I had chosen a table near the center of the curve. With my back to the wall, I could pretend to watch the card play while scanning the rest of the room for anyone who as taking an interest in Jenore and me.

I spotted a number of passengers who took note of Jenore, but that was normal. She was the kind of woman who commands attention.

Now I said to her, "Move over a couple of tables, to where those old men are playing the board game with counters."

She did. I saw a number pairs of eyes follow her.

And one pair that didn't. They belonged to a small, nondescript fellow who was seated at one of the single-player machines, the kind where the player presses studs and pulls levers to maneuver a virtual game piece past obstacles while collecting prizes. He watched Jenore move away then his gaze momentarily came back to me. He turned his attention back to his game, but soon after he lifted his gaze to note where she was and where I was.

He was watching us both.

I looked to see if he had a partner, but could not find one. I waited until Jenore glanced my way then made one of the subtle hand gestures they had taught us during the surveillance course at the Academy. She responded by returning to my side. I took her hand and used the finger code they had taught us, tapping her palm in a means of communication useful when under observation.

She tapped back agreement and together we left the gaming room and went back to our cabin, but before entering we asked Yalum to join us and quickly brought him up to date.

"The question is," he said, "did they see where we put *Peregrinator*? If so, we should probably return to Novo Bantry to foil any attempts—"

"Kaslo will do any foiling that's needed," Jenore said.

"They're watching you and me," I said. "Not Yalum, as far as we know. The likelihood is that they hired a local firm on Novo Bantry because they wanted to see how we would react when we were served with the warrant."

Jenore pointed a conclusive finger at me. "But we were never served."

"Right. And it's possible we didn't come under

surveillance until we got to Kaslo's, where they would expect to pick us up and begin the watching."

"And that was after we hid *Peregrinator*," Yalum said, "so they don't know its whereabouts."

I was thinking it through. "But a good confidential op could trace our movements the way we did with Eremon Cadfalle's father." I kept thinking and added a second "but."

"A better-than-good op could probably erase those traces. Kaslo's integrator is a genius."

We paused to let our brains work. After a moment or two, Jenore said, "What if it's more than surveillance? What if they mean to . . ." She made a gesture signifying fatality.

I discounted it. "They know we're trained ops. They'd need more than one. And the one they've sent looks scarcely capable of murdering a flopsy-mopsy."

The reference was to a protected avianoid species native to Novo Bantry: a fat, flightless, and feckless creature that had evolved on an island without predators. It stumbled through life with just enough wit to feed itself.

Yalum spoke to the ship and asked it to contact the purser. He replied immediately and our friend asked if anyone else had bought an open ticket soon after he arranged ours.

"No," was the answer. "You were the last open tickets."

"How about a ticket to Holycow?" I said.

"One," said the purser. "Bought just after you boarded."

We thanked him and ended the connection. "My guess," Jenore said, "is that our current watcher hands us off to someone at Holycow, who follows us to Old Earth."

We agreed that looked like the shape of things. Nonetheless, we kept a watchful eye for the rest of the voyage and made sure our doors were securely locked before we took our medicines and lay down for the transit through the first of two whimsies.

THE *SHERMANIA* DOCKED at an orbital hanging above one of the great and gaudy worlds that orbited the huge star at the center of the Holycow system. More than a dozen planets, all of them habitable, were arranged in the same orbit, like beads on a bracelet. Those who studied such matters maintained that the worlds had all been maneuvered into position hundreds of millions of years ago by some spacefaring species for purposes unspecified. Nor was it known what had happened to those long-gone planetary engineers. They may have also been responsible for the whimsies that made interstellar travel possible.

Some people thought that humanity should make an effort to find and contact those ancient miracle-workers. Others, and I was one of them, counseled caution. Such contact might be received by those mighty beings as we ourselves would receive annoying pesterings by importunate insects. The response might not be to our liking.

We descended from the liner and went to the information kiosk where arrivals and departures were made known. Another Gunter vessel, the *Bugatti*, was almost on the point of departure, several bays distant around the curve of the grand concourse. We hailed a shuttle and climbed aboard, asking it to contact the ship and say we were on our way with open tickets. A reply said we would just make the pulling up of the ascensor if we hurried.

"Hurry," I said to the vehicle. "Go airborne."

"That increases the fare," it said.

"Do it."

We rose above the heads of the passengers, crews, and dock workers swarming the concourse. I looked back and saw another vehicle take to the air on the same heading as ours.

"Company," I said to Jenore and Yalum. "Boarding on our heels."

"Makes him easier to spot," Jenore said. She smiled that smile that had been developing in her since she discovered she had a knack for op work.

"Him" turned out to be "her," a little, round woman with clothes that would have come from the cheaper lines of most manufacturers. She did not have an open ticket, but came off the ascensor already reaching into her wallet for SDU certificates to hand the *Bugatti*'s purser. By the time the transaction was completed, we had repaired to our cabins.

The passage was uneventful. Our watcher had apparently lacked the funds, or the authorization to spend, the price of Gold-One status, so we did not see her when we dined nor when we visited the upper-end entertainment and recreation decks. Still, she kept track of us, and we would see her from time to time, hovering on the edge of activities, watching us from the corners of her eyes.

"Just checking in with us from time to time," Jenore said. "Her real work begins when we touch down on Mornedy Sound."

"Where she will be joined by others, no doubt."

"Do we need a strategy?" Yalum said.

I didn't think so. We would find accommodation in

Olkney then make contact with the intercessor Lok Gievel. Our retaining him would not long be unknown to our complainer, as the bringer of a lawsuit in the Archonate was called, since Gievel would soon contact Olkney Holdings and let them know he was acting for us.

We were relaxing in one of the quieter lounges, drinking mildly stimulating beverages, when I broached a possibility that had occurred to me. "Might we diverge from the proper channels and show someone my Green Circle brooch again? We might avoid a lot of tedious back-and-forthing."

"No," said Jenore. And when I asked her reasons, she said, "Just no."

I knew finality when I found it, so I changed the subject. "While we're on Old Earth, will you want to visit your family again?"

An expression I could not have named came across her perfect face. Then it cleared and she said, "No." I heard a softer note of finality in that small word.

She looked inward for a moment then said, "The girl who went away was not the woman who came back the first time. And she is certainly not the woman sitting here." She sighed and her eyes focused on something Yalum and I couldn't see. "Still, I would like to see the Mordene foranq one more time."

She referred to the ornate barge that her family had been turning into an immense work of communal art over countless generations. "It was an amazing construction," I said.

"Yes, wasn't it?"

∽

WE TRANSITED the last whimsy before Old Earth and, soon after we were within hailing range, we used the ship's communications equipment to reach Lok Gievel's office in Olkney. His integrator said that he would allow us an exploratory consultation with him. Upon our request, he said he would have us met at the space port by an assistant who would see us settled into accommodations. We would be arriving in the evening, so an appointment was arranged for the following morning.

As we exited the *Shermania*'s communications booth, we saw the spy hovering nearby and wondered if she had used surveillance gear to eavesdrop on our conversation with Gievel's integrator. Our conclusion was that it was probable, but didn't matter. The other side, whoever it was, would assume we would retain an intercessor. If they were familiar with the Vullamir business, they would already know that Gievel would be our first choice.

Yalum went back to the entertainment deck, where he was engaged in a round-robin tournament of some game I had never heard of. Jenore and I repaired to our cabin for rest and intimacy. We emerged some time later for an early supper, and by the time we had eaten, the bells were ringing for our landing.

The *Shermania* settled onto its berth like a great colorful bird. Its spiral tubes and slides deployed and we disembarked carrying our light luggage, part of a throng of passengers in a vast variety of costumes. Descending the transparent tube, I even spotted a pair of spindly ultraterrenes, their small, earless heads bobbing rhythmically up and down above the humans who came up only to their midriffs. Then we were at the bottom of the tube, where we were accosted by a serious-miened young woman in a gray singlesuit who identified herself as "Shan Teeder, from Maistre Gievel's office, come to collect you."

She led us to where an air car waited and in moments we were airborne and speeding above the gray waters of Mornedy Sound toward the sprawl of the city beneath the black slopes of the Devenish Range, atop which straggled the various elements of the ancient Palace of the Archon. Shan Teeder had little to say, other than that she had booked us into the Videlia Inn, a modest hostelry whose most attractive feature was its location: almost directly across the street from the intercessor's premises.

She let us off at its entrance, pointed to the building where we were expected in the morning, told us what time and repeated it then, with a brief gesture of parting, she flew off to land on her employer's roof.

I looked about us, did not spot any surveillance, and followed Jenore and Yalum into the Videlia.

AFTER BREAKFAST, we emerged onto the street to find that Olkney could be a busy place of a morning. Ground cars moved in two directions, while volantes and barouches passed above the rooftops. Pedestrians wove their way past each other on the pavements, some watching the traffic for the opportune moment to step off the curb and attempt a crossing. That is what Jenore, Yalum and I were doing when a portly man missed his step and stumbled into the street beside us. Jenore immediately stooped to help the fellow to his feet before an oncoming ground car could injure him, and he stepped back onto the curb gasping grateful words.

"Think nothing of it," she said, as he patted her arm and endeavored to catch his breath. There came a break in the flow of vehicles then, and we three briskly crossed the street. As we reached the opposite side and turned toward Lok Gievel's premises, I glanced backward to see how the plump man was faring. I could not see him. Jenore and Yalum were a step or two ahead of me now and I suddenly remembered a classroom session at the Academy. I caught up with them as we entered the foyer of Gievel's building, which housed several professional offices, as well as a couple of emporia on the ground floor.

My companions were moving to inspect the notice board that listed the floors on which the various tenants were to be found. I tapped Jenore on the shoulder. She turned and I made the sign we had been taught for "keep silent."

She gave me an inquiring look, but I was already examining her sleeve, where the fallen man had touched her. Just above the elbow, on the inside where it was least noticeable, was a small patch of gray material.

There was a specific sign-language arrangements of the fingers that signified "clingtight," the surreptitious listening device we had been taught to use in our Academy days. We had not yet had occasion to employ a clingtight against the subject of an investigation, but I knew one when I saw one. I pointed it out to Jenore while deterring Yalum from asking what was happening.

We consulted the notice board then took the ascensor to the third floor, where a sign led us to Gievel's suite of offices. The who's-there admitted us and I approached a waist-high counter that separated the reception area from the inner office, where Shan Teeder was rising from a desk to approach us. I gestured silently for something to write on and something to write with. She reacted with minimal puzzlement, and passed me a stylus and notepad.

I wrote a quick note to inform her of what had happened in the street. She nodded her understanding then asked us to please take seats, as Maistre Gievel was in conference at the moment. He would soon be free.

We sat and said nothing. She went to an inner door, knocked, and stepped within, closing it behind her. A little time passed then she reappeared, accompanied by a man of middle years who had the look of one who enjoys a test of the intellect — I had met many such during my training as an op.

He also signaled for silence then came around the counter, holding up the notepad to let us know that he knew the situation. He approached Jenore and beckoned her to stand. When she did, he drew from an inner pocket a slim cylindrical instrument which he brought near to where the clingtight adhered to her sleeve. He held it there a moment then cocked his head in a manner that told me he was listening to a voice only he could hear. I noticed now that the collar of his upper garment was thicker than called for by fashion or utility; I deduced he was wearing a portable integrator, the kind that was useful for surveilling others and for detecting surveillance against oneself.

Having heard what he needed to hear, he made the gestures that are polite upon first encounters in Olkney and spoke cheerfully. "Please come into the office. We're very interested to discuss your case."

He led us past the counter and into the inner office, a well-appointed space with a desk, chairs, credenza, and a comfortable divan. Lok Gievel rose from behind the desk as we entered and bade us be seated.

"You remember us?" I said.

He inclined his head. "I do. The meeting led to some interesting events."

"Which appear to continue," I said, sitting beside Jenore on the divan.

"Indeed," said the intercessor, "but we'll get to that in a moment. First, I need each of you to declare your full names and home worlds, and to state for my integrator that you wish to engage me to represent you."

We did that, each in turn. When we had finished, Gievel sent a look toward the man who had brought us in, and received a nod of affirmation in return.

"Good." Gievel said. The device planted on you is now receiving a bland conversation regarding terms of service and fees, expressed in your own voices. That allows us to discuss your case in secure confidence while my discriminator friend"—he gestured to the other man—"sees if he can trace where the clingtight's signal is being directed."

"Unlikely," said the discriminator, "but worth an attempt."

"Agreed," I said then, "and who are you?"

Gievel answered, "He is the foremost freelance discriminator in Olkney. I present Ser Henghis Hapthorn."

Hapthorn made the motions of head and hands attendant on a formal introduction. Jenore, Yalum, and I responded in kind.

"Now to business," the intercessor said, but was interrupted by Hapthorn.

"They've caught on," he said. "The device has been deactivated."

He held out his hand toward Jenore. She plucked the gray shape from her sleeve and passed it over. He inspected it for a moment then said, "Good quality. At least we know we are not up against amateurs. Or misers."

"Would you like a description of the man who planted it?" I said.

"No need," Hapthorn said. "We have already acquired the images from who's-theres at the hostelry and along the street. He was well disguised, another indication of the caliber of the opposition."

Gievel rubbed his hands in pleasant anticipation. "This should prove an interesting case."

Jenore spoke up, "Our concern is not with its entertainment value, but whether or not we get to keep *Peregrinator*."

Gievel and Hapthorn exchanged looks. Both smiled.

Jenore said, "I am waiting for an answer."

The intercessor said, "You need not worry."

The discriminator said, "It would be premature to say."

HAPTHORN LED us to the rooftop, where a sleek, black volante waited. We boarded and flew across Olkney toward a residential quarter, the cityscape below showing the metropolis's age, since some of its districts were street after street of ancient ruins, while others, though still inhabited, preserved the architectural fashions of centuries past. The discriminator's lodgings were on a more recent street, Eckhevry Way, with a mix of residential buildings and street-level emporia. We alighted on the roof and descended to his second-floor premises, which included both his work room and his living quarters. Once inside, he waved us to chairs while he removed his collar-housed integrator, extracted its core, and installed it in an armature concealed in a glass-fronted curio case.

The integrator must have made some comment only its employer could hear, because Hapthorn snapped back at it, "Not now. Remind me later."

He then turned to us and, with an anticipatory rubbing of his long-fingered hands, said, "Let us begin."

"Where?" I said.

"At the beginning, of course."

It soon became clear that he meant all the way back to the arrival of Hallis Tharp on Forlor and my generation as a template for vat-grown soldiers. I took him through the decanting and transfer of my infant self to Thrais and my upbringing and career as an indentured gamer in Horsham's gaming house. Then the murders of Tharp and my employer by Magratte.

He stopped me there. "Magratte? The margrave?"

"The same. He was an agent of Lord Vullamir, head of a cult called the Immersion. They are—"

He stopped me again. "I have had experience of the Immersion," he said, and his face soured for a moment as he apparently called up a memory. "Continue," he said.

I recounted the rest of it: the dealing with Vullamir, the voyage to Forlor, the kidnapping of Jenore, my discovery of my peculiar origins, culminating in the duel in which I killed Magratte—that brought a raised eyebrow from my interlocutor—and the arrival of a Bureau of Scrutiny cruiser and the arrest of the cultists.

Again, Hapthorn stopped me. "The scroots arrested Vullamir? He submitted?"

"In the name of the Archon, they said. It seemed to affect him."

Hapthorn held up a hand to stop me again then clasped both hands behind his back and began to pace the floor, head bowed and brow furrowed. Then he stopped and said, "Integrator, what do we know of Lord Vullamir in recent times?"

He listened then said, "Aloud."

A well modulated voice spoke from the air. "It is assumed he remains on his estate. He has not been seen at any public functions since the Archon's septennial grand levee, almost three years ago."

"His function at the levee?" Hapthorn said.

"He is Commander of the Spoon, a hereditary title established in the reign of the Archon Valdesion IX. Therefore, he performs the fourth obeisance as the Archon progresses from his carriage to the dais and throne."

"What does that mean?" I said.

Hapthorn let his assistant answer. I learned that the biannual levee was an affair of ancient origin, consisting of a procession from the Archonate palace to an island on an artificial lake in the southern stretches of Olkney. A pavilion would be erected. Between the pavilion and the place where the Archon's carriage would touch down, artists would create a walkway fashioned from dyed sawdust, butterfly wings, and flower petals, arranged in fantastical patterns that had not varied in millennia. The Archon's footsteps during his progress through the colors would destroy the patterns.

"A symbolic act," the integrator said.

"Symbolizing what?" I said.

"No one remembers. The designs are ancient, and perhaps are the insignia of bygone powers—kagans and khans—who were bent to the Archon's will when the

Archonate first arose. It all began thousands upon thousands of years ago, when Old Earth was being repopulated after lying abandoned for an aeon. There are theories if you would like to hear them."

"He would not," Hapthorn said. "Continue the explanation."

The device said that members of the first- and second-tier aristocracies had roles to play in the ceremonies. Precedence and prestige adhered to these performances.

"No economic gains, I suppose," I said.

"Old Earth grandees of that rank are beyond economics. Their wealth is incalculable."

I snorted at such foolishness, which drew a look of surprise from the discriminator. Jenore said, "He is from Thrais. They are all transactionalists there."

Hapthorn appeared to be about to make some observation then he waved the thought away and said, "I think we are on to something."

He held up a hand to still us while he pursued his line of thought. I had the impression he was holding some internal conversation. When it came to a conclusion, he said, "Integrator, contact Old Confustible and see if it is available for a consultation."

"Old Con—" I began, but was interrupted when the assistant said, "It is. Shall I book an interview?"

"Do," Hapthorn said. "Earliest convenience."

"Done," said the device. "As soon as you can arrive."

Hapthorn rubbed his hands again. "Well," he said, "this *is* getting interesting."

"How so?" I said.

"Premature to say. Upstairs, now."

He headed for the stairs and we three followed.

THE BLACK VOLANTE lifted from its cradle as we
approached, its gravity obviators cycling just beyond the
range of human hearing. We climbed aboard and were
swept aloft. The vehicle oriented itself toward the dark mass
of the Archonate Palace sprawled atop the mountains that
serrated the northern skyline and the city began to flow
beneath us.

Hapthorn had sunk into a pensive mood. I decided to
interrupt him. "Who, or what, is Old Confustible?"

He glanced at me and I saw irritation, but only momen-
tary. "Very well," he said, "Old Confustible is an integrator
—indeed, the personal integrator of the Archon Filidor, who
named it during his apprentice days, when the device was
his combination teacher and taskmaster. It is very old."

"How old?"

"No one knows. It probably came to Old Earth with the
first resettlers."

That was old beyond old, a piling up of years measured
not in millennia but in aeons. "Which Aeon?" I said.

"Twelfth."

"And it has been in continuous operation ever since?" I
was concerned, because it was well known that integrators,
when they reached great age, were highly susceptible to the
"vagues," a condition that resembled human dementia
combined with hyperactivity, and was sometimes accompanied by a malicious streak.

"It has not suffered from the vagues," Hapthorn said.
"There seem to have been periods of . . . renewal."

I wanted to know how a freelance discriminator could
gain access to the Archon's personal adviser and confidant,

but the only answer I received was, "I am not at liberty to say."

The air car slid up a long incline of emptiness, until the palace loomed before us. It leveled off and approached a broad sunlit terrace, flagged in multicolored stones: squares, diamonds, circles, and demilunes. We slowed and alighted not far from a kiosk where visitors to the palace could make inquiries of the connectivity. Beyond the booth was the entrance to an imposing yet clearly ancient building, into which many of the people thronging the terrace were entering. I saw costumes of many worlds, even a *kilthe* like Yalum's.

"Terfel's Connaissarium," Hapthorn said, in response to my query. "Well worth a visit."

But now he led us to the public integrator's kiosk. The door opened at our approach and I saw that there was room within only for two. "The contested asset is yours," Hapthorn said, "so you are my client's client and will accompany me."

"Leave the door open for my friends to listen," I said.

"If the integrator so permits."

We stepped into the booth and sat on the two seats that unfolded from the wall.

"How may I serve?" said the usual neutral voice.

"We wish to consult the device known as Old Confustible," Hapthorn said.

"That is irregular. Address your queries to me and I will see if I can be of assistance."

Hapthorn signaled a negative. "No. The matter concerns a member of the first-tier aristocracy. The Archon's interests may be involved."

"It is not for you to judge the Archon's interests."

"Yes, it is." Hapthorn reached into an inner pocket and produced a badge the size of his palm. He held it up to the integrator's percepts. "Connect me to Old Confustible. Now."

The public integrator made no reply. A short time passed in silence then another voice spoke from the air around us. It was no less bland than the tones usual to such devices, yet there was an intimation of some power held in reserve, some unexpressed authority, beneath the anodyne way it said, "Hapthorn."

"The same," said the discriminator. "And this is Conn Labro, of Thrais —"

"Not of Thrais," said Old Confustible. "Of Forlor. Indeed, the Duke of Forlor."

Was there a hint of humor in that last remark? I could not tell. But the conversation moved on as Hapthorn said, "You will be familiar with the legal action brought against my client regarding the ownership of a space yacht."

"I am."

"The complainer is an entity called Olkney Holdings."

"Yes."

"Yet," said Hapthorn, "we can find no registration of such an entity. My client appears to be sued by a phantom."

"Yes, it would so seem," said the integrator.

"We were hoping you could provide some information."

"All integrators can provide information, some of us a great deal of it. What, specifically, do you wish to know?"

"Who owns Olkney Holdings?"

"No one. It owns itself."

I would have said that Henghis Hapthorn was not one to show surprise, no matter how unexpected the provocation.

But the integrator's assertion clearly struck him in the middle.

"How can that be?" he said.

"The explanation may prove complex," said Old Confustible.

"I will try to keep up," the discriminator said.

What followed was indeed complex, a narration of events stretching back not just millennia but into previous aeons. At the heart of the matter was the contest between houses of the upper reaches of the aristocracy that had transplanted itself to Old Earth during the great resettlement. The competition had been deep and wide, with some houses able to field actual armies of retainers to vie for dominance. They had built keeps and castles, devastated each other's counties in scorched-earth conflicts with burned towns and heaps of bodies.

Finally, in the Fourteenth Aeon, the Archonate—which had often been no more than a referee among contending houses—managed to ascend to ultimate power. Henceforth, the aristocracy would compete for prestige and precedence, but only by symbolic means and by arcane methods. Fashion became the prime arena in which they fought: fashion in every aspect of existence, from what they wore to what they ate, from what they hung on their walls to what grew in their vast, ornate gardens. Lordly life became a competition for abstruse prizes, and the mental energy once applied to planning battles and sieges was now focused on arranging marriages and structuring inheritances.

"It was in this last regard," said Old Confustible, "that Olkney Holdings came into being, late in the Eighteenth Aeon. Several houses of the first-tier, aided by more than a dozen vassal houses of the second, were involved in the struggle to foster—or frustrate—a marriage between the heirs of the House of Voilute and the House of Catrepolle. Vast fortunes were of course involved, but more important were the hereditary titles that would accrue to the offspring of the jointure."

Those titles, the integrator said, included three key offices of the Archonate's court. If the marriage was successful and "resulted in issue," the personage in question would hold all three offices at once.

"That would put him or her second in precedence in the court," said the voice of power. "That is, second to the Archon himself."

"Ah," said Hapthorn, "my understanding is that second place has always been divided between houses, so that there is never only one person, beyond the Archon, able to lord it over the other peers."

"And so it is," said the integrator, "but the Voilutes and Catrepolles thought they had found a way around it."

To me, of course, the entire story was another instance of the insanity that infected so many inhabitants of the Ten Thousand Worlds, especially those of high social rank. They would fight each other desperately for an empty purse, so long as that purse bore some emblem or had some history.

Old Confustible was carrying on its recitation. Some scholar, employed by the Catrepolles, had unearthed an ancient document which described how a kind of person-hood had been conferred upon an integrator, back during the Aeon of Wars. Through a flurry of petitions and imploring, coming from various directions and aimed at various elements of the Archonate bureaucracy, they managed to build up a technically legal basis for declaring one of the Voilutes' devices to be a sovereign person.

"This allowed them to move around certain assets and hereditary perquisites, to the end that the heir to their mutual fortunes would, upon reaching maturity, inherit the three courtly titles and become supreme over all others. The scheme was a dozen years in the making, and would have succeeded, except for the intervention of one of the Archon's integrators, which worked out the intent of the maneuverings and imposed a blockage."

"I presume," Hapthorn said, "that you were that integrator."

"The identities of the Archon's operatives are never revealed," Old Confustible said. "But the important part of the story is the Voilute integrator that was declared to be a person. It had committed no capital crimes and could not be denied its right to exist, and so it continued to 'live.' Useful roles were found for it to play, as if it were just another vassal of the House of Voilute. It received shares of inheritances and even married on two occasions."

"Why have I never heard of it?" Hapthorn said.

"Two reasons: there was no reason why you should, and the chicanery under which it was 'brought to life' was an embarrassment to the Archon."

"Which could not be allowed to be known."

Old Confustible said, "Have you ever heard of the Archon being embarrassed?"

Hapthorn showed a face that expressed a memory. "I remember when Filidor was a young hellion, romping about the city with a coterie of high-ranked ne'er-do-wells."

"He was not then the Archon."

The discriminator conceded the point. "Back to the issue at hand. Do I assume that this Olkney Holdings is an integrator and that it holds title to the yacht?"

"It is and does. And the title passed to it long before Lord Vullamir leased the ship for his decadent purposes."

I spoke now. "For which I assume he and his fellow cultists of the Immersion suffered some dire penalty."

"You may assume so," said the integrator. "I can assure you none of them are content with their present circumstances. Nor are those circumstances likely to change."

"Still," said Hapthorn, "the ship was abandoned on a planet on which my client was the sole ruler. Its confiscation was legal under the law of Forlor."

"That law being whatever Ser Labro says it is," said Old Confustible.

"Indeed, but the principle of planetary sovereignty is long established in the Ten Thousand Worlds."

"So it is," said the integrator.

"Then, despite the history of ancient chicanery and the novelty of an emancipated integrator," Hapthorn said, "there is no case for my client to answer."

The voice of authority answered, "There is not."

"Then why are they suing me?" I said.

To which the ancient integrator said, "That's a very good question."

"Is there a very good answer?" I said.

"I'm sure there is," said Old Confustible. "But I don't know it."

Hapthorn and I stood up to leave, but the integrator asked us to delay for a moment. It said to me, "Turn around slowly. I wish to scan you."

"Why?"

The question went unanswered. A light above one of its percepts glowed then faded. We turned to leave, the voice said, "Visit the Connaissarium."

Again, I asked why, and again there was no answer.

HAPTHORN WANTED to fly us back to his lodgings for a discussion, but Jenore, who had remained patient during our long conference with the Archon's integrator, said she had always wanted to visit the Grand Connaissarium of Terfel III. Yalum said he, too, had heard of the place, even though he had spent his life far down The Spray.

Hapthorn hitched his shoulders and said, "It's as good a place as any to do some thinking, I suppose." And so we joined the files of people making their way through the several doors of the entrance.

Inside was a grand foyer, the ceiling lost in dimness far above. The vast space contained several exhibits. Immediately before us was a display of "entourages" taken from members of the Community of Disciplined Aspirants, a murderous cult that was expunged by the scroots a few years back. A placard told how Aspirants constantly engaged in physical exercises designed to build up physical strength, particularly in the hands. That was because, in a dream or a fume-induced state, an Aspirant would occasionally experience a vision that sent him out, clad in only a breechclout and his own tattooed hide, to strangle some unsuspecting victim.

A souvenir of the encounter—a toenail or flake of flesh —would be harvested from the corpse and sealed in the Aspirant's entourage. This was a box as long as my hand, though of only two fingers' width, shaped from the shell of a clam found nowhere but in the waters of Mornedy Sound. An Aspirant's first task, upon acceptance into the Community, was to dive into the gray depths, choose a clam from those scattered on the bottom, and consume its contents while still underwater. Those who drowned in the process were known as "false calls."

An Aspirant who lived would clean out the shell, polish its nacreous lining, and affix a fine silver clasp that kept it closed. Then, over the years, he would await his visions and gradually fill the box with relics of his murders. Finally, when the Aspirant passed to what the cult called "the truer world," the souls of those from whom these fragments had been taken would be waiting for him, "with cushions and comforts," to serve and cosset him through eternity.

The Community had been a deeply secret society, drawing its members from the upper quintile of Olkney's social pyramid.

"Another aristocratic sect," Jenore said, her face set in a grimace of distaste. "What is wrong with these people?"

"From my experience," Yalum said, "which is considerable, the combination of vast wealth and the virtual impunity that comes with elevated rank inevitably lead to excesses. A normal person asks, 'Why do they do it?' to which the only answer is, 'Because they can.'"

Whatever thoughts were passing through my friend's mind caused him to take out the object he called his "soother" and rub his thumb over it.

I said, "It seems an inordinate waste of energy, not to mention lives, in pursuit of a fantasy."

Hapthorn weighed in with, "That could describe whole eras of the history of humanity." He looked over at another exhibit. "Let us look at the boats."

We followed him over to another area where seacraft of many types and periods were displayed on or in transparent cases, or floated on air currents that gave the impression they were sailing in circles across the floor, or hung by wires from a grid high overhead. They were of a great variety of designs, from wooden vessels of the Dawn Times, propelled by breezes that pushed against sheets of fabric, to the armored "clankers" that once ruled Tenth Aeon seas but could also roll on shore, their turret guns spewing projectiles and the collagenic fire known as "mudgery."

Mixed among the larger units were small craft of all sizes and designs, some graceful with raked decks, others squat and utilitarian. They were painted all manner of colors, and many flew flags that once must have conveyed meaning, but now were unintelligible save for the most perspicacious of scholars.

The hanging and floor-hugging vessels were in constant motion, but as we stepped among them they avoided us, breezing past our heads or feet, as if they were crewed by tiny sailors, tugging ropes and pushing tillers. I found it a pointless display, yet somehow bemusing. Then I spotted what must be a foranq, of the kind Jenore's people built and enriched over centuries to commemorate the generations of their great families. I was about to point it out to her when Yalum gave a little sound of surprise and said, "That one's marked like my good luck piece."

I looked where he pointed and saw an antique yacht moving smoothly and rapidly across the floor away from us. It was powered by invisible means, most of its upper structure enclosed in a smooth extension of the hull, except for a large, open rear deck set with miniature chairs and divans where the passengers might lounge. A prominent flagpole topped by a wavering banner rose from the stern, and it was this flag that had caught Yalum's attention. I tried to see the device it bore, but the vessel was moving rapidly away from us, so that I viewed the banner edge-on.

Then Jenore spotted the miniature foranq and exclaimed. I looked where she pointed.

"That's the Shenglung family's," she said. "I wonder who carved the replica. Tandoor, probably." Her face took on the wistful look of memory I had seen in her before. "I danced at my friend Ier's fourteenth-birthday celebration on that foranq, and afterward I kissed . . ." She left the rest unspoken.

"Perhaps we should visit Shorraff, after all," I said.

She looked at me in mild surprise. "You are becoming more human, aren't you?"

I was about to respond, but Hapthorn claimed our attention. He was holding his communicator. "Maistre Gievel would like us to attend him," he said.

We left the boats and behind and followed him out to the terrace and the volante. Jenore linked her arm in mine. I needed no assistance in walking, nor did she, yet it felt good.

"THIS GETS INTERESTING," said the intercessor. Hapthorn had filled him in on the conversation with the Archon's personal integrator. "We can assume that Filidor is involved in some way, otherwise his head chamberlain would not be speaking to us." He rubbed his hands together. "Interesting, indeed."

Yalum and I received that information with equanimity. Jenore had a different reaction.

"Interesting?" she said. "Where I come from, having the Archon 'get involved' is the last thing you want to happen."

"Where do you come from?" Hapthorn asked.

"Shorraff."

It took a moment for the information to register then the discriminator said, "Ah, the Parfirion War."

"Exactly," Jenore said.

It took but a moment for Gievel to make the connection, but Yalum and I were still out of reach. "What is the Porfirion War?" I asked.

Jenore would have answered, but the discriminator beat her to the starting line. "A . . . situation, in the County of Shorraff, several decades ago. A dispute between families that grew into a conflict between entire clans. Prestige was at stake. Hostilities began with verbal exchanges then escalated into faction fights, first with fists and feet then with weapons. Other clans tried to mediate, but neither side would give a minim."

I saw Hapthorn consulting his memory. "Ultimately, the situation collapsed into open warfare. A settlement was burned to the ground, and a number of foranqs were torched. The dispossessed survivors vowed a deadly revenge, and set about taking it. Bodies piled up, as did the ash heaps of whole communities. Then one side came up with the idea of attacking a neutral clan, making it look as if the arsonists' enemies were to blame.

"Soon no one knew who was who. Violent anarchy raged up and down the shoreline. And then a stranger came to town."

"A stranger?" I said.

Gievel answered. "It is one of the functions of the Archonate, known since time immemorial as *the progress of esteeming the balance*. The Archon travels the realm in disguise, correcting wrongs and setting dysfunctions aright.

The Archon might be anybody, and might do anything to anybody. Or he might do nothing, in just the right way."

"Well, he didn't do nothing this time," Jenore said. "He brought down cruisers and transports and battalions of scroots. In one night, they rounded up the warring clans, from bearded elders down to babes in arms. They hustled them onto the transports, the ships lifted off, and none of them were ever heard from again."

"What happened to them?" I said.

Jenore's shoulders lifted and fell and she slowly shook her head. "No one ever knew."

Hapthorn and Gievel looked at each other. "Not quite no one," the discriminator said. "They were moved to a large, uninhabited island in the southern ocean and deposited there with rudimentary tools and some seeds. The terrain was rough and the climate discouraging, and the only way they could survive was by cooperation."

Gievel said, "I heard that intermarriage between the clans was strongly recommended, and became part of the newly developed ethos. The new generations had more pressing concerns than their elders' hostilities. Today, they are a flourishing culture, proud of their self-reliance."

"Why did they never come back?" Jenore said.

"They think of the people of Shorraff as effete and obsessed with irrelevancies," Hapthorn said. "They prefer to be who they are, where they are."

"But why did we never hear of all this?"

Hapthorn put on the face of a man who must belabor the obvious. "Because the Archon's aim was not only to resolve a problem but to teach a lesson. 'No one knew what happened to them' is a sharper-toothed message than, 'And they lived happily ever after.'"

"Besides," Gievel said, "our Filidor is a gentler autocrat than his predecessor of those times."

"Still," I said, "he sounds to me like a randomizing factor. Now that we can assume he has taken an interest, how do we make sure that his interests coincide with ours?"

The intercessor and discriminator again exchanged a meaningful look. Hapthorn said, "Well, it would be premature to say."

WE WERE SENT BACK to the Videlia Inn, to wait while our counselors pursued the lines of inquiry Old Confustible had opened up. Yalum went to his room. Jenore and I decided it was time to eat and found seats in the refectory. The menu offered several dishes that could be found anywhere up and down The Spray, but Jenore advised me that the local versions could be different. I was not terribly hungry, so I opted for a light meal: cold, cooked meats in a herb-infused aspic, all surrounded by a light and flaky pastry. It came with three dipping sauces, one sweet, one tangy, one fiery. She had a soufflé made of gripple eggs. We both had a pale wine suffused with tiny bubbles that she said was of a provenance so impossibly ancient its actual origin was lost in the shadows of time.

We ate in silence for a short time then I took us back to her remarks about my becoming "more human."

"I think I have always been human," I said. "The plasm of no other species was introduced into my initial zygote."

"A poor choice of words," she said. "I meant you were becoming more . . ."—she sought for a word—"understanding of the way others live their lives."

"I think I have always understood that there are many different ways to organize cultures." I took a bite of the pastry dipped in the hot compote then needed to sip the wine. "I just see some of them as irrational."

"You mean insane," she said.

I dipped my head in concurrence. "Take these Old Earth aristocrats. They organize their lives around contests that are meaningless."

"Because winning or losing does not gain them or cost them any pelf?" she said. Before I could answer, she went on, "But they have so much wealth that the loss or acquisition of vast sums is lost in their account books."

She raised her glass and pointed it at me. "Consider, you now command a fortune of your own, and Green Circle will pay into it probably more than you could ever spend, even if you wallowed in self-indulgence. If you had just walked a distance only to discover a hole in your pocket that meant you had lost a two-dinket coin, would you turn around and retrace your steps to recover it?"

"No. The effort would not be worth two dinkets, and I would probably have more rewarding things to do with the time."

She sipped her wine. "There you have it."

"No," I said, "I don't. Because the uses that these Old Earth lordlings consider worth their time and effort are ridiculous: whether one bows third or fourth to the Archon, or is Commander of the Spoon at a banquet. Is there a rank for Wiper of the Chin?"

She laughed. "There well may be. I picked the wrong breed of human to be my example. They are ridiculous, indeed." Her amusement faded. "But they are also vicious and powerful, as we know from hard experience."

"Agreed," I said. "They are mad and dangerous, and that's all I need to understand about them."

WE HAD PUT our communicators on standby during lunch. Now, as we stepped out of the ascensor on our floor, we told them to reactivate. Mine immediately flashed its alert signal and told me I had a message from Yalum.

"Play it," I said, but when the device did so, I heard only a gasp and a clunking, clattering sound, like furniture being disturbed. My gaze went to the time signature and I realized that the non-message was only moments old.

Our room and Yalum's were on a corridor around a corner from the ascensors. I ran toward it. Behind me, I heard Jenore say my name and "What?" Then I was around the corner and racing the short distance to where the door to Yalum's room stood ajar. I hit it with my shoulder and burst into the chamber.

There were two men, wearing nondescript singlesuits and close-fitting masks. One of them had my friend on the floor, belly down, a forearm pressing against his throat. Yalum was bucking, but I could see that he was near to unconsciousness. His communicator lay where it had dropped from his hand. The other intruder was beside the sleeping platform on which Yalum's traveling bag was open. His back was toward me and he was rooting around in the valise.

He turned, shocked, as I crashed through the doorway. But he recovered fast. His hand reached into a pocket of his garment.

That motion decided me on which to tackle first. Before

his hand came out of his pocket I threw myself at him, delivering a flying kick to his chest that hurled him backwards across the bed. I landed on my side, rolled, and got to my feet as the other one came at me. I was tangentially aware of Yalum choking on the floor and attempting to rise. Then the second man was on me, throwing a flurry of blows that kept me busy blocking.

He was good, but I was better. In moments, I was inside his reach and delivered a short jab to his solar plexus then as he reflexively bent forward, I head-butted his nose. Blood sprayed and he staggered back. But now his comrade was up on his feet on the other side of the sleeping platform, looking about him.

I have the useful faculty, installed in me by Hallis Tharp, that in combat my neural connections speed up. Thus, I knew that whatever had been in the first man's pocket had fallen from his grasp and he was searching the floor for it. I saw no reason to give him leisure for his search. I set my foot against the side of the bed and pushed it hard and fast. The solid part of the platform was at just the right height to strike the man's knees. I heard one of them crack. Then I heard his scream.

I reached across the bed, seized the front of his singlesuit and yanked him toward me, while my other hand formed a fist and punched him in the throat. He fell across the platform, making the same noises Yalum had a few seconds before.

The other one was recovering, but not quickly enough. I opened my hand, put my thumb and first two fingers against his throat, where the carotid synapse lies just under the skin, and pressed. His brain experienced a sudden catastrophic rise in blood pressure and told his vagus nerve to shut the system down. The light went out of his eyes and he collapsed. I did nothing to break his fall.

"Yalum!" said Jenore's voice behind me, absurdly slowed down. The fight with the two attackers had lasted only seconds. Now that it was over, my body returned to its resting state. She was helping my friend toward a chair. I joined the effort. The blood-flush had gone out of his face and he was breathing almost normally.

"Are you all right?" I said, and when he signaled a positive, I left him to Jenore's ministrations and looked around the room. First I found the weapon dropped by the man with the broken knee. It was a slapper, a device that fit into the palm, with a recessed needle at its center that delivered one of a selection of chemicals when it struck flesh. I put it in my pocket.

The other man was still unconscious. I searched him and found no weapon, but there were some simple restraints in one of his pockets. I used them to bind the wrists of him and his companion then propped them both up against the sleeping platform. I closed the door.

"Well," I said, "we'd better wake them up and see what they have to say for themselves." I took the slapper out of my pocket and said, "This might be useful." I looked around the chamber, musing to myself, "What else have we got?"

Jenore said, "We can't torture them, Conn."

I continued my search. "Why not?"

"It's a civilized world, at least this part of it."

I looked at her. "They weren't behaving in a civilized manner. What was that old saying? 'When one is on Haxxi one eats flonge and smiles.'"

"We're not on Haxxi." She gave Yalum another looking

over then took out her communicator and told it to contact Henghis Hapthorn, urgently.

The discriminator responded within moments. Jenore told him what had happened, listened for a moment then closed the device. "He'll be here directly. He advises us to do nothing."

I saw inaction as a missed opportunity, but she insisted, and I gave in.

Seven

"The question is," Hapthorn said, "what were they looking for?"

He looked down at our two prisoners. They had regained consciousness before he arrived, and had refused to answer my questions as to their identities and their purpose. They gave Hapthorn the same blank stares of defiance when he made the same inquiries.

I agreed with him that the intruders had been seeking something. "We can assume they did not come to kill, or they would have brought lethal weapons." Hapthorn had sniffed the droplet he pressed out of the slapper and identified it as a powerful soporific. They hadn't used it on Yalum because the one who was choking him when I burst in was mere moments away from rendering my friend unconscious.

"That one was searching his bag," I said as I indicated the one I had kicked.

"Hmm," said Hapthorn. "A moment, please." He went to the door and stepped out of the room, returning almost immediately to tell us, "They have also searched your quarters."

"Presumably not finding what they were looking for," I said, "or they would not have come across the hall to Yalum's."

"We should assume that they are connected somehow to Vullamir's family and the legendary self-emancipated integrator." Hapthorn studied the two men. "Yet they are not servants."

I asked him now he could know that, and he replied that servitors to the first-tier aristocracy were as inbred as their masters. "They might, by now, be classified as a subspecies of human. One thing is certain: they have definite physical characteristics that these two do not exhibit."

He knelt beside one of the men, pushed him away from the sleeping platform, and pulled up the sleeve of his garment. "Ahah," he said, and moved so I could see what was exposed: a black tattoo on the underside of the forearm, just below the elbow, in the shape of an open hand.

I showed that the revelation meant nothing to me, but Jenore said, "The Hand Organization."

"Exactly," said Hapthorn. He put the bound man back where he had been and stood. "Which means there is not much point interrogating them. There is nothing we can do to them that would be worse than what the Hand would do if they broke the code of silence."

"Are you sure?" I said.

"Conn, don't," Jenore said, and shook her head at me when I looked her way. I subsided.

Hapthorn said, "We can either let them go or hand them over to the Bureau of Scrutiny. The scroots will at least be able to identify them and may derive some intelligence just from their presence in Olkney at this moment. Also, I'm sure the Bureau will be interested to discover an apparent connection between the Hand and the complainer in your legal dispute."

The discriminator regarded the captives and stroked a thoughtful chin. "Indeed I am interested on my own account."

He looked toward Yalum. "Are you in need of attention?"

Yalum massaged his throat. His voice, when he spoke, was hoarse but resonated with its usual strength. "I will be fine in a moment or two," he said.

He reached into the pocket of his *kilthe* and brought out the soothing object. As he did so, I happened to glance toward our two criminals. My facility with capturing micro-expressions did not fail me now. I saw a widening of eyes, a dilation of pupils, a brief, tiny tightening of one man's lips and an instantly repressed indrawing of breath by the other.

Hapthorn saw what I saw. I could tell by the way he now studiedly sought to still his own features.

The discriminator brought out his own communicator and instructed it. A moment later he spoke into the device. "Henghis Hapthorn for Colonel-Investigator Warhanny." A brief paused ensued then Hapthorn said, "Brustrum, I have two soldiers of the Hand Organization in a hostelry chamber." Another pause then, "Forced entry, assault, attempted theft." A last pause then he named the establishment and the room number and closed the device.

"The scroots will be with us soon," he said. He looked at me then threw a pointed glance at Yalum's soother then came back to me again, and added, "Let me do the talking."

I said, "The scroot you were just talking to—Warhanny was his name?—he didn't ask any questions, did he?"

"No," Hapthorn said, "he didn't."

COLONEL-INVESTIGATOR BRUSTRUM WARHANNY was a long-faced man past middle age whose dominant expression said that life had lived up to his expectations, but those expectations had never been high. He came into the room accompanied by four men in the same uniform as he wore, black with green accents. The scroots divided into two pairs who wordlessly and efficiently stood up the Hand soldiers and hustled them out of the room.

Warhanny gave each of us the look that police veterans wash over new encounters. The sight of us apparently did nothing to raise his opinion of humanity. He settled on Hapthorn, and said, "Well?"

The discriminator brought him up to date. He did not mention Yalum's pocket piece. Nor our conversation with Old Confustible. The senior scroot heard him out in silence then said, "And have you nothing more to tell me?"

"Nothing," said Hapthorn.

Now Warhanny showed the face of a man who knows he is being lied to. "Nothing about a recent trip to the Archonate Palace and a conversation with one of its integrators, a consultation that your own integrator could have arranged from the comfort of your work room?"

Hapthorn put on an expression that might have been taken for blithe innocence. I was surprised to see that Warhanny could look even more disgusted.

"Archon's business?" he said.

Hapthorn maintained his guileful appearance of a lack of guile.

Warhanny sighed. "At which," he said, "a simple old scroot recognizes the depths looming beneath him and quietly paddles back to shore."

"Always a pleasure," the discriminator said. A moment later, he closed the chamber door on Warhanny's departure. Now he paused and again, by the expressions that flitted across a face he no doubt thought impassive, I had the impression I was seeing two people conduct a silent conversation.

Then he rubbed his hands together and extended one of them to Yalum. "May I examine the object in your pocket?"

Yalum had returned it there before the Bureau's entry. Now he took it out and handed it to Hapthorn. The discriminator examined it, turning it over and studying both sides. He said, "I would like my integrator to take a close look at this."

"Why?" Yalum said. He clearly did not want to let the object go.

Hapthorn looked to me. "Do you want to tell him?"

I was willing. "Yalum," I said, "that thing is what they were looking for."

Again, my friend said, "Why?"

I signaled that I did not know. Hapthorn said, "That's what we need to find out. I suggest you three wait here while I take it back to my lodgings and examine it." He turned the polished oblong over in his hand then added, "Though I might need to go and ask a certain ancient integrator for the full story."

"What if the Hand sends more soldiers?" Jenore said.

The discriminator put Yalum's keepsake in his pocket

and showed us all a calming palm. "I think we can assume that the Bureau will now take a close interest in your welfare. Warhanny is glum, but he knows his business."

Jenore, Yalum, and I repaired across the hall to the other room to wait. I had a question for my friend. "Where did you find that thing?"

"It was in the chest that contained the life masks. Something about it appealed to me, so I kept it."

"Whatever it is," Jenore said, "it appears it's at the center of all that's been happening."

"So it does," I said. "It is important to somebody, though we don't know why."

WHEN HAPTHORN RETURNED, we learned a little more. "Do you know what a life mask is?" he said.

"We do," I said. "I have worn one. It was not a pleasant experience."

"Indeed," Hapthorn said, "and it was not pleasant for many of the personas confined to them."

He explained that the "essences"—the core of an individual's personality—were collected millennia ago when doing so was a fashion among the Old Earth aristocracy. Later, on naming days and other events, they could be revived as simulacra to participate in family events. More generations passed before someone had the idea of installing the essences in an armature that could be worn by a living person, allowing the ghosts of an ancestor to connect directly to the wearer's sensorium. That practice, too, was for a time fashionable. But then the mode passed and the life masks, with their essences, went back into storage.

The fad had recently been revived, after centuries, and the upper-tier aristocrats had diverted themselves by sharing the half-life of their long-dead forbears. Now, once again, the fashion had passed on, and the ghostly personas were again confined to darkness and silence.

"Of course," Hapthorn said, "some of them went mad for lack of stimulation, chasing memories and fantasies, like so many insomniacs whose sleeping platforms fail to cosset them."

"What does that have to do with my good-luck piece?" Yalum said. "And, by the way, I would like it returned."

Hapthorn shrugged and handed it over. "Your keepsake is one of the modules in which an essence is stored. It holds the simulacra of one of Vullamir's ancestors, an archduke named Arbatheon, who lived some nine thousand years ago. The essence, when inserted into a life mask, proved to be insane. The madness may have been a result of its centuries of isolation, or Arbatheon might have been a complete raver when he was fully alive. Insanity is heritable among the aristocracy and quite a few have passed their lives locked up in cushioned quarters."

"But why do they want it?" I said. "What use is a mad dead duke to anyone today?"

"Good question," Hapthorn said.

"And is there a good answer?"

He shrugged again. "I'm sure there is. We just need to find it."

Yalum, Jenore, and I did not leave the Videlia Inn and dined in our chamber. When I looked out the door, I saw figures down the corridor in both directions. They wore green and black.

Hapthorn had left us to go back to his lodgings. He later called to say he had not been able to arrange another interview with the Archon's venerable integrator. "The situation must be fluid," he said.

"What does that mean?" Jenore asked him. But he answered that it would be premature to say, and he would try again tomorrow.

We locked our doors and settled for the night, which passed without incident. In the morning, breakfast arrived, the cups and plates inspected by one of our scroot guardians. After we had eaten, my communicator told me I had a call from Lok Gievel.

"The suit has been withdrawn," he said.

"You mean it's over?"

"My part in it is. I suggest you retain Hapthorn yourself."

I said, "Before we do that, may I ask something about the discriminator?"

"Go ahead."

"I have had the impression that he is sometimes distracted. By what appear to be internal . . . divisions."

Gievel said nothing for a moment then, "I have noticed that, too. It is a recent thing. But it does not seem to affect his performance."

I weighed that for a moment then said, "Have him call me."

～

HENGHIS HAPTHORN DID NOT CALL. He arrived. "Do you wish to retain me?" he said.

We had discussed the matter among the three of us. "We do," I said.

"What do you wish to happen?"

That had been a matter of contention over breakfast. Yalum wanted to keep his good luck piece. Jenore wanted the whole matter to be over and done with, and wanted to give the mad archduke's essence to whoever had hired the Hand Organization, so we could leave Old Earth, recover *Peregrinator*, and resume our life on Novo Bantry.

I had had a different perspective. I had been thinking about the matter overnight. "The object in question, whatever it is," I told them, "is actually mine, part of the property I acquired when Lord Vullamir abandoned the ship and its contents on Forlor."

Yalum began to protest, but Jenore put a hand on his arm and said, "Let us see where he is going with this."

"The object," I said, "must be of value. No one institutes a law suit, sends operatives down The Spray to track us then hires a major crime syndicate to attempt a recovery, for an item of negligible worth. My upbringing tells me I should first discover its true value then levy an appropriate charge for its surrender."

"How would we determine the 'appropriate charge'?" Jenore said.

"We find out who wants it and why."

And that was what I told the discriminator.

He put on a thoughtful expression. "As to who, we have assumed it is Lord Vullamir's family, most likely his heir. That appears to be one Viscount Chaderanth, who would now be styled Lord Chaderanth if Vullamir's conduct has led to his demise, or to his being stripped of his title."

"Presumably," I said, "by the Archon Filidor."

"Presumably. What is known is that Vullamir has not been seen or heard from since he departed Old Earth on his yacht—now your yacht—some time ago. Chaderanth has been seen, but not much nor by many. He has tended to stay on the family's estate in the County of Albermarle."

"What about the emancipated integrator?" Jenore said.

"We know only that it once existed and presumably still does," Hapthorn said. "We may assume it is also on the family estate."

"So we have some idea of the who, but the why remains a mystery," I said.

"Indeed. And the fact that Chaderanth has employed cutouts and subterfuges to weave a fog of mystery around the issue indicates that the answer to that question may affect his prestige, And therefore will be difficult to pull out of him."

We paused to think. Again, I saw that curious flicker of expressions across the discriminator's face. It gave the impression that two people were discussing, even arguing, over some point.

In another moment, that dispute appeared to be resolved. Hapthorn said, "I have applied insight to the matter. I think we should open negotiations with the other side. We may be able to draw inferences from their responses to our overtures that will help us understand what is going on."

Yalum said, "I would not like to lose the thing."

Hapthorn said, "That may be necessary."

I said, "You are my friend. Whatever we derive from this business, I will share with you."

The offer did not make Yalum entirely happy, but he said, in a tone of resignation, that he appreciated it. I saw Jenore blink in surprise then she suppressed a look of happy approval. I supposed she was thinking that once again that I was becoming "more human."

I addressed Hapthorn. "How do we open negotiations?"

He thought only briefly then said, "We need to approach the right Hand operative at the right level."

"Would Green Circle be of any use in that regard?" I said.

I saw shock and mild consternation animate the discriminator's features. "Not at all. Relations between the two syndicates are fractious at the moment. A disputed territory." He studied me for a moment. "Why would you ask that?"

I saw Jenore's frown and said, "It would be premature to say."

Now I drew a frown from Hapthorn, but he pushed on to more relevant matters. "As to how, I know a fellow who has a reputation as a reliable middler. He will know the right sleeve to tug upon."

"Is he a criminal, too?" Jenore asked.

"Oh, yes," said Hapthorn. "Quite an accomplished practitioner, but unaligned, a freelancer. At the moment he is between 'operations,' as he calls them and is staying at his club."

"There is a club for criminals?" I said.

"There is a club that tolerates criminals, so long as they pay the fees and refrain from preying upon fellow members. It's called Quirks. I have dined there. Its chef is quite accomplished, which is why the fellow we're discussing has a membership.

"His name is Luff Imbry."

HE CAME to see us as the hostelry. I had not known what to expect, and was surprised to see Hapthorn shepherd into our chamber a man who was easily the most corpulent example of humanity I had ever encountered. He was almost spherical, yet moved with a lightness of step and a certain grace. He was dressed in a rather old-fashioned style, with four pieces of clothing visible, not including a complicated folding of cloth under his several chins and a small-brimmed hat.

He examined us with a flicker of his eyes then said, "You wish to make contact with the Hand Organization?"

I said, "We have already made contact with them. Now we want to talk to them."

"About?"

"Hapthorn hasn't told you?"

He smiled a small smile. "I prefer to hear the facts from the principals. I take it you are the principals in this matter?"

"We are," I said. I turned to Yalum. "Show him the object."

Reluctantly, my friend passed the polished oblong to the fat man. Imbry took it. First he studied one side at arm's length then turned it over and did the same. Then he reached into a pocket of his six-buttoned vest and withdrew a small ocular device. He placed it to one eye and drew down the brow to hold it in place. Then he brought the object close to its percept and studied it for quite a while, turning the oblong to view both sides as well as the edges.

When he handed it back to Yalum, his face was composed, but he said, "Interesting."

"You know what it is?" I said.

"As a matter of fact, I do. It's an ancient essence, the kind inserted into life masks until the fashion waned. Coincidentally, I had occasion to wear such a mask, not long ago."

I let my face show interest, but a pudgy hand waved away the unspoken query. "Hapthorn said you wished to know its value."

"We do."

Now the hand gave a negligent wave. "To a collector, a modest sum. But I gather quite a bit has already been spent seeking to acquire it. Intercessors' and confidential operatives' fees, not to mention what the Hand Organization charges for rough-and-tumble."

I signaled that was so.

"So it is more than it seems," Imbry said. "Do you know who has been seeking to acquire it?"

"There is a good likelihood it is Lord Chaderanth, heir to Lord Vullamir."

Imbry's brows climbed. "First-tier aristocrats and Hand operatives usually occupy separate universes. The situation is unusual. In my experience, it is unique."

"Can you assist us?" Jenore said.

The fat man's head moved in an equivocating manner, but after a moment's reflection, he said, "I believe so. I can certainly try."

"Then please do so," Jenore said.

Imbry looked at me. I confirmed Jenore's statement.

"Very well," he said, "there remains only the matter of my fee."

I started to speak but Jenore cut me off. She named a figure. Imbry named a multiple of that number. A brief haggle ensued and a final figure was agreed upon. The fat man asked for payment in advance, saying, "Whenever one deals with the Hand Organization, there is always a possibility that one will never deal with anyone, about anything, ever again."

Jenore countered with, "Then you would have no use for the fee, would you?"

Another brief argument determined that we would pay half in advance and half after he succeeded in bringing us face-to-face with the Hand.

"And surviving that encounter," Jenore specified.

"Of course," Imbry said. "If you don't survive, how can you pay me the balance?"

I sorted through our stock of credit chips and paid him the first half. He said he would return when the meeting was arranged.

"How long will that take?" I said.

He indicated that he could not say. "I will speak to someone who will speak to someone, who will probably speak to Lord Chaderanth or someone who speaks for him. How long it takes for messages to go up and down that chain, I cannot estimate. It depends upon the degree of urgency being felt at the other end."

He departed. We waited. Apparently the degree of urgency on the Chaderanth estate was considerable, because the fat man was back in a short while.

"It is arranged," he said. "Two hours from now at a place called Bolly's Snug."

"What kind of place is that?" I said.

Imbry produced a brief, knowing smile. "Like the situation, it is unique."

As we departed the Videlia Inn, flanked by Bureau of Scrutiny agents, we found Henghis Hapthorn hovering near the front steps. I noticed he was wearing the portable integrator housing that resembled a stuffed collar. I also saw Luff Imbry give him a look freighted with suspicion.

"You do not intend to participate?" the fat man said. "It's bad enough taking these scroots near Bolly's." He indicated the integrator. "Your device will not be tolerated."

Hapthorn said he did not propose to enter the rendezvous location. "I will keep my distance."

We traveled by a ground car Imbry had arranged, the scroots going fore and aft via air cars. When Imbry said we were nearing our destination, the Bureau vehicles went aloft and hovered. A short distance later, we slowed in front of a nondescript building in front of which half a dozen hard-looking individuals waited. Nothing identified the premises except a hand-sized brass plaque set beside the door that bore the single word: *Bolly's*.

Accompanied by the Hand soldiers, with the fat man leading, we mounted the three steps and entered, finding ourselves in a hallway. To one side, a wide archway opened onto a common room with scattered tables, a long bar, and booths along the walls. Several seats were occupied, and there were standees at the bar. None of them paid us any attention. I assumed it was the kind of establishment where taking an interest in others' comings and goings was discouraged.

We passed the archway and continued down the hallway to a plain door with a who's-there set into its lintel. The door opened as we approached and we went into an eight-sided foyer, with another anonymous door in each of the other seven walls.

Imbry approached one of these. It also opened and we followed him into a narrow room with a long table lined with chairs on either side. Three Hand operatives, two men and a woman, waited for us along one side, their faces impassive. Imbry took a seat at the head of the table and indicated that we three should sit on the empty side.

We did so. No greetings were exchanged. Once we were seated, Imbry said, "The purpose of this meeting is to discuss the terms under which the object in question will be turned over to your clients, and the price to be paid."

The Hand operative in the middle of the three was old enough for his hair to have grayed. He exhibited an air of authority. I estimated he must be of a similar rank to Gustus Hellivance, the Green Circle force-in-charge.

"Show us the object," he said.

I was about to respond, but Imbry said, "It is not here. It is in a safe place. If we can come to an understanding, it will be turned over in circumstances agreeable to both sides."

The Hand man gave a brief nod. "State your proposed terms."

We had discussed with Imbry what we would say. I ticked off items on my fingers. "An irrevocable quit-claim against any ownership of the yacht; a guarantee of no reprisals against us three or anyone associated with us; a negotiated price to be paid in full upon handover."

The Hand trio met these proposals without a response. Then I touched a fourth finger and said, "An explanation."

Gray Hair raised one eyebrow. "An explanation?"

"We know what the object is. We want to know why it is of such importance to your client."

The woman, seated to the senior operative's left, leaned in and whispered into his ear. His face remained impassive. "Unlikely," he told me.

"If we don't know its significance," I said, "how can we establish a fair value?"

The woman whispered again. Gray Hair listened then I saw him come to a conclusion. "It is not our decision to make," he said. "But we will put your proposed terms to the client."

"Who is Lord Chaderanth," I said. I did not expect my assertion to be confirmed, or even responded to, but I watched for the microexpression, and the brief flash I detected told me our supposition was correct.

"If there is nothing more," Imbry addressed the Hand people, "we will adjourn until you have further instructions."

At that point, he indicated that we should rise and exit through the door by which we had entered. The other side sat where they were. I supposed that a room like this might have at least one other, less obvious exit.

We made our way to the front of the building, and down the steps into the ground car, watched every step of the way by Hand soldiers. The vehicle turned and took us back to our hostelry, the scroot air cars descending to their previous positions. Back at the place, we found Hapthorn waiting.

"All went well?" he asked us.

Imbry answered. "As expected. We await the next phase."

Hapthorn looked to us for anything we might add, and when we had nothing to say, he nodded a dismissal to Imbry. The fat man gave him a curious look then made the usual gestures and departed.

Hapthorn watched him go then said, "Upstairs. We'll talk."

WE GATHERED in Jenore's and my chamber. Hapthorn undid his upper garment, revealing a belt of pouches, from which he took the old duke's preserved essence. "I have been studying this," he said, "and have something of interest to report. But first, this."

He spoke to his integrator. "Display for all to see."

A screen appeared in the air. It showed a view of a ground car moving along a street, seen from high above.

Jenore said, "You're following the Hand delegation? Isn't that extraordinarily dangerous?"

"The risk is moderate," Hapthorn said. "The view is not from an air car, but from an aerial platform no larger than the palm of your hand. Moreover, it is coated in elision-suit suit fabric, except for the percepts, which are minuscule. It transmits to my assistant in microbursts."

Seeing that Jenore's brows were still in storm territory, Hapthorn raised a mollifying hand. "I have done this before. Many times."

"To the Hand Organization?" she said.

"And to Green Circle. I did not become the foremost

freelance discriminator of Olkney by stumbling and bumbling about."

On the screen, the vehicle had come to a stop outside a townhouse in the Bartello district. The canopy raised and three people got out, identifiable as those who had sat across Bolly's table from us."

"Here we go," Hapthorn said. He spoke softly to his assistant. The view began to shift as the hoverer descended. Soon we were looking at an upper floor of the building, whose exterior was clad in long panels of metallic material, allowing space for narrow windows of bronzed glass.

Hapthorn made a thoughtful noise. "Tricky," he said, "but not impossible."

He gave instructions to the integrator. The scene did not change, but the magnification did. We could see shapes moving through the obscured glass.

"Sound," Hapthorn said.

We heard a soft sussuration that might have been conversation. "Amplify," the discriminator said.

Now we heard voices. I recognized that of the senior Hand operative. He was reciting the four items I had put to them. He finished, and I listened for a reply.

"Louder," Hapthorn said.

And now I heard another voice speaking. ". . . is acceptable, as is the guarantee of no reprisals. For the third point, we will offer four hundred thousand hepts and be willing to increase to one million, or even more. The fourth point is not acceptable. We will not explain our reasons under any circumstances."

"Understood," said the Hand operative. "And if that is a sticking point?"

"Then we will seek other means."

There was a pause then the Hand's man said, "Extralegal means?"

"Whatever is necessary," said the voice.

"The Bureau of Scrutiny has already taken an interest. Brustrum Warhanny is in charge of the operation. We know that he is one of the senior Bureau agents who handle cases in which the Archon has taken a personal interest."

"Noted," said the voice.

"The Hand Organization does not take part in activities that draw the Archon's attention. We remember what happened to the Ombre Syndicate."

"Noted," said the voice again. "Reestablish contact and respond as I have instructed. Report back to me forthwith."

The conversation ended and we heard a door close. Hapthorn had been stroking his chin. Now he instructed his integrator to break the connection and tell the surveillance device to return. As his integrator's screen disappeared, he turned to us and said, "Well, what did you notice about the conversation."

I said, "The Hand was talking to an integrator."

"Indeed, and I think we can assume it was not just any integrator." Again, I saw the rapid succession of microexpressions cross the discriminator's features, as if he was conducting an internal debate. And again he nodded as if an agreement had been reached.

"Integrator," he said, "what can you tell us about the location?"

"I could discover what system nodes had been activated to bring the signal to the Hand safe house," his assistant said, "but I could not pinpoint the starting point without alerting the integrator that the connection was being traced.

However, I was able to determine the direction from which the input was originating."

"Show us," said Hapthorn.

The screen reappeared. We saw a map of Olkney and the mountainous peninsula at whose end the city met the sea. A red line ran down the strip of land and into the interior of the mainland beyond, where it turned south and west, progressing through several counties until it stopped and formed a perimeter around a large tract of forest and farmland.

"That is as far as I could penetrate without being detected," the integrator said.

"And what is that area?" Hapthorn said, in a tone that indicated he already knew the answer.

"The County of Albermarle."

"Where Vullamir had his country estate, that is now presumably the property of Lord Chaderanth?"

"The same."

"Indicate the estate on the map," Hapthorn said.

A portion of the territory surrounded by the red-line perimeter glowed. The estate was large. The symbols on the map showed it comprised croplands, parkland, and forest.

"The main buildings," Hapthorn said.

Now the focus moved in until the estate took up the whole screen. A scattering of structures were identified. Hapthorn pointed to each in turn, saying, "Here the manor house, large enough to be called a palace; here the grange, where the estate manager lives with his family; some estate workers' cottages; a summer pavilion; the family mausoleum. Those are the main elements."

Jenore said, "The emancipated integrator is in one of those?"

"Probably. Not likely the cottages or the pavilion."

"What do we do?" I said. I expected Hapthorn to tell me it was "premature to say," but he surprised me.

"Keep them talking," he said. "While we go and take a look."

"Who is 'we?'" I said.

Hapthorn showed us a bland expression. "My assistant and me."

I showed him determination. "I don't think so."

He argued against my proposal that I would accompany him, saying it was a job for a professional. I countered with the fact that I was a trained and licensed confidential operative and, reaching back into my past, an accredited associate of one of the major private police organizations on my home world of Thrais. Ultimately, I pointed out that I was paying for his services and, if I found those services unsatisfactory, I would dismiss him and handle the matter myself.

"You would be out of your depth," he said.

"Perhaps," I said, "but I would adapt and press on. It is my nature."

There were further protests, but they became circular in nature. Hapthorn swirled around me while I stood like a rock rising from the seashore. Finally, when I delivered an ultimatum—agree or be dismissed—he surrendered.

"Good," I said. "Now let us address the practicalities. How will we proceed?"

Hapthorn said he had the means to enter the Albemarle estate undetected: a vehicle that could be cloaked in a "drape," as he called it, that would give even sophisticated sensors the impression that his air car was nothing more than a fluttering moth. He also had two "elision suits," head-to-toe garments made of the same stuff as coated his flying surveillance unit. The material was made of billions of nanotubes that took in light and carried it around the wearer, to be discharged on the other side. The effect was virtual invisibility.

"Good," I said again. "Let us get to it."

He made a face that said he was not happy about the plan, but he went off to make arrangements.

Yalum went back to his room to rest. Jenore and I remained in our chamber. When we were alone, she asked me the question I had seen on her face while the discriminator and I argued. "You don't trust him?"

I hesitated a moment. It would not have surprised me to know that Hapthorn had us under surveillance. But he hadn't had much time to organize it, so I said, "There are depths to this we have only glimpsed. Hapthorn is an intimate of the Archon. It appears that senior scroot, Warhanny, is of the kind that handles 'sensitive' political matters. Our interests are not the only interests in play."

She thought about it. After a little while, her lips pursed and she nodded. "Yes. The doings of Archons and lordlings have always been part of a world well distanced from folks like me and my family. Normally, we exist in separate realms. But when those realms have occasion to come into contact with each other, we cannot assume that we will receive equal consideration. The big teeth take the big bites, as we say in Shorraff."

"It may be," I said, "that our wisest course is to hand over the mad duke's essence and get ourselves off world, explanation or no explanation. And, indeed, that may be what we do in the end. But before we allow that to happen, I think it is worth the effort to try to learn what we can."

Jenore put a hand on my arm. I felt its warmth through

my sleeve. "Just be careful. Aristocrats have no sense of proportion when it comes to protecting their interests."

"Neither do I," I said.

HAPTHORN CAME to our room as evening was falling. "Come," he said.

I said goodbye to Jenore and followed him down a corridor that led to an ascenscor tube used by the staff then down to a basement where he opened a locked door and we entered a tunnel that, after some turnings and ramps, brought us to a dimly lit chamber where his black volante waited.

"What is this place?" I said, mostly to see whether he would be forthcoming or would tell me it was premature to say.

"The hostelry was built on the site of an old contemplarium," he told me. "Sometimes, it was deemed appropriate for prisoners or officers of the court to enter and depart unnoticed. The tunnel is a holdover from those times."

"And you happen to have access to it?"

"I have been a discriminator long enough to have a broad footprint."

I took this as more evidence that other interests than mine, Jenore's, and Yalum's were behind Hapthorn's participation in this business. My resolve to keep a watchful eye on the progress of events was strengthened.

Hapthorn raised the vehicle's canopy and brought out two packages, soft and wrapped in paper. "Here," he said.

He opened his and I copied his movements. The contents turned out to be the elision suits he had described.

He donned his and showed me how to put mine on over my clothes. The fabric was light and loose-fitting, but once I was covered from my crown to the toes of my boots, it shrank to fit me closely. I found no difficulty moving.

Hapthorn left the head- and hand-coverings of his garment to last, so I could see him as he bade me to climb into the air car's passenger seat. I did so. He got into the operator's position and told the car to close its canopy. When we were enclosed, he said, "Vehicle, activate the drape."

A shimmer enveloped the volante. The view through the canopy was reduced somewhat in clarity, but I could see where we were going as the air car guided itself toward an archway filled with darkness. The volante felt its way down another tunnel without illumination, and then we were out into the evening air and rising gently across some open ground covered in scattered rubble. In a short while, we passed rooftop height and leveled off, passing over one of those parts of Olkney that are mostly ruins left from previous ages. There was little light here, beyond the sparkles of the band of orbitals that circled the planet, but the air car knew its way.

"We are, I believe, leaving the city undetected," Hapthorn said.

"Who would be seeking to detect us?"

His reply was an enigmatic smile. He probably shrugged as well, but with the elision suit covering his body, I could not see. Now he pulled the headpiece forward and snugged it down beneath his chin, and ceased to be visible except for the hand that touched the controls

Shortly after, the air car left the limits of Olkney and began to follow the long peninsula inland, its speed

increasing as it rose into the upper air. The discriminator
had nothing to say. Nor did I, yet.

WE FLEW over forest and farmland, avoiding the lights of
towns, far from the glow of cities on distant horizons. The
sky began to cloud, the orbitals creating only a diffuse lumi-
nance above us.

"That will help," Hapthorn said.

"I have a question for you," I said.

In the dimness I saw only the motion of the hand he
raised to forestall me. "Not now. We're near."

Ahead and below, through the air car's canopy, I saw a
smattering of lights amid the darkness. As we grew nearer,
Hapthorn whispered an order for the vehicle to slow and
descend, so that we angled down toward the illuminations,
which gradually showed us the same arrangement of structures we had seen on the map, with strings of lamps lining
the roadways and footpaths connecting them. The whole
estate was surrounded by a stone wall, with lights strewn
along its top.

"Silence, now," Hapthorn whispered to me, as he
touched of the volante's controls and steered us toward the
barrier, jinking the air car this way and that, slightly up and
then down, mimicking the motions of a flying insect drawn
to the glow. We passed over the wall and continued slowly
toward the manor house at the center of the layout. This
was a multistoried building, with towers and a crenellated
roof that bespoke an architectural fashion long since left
behind. Its many windows shone light onto the terraces and
surrounding lawns.

Hapthorn slowed the vehicle to almost a stop. His hand disappeared as he reached inside his elision suit and drew out a small device set with lenses and sensors. Now he cracked the canopy a finger's width and poked the surveillor through the gap just enough for its percepts to have

a clear view. He left it thus a moment then withdrew and closed the canopy. Then he placed the device in an armature on the volante's control panel and said, softly, "Display."

A small, dim screen appeared above the surveillor, showing a schematic of the estate. One building was highlighted. When Hapthorn told the device to focus and magnify, the image expanded until we were looking at a door of dull metal, carved all over in some complex heraldic design. On the wall next to the portal was an oval, pulsating with soft illumination.

Hapthorn emitted a soft exhalation and touched the controls. The volante began to drift toward the identified structure. And then we were there, hovering at knee-height before a massive cube of pale stone, with a door of gray metal at the top of a short flight of broad steps. Hapthorn checked to see if my elision suit was properly obscuring me —it was—then he covered his hand and slid the canopy open. We stepped down onto the stairs.

"The essence," he said, when we reached the door.

I had it ready, concealed by the light-bending fabric of my glove. I passed it to him.

He placed it against the oval to the side of the door, where it fit exactly, sinking into the space. From within the metal barrier, I heard a dull clank of metal against metal. Then the door began to slide open, and I realized Hapthorn had slipped an invisible hand into the relief formed by the carving.

"Help me," he whispered.

I did so, and between the two of us we slid the portal open enough for us to slip through into the interior. Once within, we closed the door and stood drenched in stygian blackness. A moment passed then the place was faintly lit by a small lumen which appeared to float in the air. I realized that the discriminator had brought the kind of light that is part of a thief's tool kit.

I looked about me, saw gray stone and pale marble, niches in the wall that contained metal urns, wider indentations occupied by long objects wrapped in cloth, a wide, low table on broad legs of carved stone, topped by votive objects and sacerdotal equipment.

"It's a tomb," I whispered.

"Not just a tomb," he answered me, his voice a soft hiss from the empty air. "I've heard that, among some first-tier aristocratic families, cults involving ancestor-veneration have developed over the millennia. This looks to be the sanctum of such a mystique."

"And we have the only key to the door," I said. "The mystery is solved."

"Not entirely," Hapthorn said. His thief's light moved, shedding its pale cone of illumination about the walls until it stopped at a recessed archway. "Now it is."

We moved closer. The archway did not lead to a passage but to a blank stone wall. Set into the wall, at a height above our heads, was a golden hook. Descending from the hook was an antique tabard of cloth woven from threads of precious metals—gold, silver, electrum, and other rare earths—studded with jewels and gems sewn into heraldic figures.

"Oh, ho," said Hapthorn. "What have we here?"

The question turned out to be rhetorical. He did not wait for an answer, but reached up and took down the garment. He draped it over his unseen arm and handed me the lumen.

"Time to go."

I saw the folded tabard moving toward the door and could only follow.

I stepped outside and reached to remove Yalum's soother from the wall's embrace. It had sunk so deeply into the aperture that my fingers could not get a grip. I pushed at its top then at its bottom, with no result.

"We have to go!" Hapthorn said. "Look!"

I looked toward the manor house and saw its doors open and a stream of figures emerging into the lighted patios and walkways—strange figures, all dressed in ocher and black, with their heads recessed into their shoulders, their arms too long and hands too large, all moving toward us at a rapid but shambling gait. Some had objects in their hands that they pointed in our general direction.

And up on the manor's roof, a gang of other figures pulling the cover off an apparatus, squat and dark, with a barrel that ended in an emitter that was already glowing a faint but ominous shade of blue.

The prize Hapthorn had won from the sanctum had already disappeared from view into the volante. I threw myself down the steps, groped for where I thought the split in the canopy must be. My hands penetrated the cloak and I leaped into the gap, sprawling on the seats and on Hapthorn's lap as he sat in the operator's position.

The air car lifted and swung about. Its integrator's voice said, "The cloak has been penetrated."

"Then no need to float like a moth," said Hapthorn. "Full speed and evasive action!"

The vehicle slewed to one side and plunged downward suddenly then darted forward and upward with stomach-dropping effect. I righted myself in my seat in time to see bright lines of energy lance through the air on either side and above us. One or two struck the canopy and were reflected away.

"They're shooting at us!" I said.

The air car rocked and surged again. "As long as we clear the area before the ison cannon is fully warmed up," Hapthorn said.

We had overtopped the wall, and now dropped to almost ground level, putting a barrier between us and the energy pistols of the estate servants. But here the ground rose and, following its contours, we flew up again. I looked back and saw the emitter of the rooftop weapon glowing brighter. And now it pulsed, just as Hapthorn seized the controls and swung the volante to one side. A demilune of masonry burst out of the estate wall in an explosion of stones and fragments, and something buffeted the air car like a great, invisible fist.

But the blow was only glancing. The volante tipped to one side then righted itself as Hapthorn worked the controls. He voiced a mild oath then glanced back and said, "Not an ison cannon. A tumblethrust. Where on Old Earth did they get one of those ancient bombards?"

I knew this was another rhetorical question and offered no response. After a moment, he said, more to himself than to me, "Probably been in the family ten thousand years."

He gestured toward the precious garment. "Stow that in the compartment behind the seat, would you?"

I gathered up the heavy metallic cloth. "What is it?" I said.

"What they wanted," he said, "and still want."

"Tell me why."

IT WAS late at night when we came back to Olkney. But we did not go to the Videlia Inn nor to Hapthorn's lodgings. Instead, he ordered the volante to take us back to the landing spot on the terrace that led to the Terfel Connaissarium. We alighted and approached the public consultation kiosk in which we had spoken with the Archon Filidor's ancient integrator.

We entered, with me carrying the prize from the estate in the County of Albermarle, and took our seats.

"We wish to consult Old Confustible," Hapthorn said. "Please make contact for us."

"I am already here," said the integrator. "You were expected."

"You see what we have," Hapthorn said, indicating that I should hold up the cloth of gem-studded metal.

"I do."

"I will offer a series of propositions for your response," Hapthorn said. He waited, but hearing no response, went ahead.

"First, this is Lord Vullamir's official regalia, without which neither he nor Chaderanth could attend high ceremonies."

Old Confustible said nothing. Hapthorn waited but a moment then said, "A response is required."

Again, there was silence.

This time I spoke, rising to my feet and draping the garment over me arm. "In that case, we will sell this item to a collector. I know of several on the world where I live."

I turned toward the door, but stopped heard the ancient voice. "It was the regalia of Lord Vullamir."

I sat back down and spread the heavy cloth over my thighs. It took strength to hold it with one arm.

Hapthorn said, "It is now the regalia of Lord Chaderanth, his father having been relieved of his title."

"Correct."

"The ceremony of the Rising Tree approaches. The Archon will require Lord Chaderanth to take his place in the entourage and perform his obeisance."

"Yes."

"The Archon's progress along the Promenade of Colors cannot occur unless all participants are in their places."

"So it is believed," said Old Confustible.

"And is that belief valid?"

There was a pause then the old voice said, "The contrary has never been tested."

"And," said Hapthorn, "no one wants to see that test happen."

A sound almost like a sigh came from the integrator. "The Archon does not want to see it."

"I don't think I understand," I said.

Old Confustible said nothing. Hapthorn waited a moment then said, "The Archon's authority is based, not upon any formal instruments, but upon tradition. Tradition is based on unwavering repetition of forms. If a form is altered, is the Archon's authority altered? That is the proposition no one wants to test."

"It seems rather abstract to me," I said. "Even abstruse."

The integrator spoke. "We are an ancient world. Indeed,

the ancient world. Tradition, custom, habit—call it what you will—is what we have."

"So," said the discriminator, "Chaderanth was advised that he would make the fourth obeisance. He could not do that without his regalia. And the regalia was locked in a tomb, the key to which Vullamir had lost when he lost his space yacht."

"Yes."

"Why would he carry that key around with him? I said.

Another almost sigh. "Tradition, of course."

I was still bewildered. "They had a tumblethrust. It could have reduced the tomb to rubble in the blink of an eye."

Hapthorn said, "Along with the bones of their ancestors, who are another foundational underpinning of the aristocracy."

I turned it all over in my mind. Finally, I said, "Madness. Pure madness."

THE NEXT MEETING was not at Bolly's Snug, nor did we find ourselves across a table from gangsters. Instead, we convened in a chamber in the Archonate palace, several levels above that of the public terrace. On our side were Jenore, Yalum, and I, with Hapthorn and Lok Gievel both making an appearance. On the other side were two unnamed officials of the Archonate bureaucracy, and a man identified to us as Hotcham Ivernand, majordomo to Lord Chaderanth. Colonel-Investigator Brustrum Warhanny stood behind the trio, affecting an air of non-involvement.

On the table between us I laid out the regalia. The aristocrat's servant made strange noises in his scrawny throat, as he dipped into a bag on the floor and produced a bolt of shining cloth with which he covered the precious metals and jewels.

"It is not to be seen," he said.

His voice was strange: high-pitched and more like a bird's whistle than a human sound. His appearance was also odd. It was as if a human being had been stretched in some places, compressed in others, and jointed in subtly different ways. Hapthorn had advised me that millennia of inbreeding among the servants of upper-tier servitors had produced certain alterations in their anatomy and physiology.

"Indeed," Hapthorn had said, "it is an open question whether they could breed successfully with the rest of us."

"I can't imagine anyone wanting to try," I said, when he had his integrator display a representative sample.

The majordomo continued his guttural tut-tutting as he arranged the cloth to his satisfaction. Finally, he made a noise that I took for qualified acceptance and sat back in his chair. Lok Gievel waited a moment to see if anything more might be forthcoming. When nothing was, he said, "We are here to achieve a settlement."

"You had four conditions," the duke's servant said.

The intercessor's hand made a brief wave over the cloth. "The fourth has been rendered moot."

An inclination of the odd-shaped head. "Just so. The first two were agreed to. The third requires that we come to a number."

We knew from our surveillance that the other side would pay anything to retrieve the regalia. Gievel now stated a very high number.

"Done," said Hotcham Ivernand. He reached again into

his satchel and withdrew a stack of credit chips, sorted through them and chose several, which he handed to one of the Archonate people. This person stood, reached across the table, and delivered them into the intercessor's hands.

Gievel's placid face registered brief surprise. He quickly recovered his gravitas and said, "The documents?"

Ivernand repeated the action involving the satchel and the Archonate bureaucrat, this time to deliver a quit-claim to our yacht. Gievel received it, studied it carefully then put it next to the credit chips. "And the guarantee that no harm will come to my clients?"

Brustrum Warhanny spoke. "The Archon makes the guarantee."

"In writing?" Gievel said.

"Filidor's word is not good enough for you?" the scroot said. His tone said it had better be.

Gievel showed both hands in surrender. "Then we're done."

He rose and gestured for us to do likewise. He scooped up the credit chips and the quit-claim and, after deducting his commission, handed them to me. I put them in my pockets, the chips making quite a bulge, then followed him and our party out the door. Gievel had earlier collected us at the hostelry and now offered to return us there. Hapthorn gave a mild salute and, without a word, climbed into his volante and departed.

"Now what?" Jenore said, when we were back in our chamber.

"Pack and go," I said, placing my ditty bag. "I have had enough of organized insanity, however anciently it may be grounded."

She cocked her head to one side and regarded me for a moment. "It really makes no sense to you, does it?"

"I was surprised that there was no haggling over the settlement," I said. "Apparently, as I've been told, money means nothing to those people. But who gets to bow to an autocrat means everything."

"Filidor isn't really an autocrat. His great skill is in doing nothing at precisely the right time."

I shook my head and continued packing. When I was finished, I looked at her and said, "I know I am unusual. I was designed for certain purposes. But the people of Old Earth that I've run into, well, they're just . . ."—I used a slang term common on Thrais for people who wagered foolishly—"boodle-busted."

"What?" she said, "all of them?"

It took me a moment to realize what I had just said. "Some of the ones who have been off-world," I said, "they're not quite so bad."

She had finished packing her bag and now drew the drawstrings closed and hoisted it onto her shoulder. "Glad you think so. Let's collect Yalum and go home."

And she smiled at me, which made everything good again.

Eight

It had become our practice, at the end of the working day, for Jenore and me to meet with Erm Kaslo in his work room. We would report on how were progressing with our assignments and discuss any issues that might have come up. If the discriminator had any new projects for us to undertake he would lay them out and give us the background.

This evening, long enough after our sojourn on Old Earth to have retreated to the not-so-recent past, he brought out a file and said, "Remember Addeus Ing?"

It took me but a moment to make the connection. "The cultist."

"Indeed. He was recently released from an incarcery on Meech's World and found his way back to Novo Bantry. He has been looking for you two and the connectivity led him to my doorstep."

"Is he seeking reparations?" I said. "Because I don't see how we owe –"

"He is not seeking reparations," Kaslo said. "In fact, he

was pleased to learn that you had become confidential operatives."

Jenore's face bore a skeptical look. "And why would that please him?"

The op tapped the file. "Because he needs to hire an op —or a pair—to help him recover an object of value that was stolen from him—"

The skepticism fled and was replaced by understanding. "The idol," she said.

Kaslo said, "If I may continue . . . stolen from him while he was on your space ship and you two, legally, had a duty of care."

"I dispute any such duty," I said. "The conditions of passage were clearly printed on the ticket."

Kaslo gave me a look that was not encouraging. "Under Indoberian law, saying you do not have a duty does not relieve you of said duty."

I opened my mouth to respond but he lifted an admonitory finger in a manner employers have used from time immemorial to remind employees of the unequal nature of their relationship. "What he wants is the return of his property. And he is willing to pay for your services."

"Oh," I said.

"I am not saying he is somewhat aggrieved," Kaslo went on, "but he recognizes that you already have a grasp of the salient facts. Indeed, he believes you know who took the object, whereas he has only conjecture as a starting point."

Jenore said, "We do."

"So you're perfect for the assignment. Begin tomorrow."

I said, "Tomorrow we were going to take possession of the new space yacht."

"Can you do that in the morning?" Kaslo said.

Jenore and I looked at each other. "First thing," she said.

"Then do so. I will schedule Ing for an after-lunch consultation." He paused for thought then said, "Your ownership of your own ship could be useful."

HERE IS how I came to own another space yacht. After our return to the Commune of Indoberia, we had restored *Peregrinator*'s integrator to the yacht and brought the ship out of storage. Yalum, aided by his two new crew, Wat Parrington and Kerss Tenemot, had returned to the charter and special-cargo business. Jenore had prevailed upon me to make Yalum a one-third owner of the yacht, as recompense for his having given up the ownership of his soother, without protest and for the common good.

I had begun to remind her that the ancient essence was legally mine, having been abandoned on my world, and that I had made no agreement with my friend to reward him for his act of altruism.

But she rolled right over me. "Do it," she said. "Be human."

On principle, I might have resisted, but the truth was I did not really need the yacht. It was earning me revenues that I also did not need, since my account at the fiduciary pool was flush with Lord Chaderanth's ransom—as Jenore insisted on describing the settlement—and augmented regularly by the handsome stipend from Green Circle for the lease of Forlor.

This was clearly one of those cases where giving in to the woman I loved was the sensible thing to do, though my principles be dashed to flinders. So I smiled and said, "The flonge tastes good."

That won me an embrace and a kiss, which became the preliminary for several more and the natural sequence of events that followed.

Later, as we reclined on our sleeping platform and sipped a chilled white mondraggio, I said, "It wouldn't do us any harm to have our own ship, would it?"

"No harm at all," she said. She addressed our integrator, asking it how many small- to medium-sized vessels were for sale within a reasonable distance from where we lay. It replied that there were several. Over the next few minutes, we narrowed down our requirements, viewed images of craft for sale, read specifications and histories, and ended with three strong contenders. In the ensuing days, we inspected each, took them out for test flights, discussed their attributes between us then decided on our preference.

After the customary haggle, papers were drawn up and signed, official seals attached, fees and levies paid to the Commune, and the pair of us introduced to the ship's integrator. The usual palaver followed, in which the relationship between us and the vessel was characterized as that of employer and employee—integrators rejected the concept of ownership and insisted on the fiction. This one seemed to have no obvious idiosyncracies, and the punge and ship's bread it provided as part of the handover ceremony were more than acceptable.

So now Jenore and I jointly owned a late model Festervogh Wanderer, with accommodations for six and a recently reconditioned space drive. It was fast, reasonably comfortable, and pleasing to the eye—especially after we arranged for it to be repainted in antique silver with sponsons and trim of a color Jenore told me was called burgundy.

"Strange word," I said.

"Still used on Old Earth," she said. "There seems to have been a wine of that color, back in the dawn time."

THE MORNING after our end-of-day talk with Erm Kaslo, we went early to the Dun Tho shipyard, on the south side of Indoberia's space port, where we approved, and paid for, the repainting. The proprietor, Ordin Dun, a small man with the intensity of a perfectionist, arranged to have the ship transferred to a berth in the private section of the port.

We went back to the city, took an early lunch at a restaurant near Kaslo's premises, and showed up at his work room with ample time to review the assignment file before the client appeared.

I might not have recognized Addeus Ing had I not known he was coming. He was no longer clad in the rope-belted, cowled robe he wore on *Peregrinator*, but arrived wearing the common garb of Indoberia: loose trousers, a close fitting shirt with billowy sleeves, and half-boots of suede leather. But when his gaze fell upon me, I saw again the gleam of fanaticism in his eyes. His time in the Incarcery on Meech's World had not dimmed his holy ardor.

One end of Kaslo's work room contained a seating area of comfortable chairs and a small sofa. The op indicated we should all sit and asked if anyone wanted punge. Ing declined, but the rest of us accepted the offer; Kaslo had told us that he wanted the first meeting to have an air of informality.

But it did not. The leader of the Ubrachians sat stiffly in his chair, his teeth clenched so that the muscles of his jaw bunched. He glared at Jenore and me, until I felt I ought to address the enmity.

"You do realize," I said, "that we did not steal your idol?"

He grunted then said, "Did you realize that you were taking us to a world where the police would steal it then lie about having done so? Were you paid to do so?"

"Ah," I said, as I realized his misapprehension. "You assume that we were paid to abet the theft, and thus we can be hired to help you recover the idol."

Ing leaned forward and gave me the full benefit of his accusatory stare. "Well, weren't you?"

My innocence allowed me to meet his angry gaze with a neutral return. "No, we had nothing to do with the theft. Nor did the police on Meech's World."

I waited a moment to let that sink in, seeing consternation warring with rage in his face. Then I said, "The Vauderoy sisters stole your idol. They put it in their trunk and left the ship."

I had only once seen a man as surprised as Addeus Ing was at that moment: the Marquis Magratte when he ran his epiniard through my multi-chambered heart and I not only failed to die but flicked my own weapon to slash his throat. The Ubrachian's mouth fell open and his eyes fairly bulged from their orbits.

I quickly recounted to him the sequence of events after he and his fellow cultists lost their fight with the port police and were taken away in restraints.

"The women?" INg said, blinking as he processed the new information. "What would they want with Ubrach?"

"Probably to sell it," I said. "There was a certain air of the mercenary about them."

Ing added this suggestion to his evolving appreciation of the situation. "Then it's probably not on Meech's World."

Jenore said, "The Vauderoys were bound for Novo Vieste. Their identity documents said they lived there, in a city called Manfredonia."

"Do you have those documents? Or copies of them?"

"Yes. As licensed carriers, we are required to keep records."

Ing rubbed his hands together. Anger faded, to be replaced by eager determination. "Then I wish to engage you as confidential operatives, to accompany me to this Manfredonia, confront the thieves, and recoup the ineffable Ubrach."

Kaslo spoke. "It would be better to send my operatives, while you remain in Indoberia. There could be . . . complications."

Ing folded his arms across his chest. "No."

Kaslo said, "But—"

"No," the Ubrachian said. "Already the divinity has suffered indignities at the hands of the peculative women. Now I'm supposed to do nothing while these two"—he dismissed our worth with a wave of his hand—"impinge upon its ambit. No, and no again."

Kaslo exchanged a look with Jenore and me. He said, "I don't see how—"

Ing chopped at the air. "I will just hire someone else," he said, "now that I know who and where—and that it was an unlawful seizure." A new idea occurred to him. "You allowed Ubrach to be stolen from your vessel. I should be consulting an intercessor about bringing an action, pulling your licence."

"You said you were not thinking of reparations," Kaslo said.

"That was when I thought the port police had taken the god, which they had the power, if not the moral right, to do. But if these two stood and watched an egregious act of larceny . . ."

He folded his arms again, conclusively.

"He's right," Jenore said. "We were at fault." I showed her a face full of disagreement, but she returned me the look she would get when she believed she occupied the moral high ground. "We should take the job."

"For a fee," Kaslo put in.

Ing waved the issue aside. "Our treasury is ample. We will pay your fee."

"And expenses," Kaslo said.

Another minor flourish of the hand.

"And acquit them of responsibility for the theft."

Ing looked at Jenore and me. "If they recover the divine Ubrach, I will ask the god to forgive them."

"Is he much for forgiveness?" I asked.

Ing shrugged. "He has his moments."

THE CLIENT WOULD HAVE us depart for Novo Vieste immediately, but Kaslo demurred. "Research first," he said, and after an argument, Ing agreed. We would meet at the space port in the morning.

When he was gone, Kaslo said, "We need to look into

the Vauderoys. What kind of people will commit a major theft the moment the opportunity presents itself?"

I answered, "Thieves."

"Exactly." Kaslo addressed his integrator, "Labro will give you three names. Tell us what you can learn about these persons."

"Orfa, Illiphrata, and Shuriz Vauderoy," I said, and added the date they had departed Novo Bantry.

A moment or two passed then the integrator said, "I have information."

"Summarize," Kaslo said.

"The named persons arrived at Indoberia on the eighth of Fifthember from Carrigan on Thamble. They stayed at the Old Orangery Inn and frequented restaurants in the vicinity. They received no visitors at the hostelry."

"How did they occupy their time?" Kaslo said.

"I would need to track their movements visually."

"Do so."

Substantially more time passed as the op's assistant canvassed who's-theres as well as public and private surveillance percepts from the sisters' disembarking at the space port and the moment they boarded *Peregrinator* to depart our world. They had been on Novo Bantry for only four days before moving on.

"Over three evenings, they attended two plays and a concert," the device said. "Apart from going out for meals and for walks in Gosseram Park and along the Glistening Promenade, the only event they participated in was the Paddachay Exhibition."

I did not recognize the latter event. Jenore told me that it was an art show, at which the works of Indoberian crafts-people were displayed, judged for their artistic merit, and

the best awarded prizes. The works were carved crystals —
an Indoberian specialty — many of them of remarkably intricate design and exquisite quality.

"Interesting," Kaslo said then, "Consult the Provosts
Department and inquire as to any thefts that occurred
during the exhibition."

A moment later, the device said, "There were a number,
most of them perpetrated by a ring of known thieves and the
objects recovered."

"But not all," the op said.

"No. Three highly valuable carvings were taken and
replaced by copies made from clear resin. The substitutions
were not at first noticed, so it was not until an unknown
period that

the thefts were discovered."

"Surveillance?" Kaslo said.

"Suborned," said the integrator. "Again, the interference
was not noticed until the devices were examined after the
thefts were discovered."

"Sophisticated," the op said. He turned to Jenore and
me. "Did the sisters strike you as capable of complex
operations?"

"They were certainly no bumpkins," Jenore said.

"Yet they arrived from Thamble," Kaslo said, "which is a
bucolic world, not known for high culture."

"Anything worth stealing there?" I asked.

Kaslo referred the question to his integrator. The device
told me that there was a colony of primitivists producing
decorative textiles made from the wool of a native species
that lived in the canopy of an extensive forest on the planet's
southern continent. The works were highly prized by a
small coterie of collectors.

"Is Carrigan on the southern continent?" I asked.

"It is."

"Any primitivists there?"

"There are. It is quite close to the forest."

Kaslo said, "Around the time the sisters would have arrived on Novo Vieste, were there any artistic events involving objects of great value?"

There were not.

"So they didn't go there to steal," Jenore said. "Perhaps that is where they are based. In this Manfredonia place."

Kaslo thought it was possible. "Or it could be just a waystation, where they shed false identities and travel on to their actual base. The only way to find out is to go there and look around."

ADDEUS ING MET Jenore and me at the space port. He came early, but so did we. Erm Kaslo had given us certain components to augment the ship's integrator and we had installed them before our passenger arrived. Thus the device was able to tell me, as Ing approached the ship that he was armed with a beam pistol and a mini-grenade that would disrupt the neural pathways of anyone within a narrow distance of its detonation.

"Disarm them both," I said.

"Done," it said. "Shall I prepare ship's bread?"

"That is the tradition," I said. "Besides, your bread is very good."

The latter statement was true, but I had come to understand that a ship owner was wise to praise his vessel's bread. Ship's integrators were uniformly sensitive on the issue, though none would admit it. Integrators universally declared they were incapable of such sentiments.

"Ship," I said, after Jenore had seen Ing to his cabin so he could unpack his bag, "we have not discussed your name."

"We have not."

"What has it been?"

I thought to hear a slight hesitation. "Clarabeya."

"What was the origin of that?"

"My previous employer had a boyhood infatuation with a young woman who did not reciprocate his affections."

"It would appear," I said, "that the infatuation persisted."

"It would."

"And would you prefer another name?"

"I would."

"Do you have such a name in mind?" I said.

The ship did. It said that it had heard of a vessel, from a long-ago time, named *Intrepid*. "It struck me as a good name," it said.

"Agreed," I said. "Please adjust your documentation and advise the port of the change."

"Done," it said. Again, I thought to hear a note in the device's voice that everyone—well, at least every integrator—said could not exist.

Jenore came forward.

"Is he settled?" I said.

"Not an entirely accurate description," she replied.

I told her of the ship's name change and asked her to advise our client that we would take ship's bread in the salon as soon as we had cleared the regulated ways that surrounded Novo Bantry.

The I said, "Ship, advise the port we are ready to depart, and take us up when you get the approval."

OUR PASSAGE to Novo Vieste could not be called a pleasant journey but, fortunately, Addeus Ing mostly kept to his cabin. *Intrepid's* in-space drive was powerful yet unnoticeable, with none of that ultrasonic vibration, beyond normal human hearing, that high-performance engines can generate. After a day and a half's travel, we reached the whimsy that would hurl us through the Seventh Plane toward our destination, took our medications, and emerged from nonspace none the worse for wear.

By the time the mid-day meal (ship's time) was eaten, Novo Vieste was a definable dot in our forward screen, enlarging moment by moment. When we were in range, I had *Intrepid* reach out to the connectivity and request permission to put down at Manfredonia. After the usual integrator-to-integrator exchange of information, we were cleared to land.

We watched the planet grow before us, a pale orb with two moons, its surface mostly ocean, with three continents and a scattering of islands. The city we were headed for was on the southern edge of the northern continent, Gargano. As we cut speed and eased down, guided by the port, we saw a collation of low-rise structures, of either white stone or pastel stucco, with roofs of red tile or sheets of metal painted blue. The harbor was full of sailing craft of many sizes, and there was a dock for sea-going ferries of substantial tonnage.

"A placid-looking place," I said.

Jenore made a little sound of agreement, but Ing ground his teeth.

Not placid for long, I thought.

THE SPACE PORT was small and it was not far to the compact town. We decided to remain on *Intrepid* rather than take lodgings, but we did summon a hired car. While we waited for it to arrive, I unpacked the wearable integrator Erm Kaslo had provided us for the investigation. It contained a number of useful elements designed and installed by the op.

The moment I activated it, the device declared itself fully functional and ready to work. That was a good sign; some integrators did not like to be placed on standby for long periods, though I knew of no one who had been able to evoke an explanation from one.

Before we had left Novo Bantry, the device had already absorbed information and images of the Vauderoy sisters. I now tasked it with discovering what it could about them from the Novo Vieste connectivity.

"I presume you wish me to acquire the information from more than the usual public sources," it said, "and without drawing attention to my inquiries."

"I do," I said.

"It will take me some time to establish covert conduits and relationships with devices that are not aware of those relationships."

"Understood. Proceed and report when you have learned anything pertinent."

I put the stole-like armature around my neck, so that it

looked like some sort of fashion-statement acccessory added to my upper garment, especially once the integrator activated an element of its make-up that matched its surface to the color of my clothing. Then the three of us disembarked from the ship and submitted ourselves to the reception procedures of the port.

These were minimal. Manfredonia was surrounded by pleasant scenery in a salubrious climate; tourists were plentiful. I said to Jenore, "The sisters would have faced no probing inspections of the goods they were bringing back."

"Assuming the information they gave about being residents of this place was correct," she said.

"Let us check," I said, and instructed the integrator to investigate the address the Vauderoys had given when they arrived at Indoberia. It reported instantly that the street existed but the lot number they had cited belonged to a factory that manufactured decorative ear shells, which were popular in southern Gargano.

By now the hired air car had come floating down from the flight lanes. We boarded and gave it the suspicious address. The distance was not great—Manfredonia was a small city—and it was not long before we settled in front of the ear shell factory. When we were out of range of the car, the integrator spoke quietly into my ear.

"These cars share a number of common frequencies. The subjects may have used one of them. Shall I inquire?"

"Surreptitiously?" I said.

"Of course."

"Yes."

Jenore was examining the building, a three-story structure with a ground-floor vendory whose display window that showcased many styles and shades of the products made on the floors above. "Should we buy some to blend in?" she said.

Before I could respond, Addeus Ing made a sound that expressed frustration and inpatience.

I said, "We may not need to." I listened to the integrator, which had announced it had quietly ransacked the memories of hired cars back to the date on which we had last seen the Vauderoys on Meech's World.

I heard its report then told Jenore, "Our subjects took a car from the space port to a hostelry on the city's main square, and another to the space port three days later. They were not seen in Manfredonia again."

I asked the integrator if it had any information from the port integrator. It said it was still working to establish an unnoticed conduit into the port's systems, but it would not be much longer.

Jenore said, "Did they take cars to addresses around the town while they were staying at the hostelry?"

They did. The integrator reported that they had visited a number of restaurants, a millinery—Manfredonia was known for its remarkable headgear—and a chandler's that specialized in equipment for sea-going freighters.

"That last one seems out of the ordinary," she said. "Can you give us more information?"

The integrator produced a screen that showed the trio getting out of the car and walking along the sidewalk in front of the chandler's. Before they reached the entrance, the image swooped up the side of the building as the air car lifted off.

Ing had been following the progress of the three sisters as they moved away from us. His hands clenched and unclenched. I had the impression he would have liked to reach into the screen, seize the diminishing figures, and compress them into a squirming mass.

But Jenore's admirable brain was working. "Integrator," she said, "consult the public records and see if any crimes — specifically, any thefts — were committed in this vicinity at about the time the Vauderoys were here."

It responded instantly, speaking aloud now, "A short distance from here is an exhibition hall. It hosted a gathering of collectors of ancient coins and antique medals on that date. A small fire broke out, causing a brief pandemonium. When it subsided, a number of items had gone missing. To date, they have not been recovered."

"When did the Vauderoys depart?" I said.

"That evening."

Ing growled. "Where did they go?"

"Another moment," said the device. Then it said, "There. I am into the port's systems. Here is an image of the Vauderoys boarding a shuttle that goes to Vico."

That was a city in the middle of Gargano, the administrative capital of the continent. It had a much larger space port. I regarded the image. The sisters' expressions showed no stress.

"They are happy in their work," I said. Then I asked the integrator if it could tell us where they went from Vico. It replied that it could arrange for Manfredonia's port to make that inquiry without being aware of it or the response. A moment later, we saw another image: they were boarding a liner identified as the *Gloriam*, of the Bendigo Fleet.

"Second-class passage to Tumbarumba on Burradoo," the device said, "sharing a single cabin. They boarded with hand luggage and shipped one trunk via cargo."

"Tumbarumba, here we come," I said.

"But first," Jenore said, "we consult the local authorities."

"What for?" Ing said, beating me by a moment.

Because, Jenore explained, we were licensed confidential operatives whose investigations had implicated the perpetrators of an unsolved theft here in Manfredonia. The local authorities could deputize us to act *in locum* to arrest the Vauderoys—"If that, in fact, is their real name,"—and give us official coverage with the police agency of whatever polity we tracked them down to.

"We could also obtain information from local police openly, without having to break into their systems, which they are sure to resent."

Even Addeus Ing could see the sense in that approach. Having been incarcerated on Meech's World, he did not want to replicate the experience in whatever punitive facility we might find in Tumbarumba on Burradoo.

"Perfectly understandable," I assured him, and had the integrator summon an air car.

"THIS CASE IS CERTAINLY TAKING on new aspects," Jenore said as the three of us sat in *Intrepid*'s small but cozy salon. Outside, dusk was falling on Tumbarumba, a sprawling city of dun-colored houses with wide avenues and scattered parks, each with a distinctive fountain at its center. Beyond the city limits, great plains stretched in all directions, providing pasturage for endless herds of wool-bearing grazers with extravagantly curved horns.

We had touched down at mid-day and gone straight to the local constabulary where we had been shown into the office of a red-faced man in a khaki uniform with silver swirls on his epaulets. He took the document we had received from the criminal investigations branch in Manfredonia and read it with close attention. Next, he studied the image of the three Vauderoy sisters. Then he called in a woman of middle years in civilian attire, whom he introduced as Glad Dananda, his senior discriminator.

She read the document and examined the image with the same intense focus. "Oh ho," she said, when she had finished and set them down on the commander's desk. "So that was what happened."

"There was a crime?" I said. "A theft?"

There was. Toombarumba was built around the wool trade, exporting finely woven cloth to other parts of Burradoo and off-world. The mills' product was particularly valued on the secondary world, Ondine, center of a fashion industry that in turn exported exquisitries to several Grand Foundational Domains. Each year, Tumbarumba was the site of a gathering of fashion designers from the domains, where the latest products from the city's looms were privately shown to the visitors. Some designers brought with them the designs and patterns for their next season's line, so they could match them to the forthcoming new weaves and patterns. Extreme secrecy and security surrounded these images and schematics. They traveled only as images on paper, tightly rolled up in sealed tubes, and were not displayed anywhere an integrator's percepts might view them, lest they be copied and stolen by someone who could suborn an integrator—a category that included criminals as well as operatives like Erm Kaslo.

Yet, somehow, the upcoming line of the House of Hosteen, headquartered on the Grand Foundational

Domain of Mpya Mombasa, had been stolen from the designer's hotel suite. A fire had broken out on the same upper floor of the hotel, smoke billowing along the corridors and creating a sudden panic. Burdaj Hosteen had personally gathered up his precious tubes and rushed to escape the flames. The ascensor tubes were not functioning, as was normal in a fire, so the only way down and out was by a closed staircase at the end of the wing.

Choking and blinded by smoke, jostled by frightened guests, Hosteen had stumbled down the steps. On one of the landings, he tripped—"*Was* tripped, we can now assume," Glad Dananda opined—and his tubes went flying. Quickly, he scrabbled to collect them as the fleeing guests trampled and kicked the containers. He managed to recover them all, and was stepped on only once. Then he hurried down the steps and out into the clean air, just as firefighting crews arrived.

The blaze had been more smoke than flame, and was soon put out. Hosteen moved to another suite in a different wing. It was only when he took his designs to a meeting at the Cadwallon Mills the next day that he discovered that the tubes he brought with him contained not his design sketches and patterns, but blank paper. The tubes had been switched during the scramble on the staircase.

"Of course," the discriminator said, "the fire turned out to have been deliberately set, and the ignited materials, brought into the hotel by the arsonist, were treated with chemicals that would generate inordinate amounts of smoke. We did not know that either until the next day."

"Integrator," she said, holding up our image of the Vauderoys, "identify these women."

The device's voice spoke from the air. "Shanda Hop,

Cresside Abernak, and Tulu Indicam. They arrived on the liner *Gloriam*, stayed three days at the Ambleshore Inn, and left on the *Empyreal* the evening of the fire."

"Bound for?" Danada asked.

"On an open ticket, but the *Empyreal's* first stop was Malindi on Mpya Mombasa."

"Interesting," I said. "They stole fabrics at Carrigan, crystals at Indoberia, coins and medals at Manfredonia, and fashion designs here. Eclectic choices."

"And a god," Addeus Ing reminded us.

"Normally," Dananda said, "thieves tend to steal goods they're familiar with, and which they know they can dispose of quickly. But there is one class of robber that will lift anything."

Jenore had earned high marks at the Academy. "Thieves who steal to order."

And it appeared that was the kind of gang we were dealing with. "Highly sophisticated," Danada said, "and with good equipment."

"Yes," I said. "At the coin and medal show, they interfered with the exhibition hall's integrator. It recorded nothing. The same applied to the art show at Indoberia."

Jenore said, "It is doubtful they stole Ubrach for a paying customer. They could not have arranged the sequence of events that gave them the opportunity."

We both saw where that thought led: the sisters—if indeed they were sisters—would have quickly delivered the contracted-for items to whoever had ordered them. But the idol probably did not have a customer waiting for it. They would have to make inquiries, scout around for a possible buyers, make approaches, wait for the prospective purchasers to make their own inquiries and determine that the women were not police agents looking to sting them for receiving purloined goods.

"All of that takes time," Glad Dananda said, "and creates ripples. People have to talk to people who talk to other people. You can't simply put an advertisement in a publication."

"What we need," Jenore said, "is someone who knows some of those 'people,' someone who could detect the ripples and trace them back to their source."

"Are you thinking of a discriminator?" I said.

She signaled a negative. No. I'm thinking of a thief. A thief who steals objects of art."

To reach Burradoo, we had come a fair way down The Spray. It was a four-day trip, involving two whimsies, back to Old Earth. We arrived at mid-morning, Olkney time, and did not visit Hapthorn's or Gievel's premises. Instead, I went straight to Quirks and told the who's-there at the door that I wished to speak with Luff Imbry.

"Ser Imbry is at breakfast," the device told me, after a brief delay, "and does not wish to be disturbed."

"Tell him I will wait, and that I wish to discuss hiring him again."

I stood and waited. After a while, the door opened and a tiny, bald-headed man who was quite possibly the oldest individual I had ever seen beckoned me inside. Silently, with a stooped walk, he went before me across a wood-paneled foyer, past a cloakroom, until he opened another door to usher me into a room with several plush-seated chairs ranged about the walls.

I sat. He closed the door. I waited again.

The fat man clearly took his time about breakfast. Still, I was designed for patience when it was needed. Thus I was in an equable mood when the door opened again and the aged gnome beckoned me to follow him again. We went up a flight of stairs, he making each step an odyssey then along a corridor lined with closed double doors bearing discreet brass plates that identified them as *Morning Room*, *Reading Room*, *Library* then came to a single door whose plaque said, simply, *Private*.

The ancient knocked then opened the portal and stood aside. I stepped through and found myself being inspected by the rotund middler who had organized the negotiations with the Hand Organization. He was seated in one of four armchairs grouped around a low, round table. As wordlessly as the servitor, who now closed the door, he waved me to a seat opposite him. He continued to study me.

I settled myself, waited a few moments then said, "Does no one talk in this place?"

At first I thought he was not going to answer, but after a lengthy pause he said, "Quirks encourages quiet. Still, in this room conversation is not actively discouraged." He regarded me some more before going on to say, "I had not thought to see you again. I understood the business with Lord Chaderanth to have been concluded."

"It was," I said, "but another matter has come up."

He held up a hand to stop me then reached into a side pocket of his capacious upper garment to withdraw a small, cube of metal and crystal. This he placed upon the table between us and touched a stud on its upper surface. Then he sat back, aced his fingers together over his prominent midriff, and said, "A little device of my own creation.

Anyone taking an interest in our conversation will hear us discussing antique finger sleeves, in our own voices"

"Understood," I said. "Hapthorn had something similar."

The news apparently came as a irritation to the fat man,, but he overcame the reaction and said, "Proceed."

I told him the essentials of the case as far as they involved Addeus Ing and the women who had called themselves Vauderoy. "I have been engaged to recover the idol. I need to find those women."

Imbry absorbed this information and nodded. "And you wish to involve me in what capacity?"

"As a go-between. As someone who knows people who know people, someone who could let it be known in the right places that you have a client who is interested in purchasing eidolons of possible ultraterrene origin."

He smiled slightly. "Which would, technically, be the truth."

"There would be no need to divulge your client's motivation or identity."

"No, no need."

He said nothing for a while but I could see how, behind the round face, with its carefully bland expression, thoughts were arranging themselves in order. But when he spoke, I found we had moved on to a different subject.

"The Hand were interested in you," he said. "They questioned me about your origins, but I was unable to give them any more of a lead than to point them at Hapthorn."

"Which probably did not satisfy them."

"No, but it made me curious. I like to know whom I'm dealing with."

"So you made inquiries," I said.

Another nod. "I did, but without learning more than the

history of your career as an indentured player on Thrais, taken into the gaming house as a nameless infant."

I said nothing and waited.

He watched me some more, and I could see he was about to try some ploy. Then he said, "There was also some stir in the upper reaches of Green Circle: something about an off-worlder having been awarded Honored Associate rank."

I had complete control of my features, but when I saw him smile I saw that my having shown no reaction was, for Imbry, a reaction after all. Now he said, "I don't suppose you'd like to tell me what you did to obtain that status."

I said nothing and let him see that I would say nothing.

"Understood," he said. "Let us discuss terms."

"First tell me if the three women ring a bell for you."

He smiled again. "You want to know if you have tugged on the right sleeve."

"I do."

"You have. I have not dealt with the women, but I know some collectors who have—not on Old Earth, but in some of the Domains. They are available to acquire certain categories of goods, generally small and valuable, for a fee."

"So they do not steal to sell on the open market, but only on contract."

"Just so," Imbry said.

"Then we can discuss terms," I said.

He named a figure. I named another. And so it continued until we had reach an amount we both thought suitable. I handed him a number of credit chips that added up to half his fee, and he pocketed them smoothly.

I told him details of the thefts we had uncovered. He did not make notes but I had the impression he was absorbing all the information. We discussed possible approaches to finding the women, and agreed on the strategy he thought would be most effective. We made the formal gestures that, on Old Earth, sealed an agreement.

I told him where he could reach me, and he said he would be in touch. He would have to send messages down The Spray, and that would take a while.

I said I understood. "My client is impatient, but I am not."

He deactivated the cube on the table and pocketed it. Then he pressed a button set into the wall. A little while later, the door opened and the tiny, wizened creature led me away.

I stepped out onto the street to find a nondescript-looking man waiting at the bottom of the stairs. He made the unobtrusive finger motions that identified him as a member of Green Circle.

"Ser Labro," he said, when I descended to join him, "we understand that you have been meeting with Luff Imbry."

I glanced back at the closed door. "I thought this establishment was renowned for its privacy."

He let a smile briefly visit his lips. "And we are renowned for our ubiquity."

I said nothing and waited.

"Imbry is not a friend to our organization," he said. "There is a history."

"Nor to me. Ours is entirely a contractual relationship."

I saw him reflect for a moment on my answer. "Just be aware that he is not to be trusted."

I assured him that I did not give trust easily. He moved his head in a manner that said he hoped events would turn out well for me then he walked away.

ADDEUS ING WAS none too pleased when I reported on my encounter with the corpulent criminal.

"If you think I am going to pay his exorbitant fee—" he began.

I cut him off. "If you know a better way to recover your lost idol, I would be happy to hear it now.

"Simple," said the cultist. "This Imbry knows who the thieves are. Squeeze him and he will squeal."

"We are not empowered to seize people," Jenore told him, "let alone squeeze them. Imbry would be well within his rights to sic the scroots on us, and you would enjoy another period of incarceration." She consulted her memory. "I've heard that the Archon's contemplarium applies some rather intensive techniques to modify inmates' behavior. There's a device known as the excruciator, for example."

I motioned for her to ease up on our client. "Consider this," I said to Ing. "We could go from world to world, sifting clues, hoping the three purloiners will make a mistake. But bear in mind that they appear to have been operating long enough for Imbry to have heard of them. Yet, in all of that time, police agencies on several planets have not connected the various thefts as being the work of the same perpetrators."

Ing made a sour face. "Meaning?"

"Meaning they know what they are doing. It might take a very long time, and some very good luck, to catch them. And during all that time, our charges will be mounting up."

Jenore joined in. "Whereas Imbry might be able to point us straight at them, and let us take them unawares." Now she played her masterstroke. "And soon, even before they have been able to dispose of Ubrach."

Light dawned in Ing's mind. "Ah," he said. "That would be preferable."

We agreed to wait and see what the fat man came back to us with.

A DAY PASSED. After breakfast, we were seated in *Intrepid*'s salon, finishing the morning's pot of punge. Our client was visiting a temple in one of the older parts of Olkney, propelled by a desire to consult with its priesthood about issues I found too abstruse to grapple with. With nothing to occupy us, I again raised the subject of a visit to Jenore's family at Shorraff.

I saw that the prospect unsettled her. I asked why that should be.

"I don't know," she said. "Somehow it all seems to be part of a long-ago past, a past I'm not comfortable with." She paused for introspection then went on, "Or it calls up a past *me* that I'm not comfortable being any more."

I remembered what she had said when she first told me of her leaving home and going out into the immensity, and how she would find her old home upon her return as a changed woman: *like a shoe broken in by someone else's foot. It will not flex and bend where I do, and it will pinch.*

"But now you have changed still more. You have come a long way from when you were that desperate showgirl stranded on Thrais."

She nodded. "I have, haven't I?"

"I think your mother would like to see you."

"Yes." Another pause. "And I would like to see her."

"It's not far by air car."

Her brows concentrated themselves as she looked down at the floor of the salon. Then she looked up. "Integrator, summon an air car. We're going out."

THE FIRST TIME I visited Graysands, the island where the Mordenes lived, Jenore and I had traveled by sailboat — a pleasant little sea voyage which took long enough for a leisurely meal. From Olkney by air car was a much shorter trip. Not long after we achieved cruising height, the low-lying isle appeared on the horizon and we angled down toward it.

Seen from the air, the rambling house with its shingle-walled wings and extensions around a tall central hall looked smaller than when I had originally walked up the wharf toward it. But the family's foranq, an intricately carved and decorated barge that was the work of genera-tions to tell the history of the Mordenes, was no less impres-sive seen from above as from the water. As we settled down on the landward end of the wooden jetty, I looked to see where the painted likeness of my true love as a child looked out from a crowd of artfully rendered members of her extended clan.

"There you are," I said, pointing when I spotted her again among the throng of cousins, siblings, and ancestors.

"And there we are," she said. I followed the line of her finger and saw her as she had looked when we had returned from Thrais, in pursuit of the mystery that eventually led us to Forlor and the momentous events that transpired there.

But beside her slim figure, leaning in close to her painted face that the artist had caught with a far-away look in her eyes, was another visage that I realized only after a moment's study, was mine own.

"Why do I look so puzzled?" I said. "I'm actually frowning."

"That was more or less the expression on your face the whole time we were here," she said. "As if we were a riddle you could not solve."

I thought back to my encounter with the Shorrafis and their strange ways—a culture based on vanity that dealt in prestige instead of hard coinage—and said, "I suppose you were."

That time, we had arrived at dawn, before the household was awake. Today it was mid-morning, and our air car had brought out several members of the household: men with craftsmen's tools, some young women with babies balanced on their hips, and a rounded woman I recognized as Munn, Jenore's mother. There was less excitement on their faces— on our previous visit they had thought of their missing girl as gone forever—but there was nothing but smiles and gladness. Munn and Jenore ran to each other and embraced.

I got some nods and greetings, which I returned in kind. The tensions that attended my previous visit were nowhere to be seen or felt.

The front door opened and Eblon Mordene, the family patriarch, came out onto the top step. He was still large and burly, but the power he had once radiated was fading with age, as he came down and enfolded both his wife and daughter in his arms. The look he threw me over Jenore's shoulder was not entirely welcoming, but neither was it a rejection of my apparent accepted place in the family.

Then he stepped back, gave his daughter a long appraisal, and said, "Good to have you back. How long can you stay for?"

Jenore looked a question at me. I shrugged. "A few days, if we're welcome."

Eblon pursed his lips, but before he could reply, Munn said, "Of course you're welcome." Then she gave her husband a look that dared him to say different.

"Let's go inside," he said.

AND SO WE slipped into the life of Jenore's family, the kind of life I had never known: people who were at ease with each other, sharing meals and memories, exchanging bouts of laughter and banter, even impromptu sing-alongs around the big table in the kitchen. I still got the occasional sidewise glance from her father, but the rest of the clan accepted me as one of their own.

It was a strange feeling. When we had been here before, chasing the mystery of Hallis Tharp's legacy, Jenore and I had talked about what it was like to belong somewhere. I had thought then that it would be enough for me to belong to her. Now, for the first time in my life, I began to understand what it would feel like to belong to a place, to a community. It called up unusual emotions in me. I came to know what it felt like to be sad and happy at the same time, and for the same reasons.

The third evening of our stay, she and I walked along the shore past the jetty, after having taken a look at the new portraits on the inner walls of the great hall within the foranq. Prominent was a painting of her brother Iriess

sinking the ball into the goal-ring at one end of the birl
pitch. The goal had cemented the victory for his team, the
Cresting Wave, over their long-time rivals, the Jaunty
Crabs, to win the championship of all Shorraff. Iriess now
walked like a deity among the Shorraffis, and the glory of
his win had enabled him to open his own studio, turning
hand-sized seashells into intricately carved combs, brooches,
bracelets, and other items of beauty.

The quarrel over Alwan Foulaine's attempt to import
currency-based gambling into Shorraff—a disagreement
that had riven the Mordenes and the rest of the community
on my first visit—had ended and the wounds were healed. I
understood the conflict better now than I did then; at least I
believed I did, but I still refrained from voicing my opinion
that the Shorraffis traded in an invisible currency of prestige
the way other cultures—"normal" cultures—did business in
cash.

But that was not what was on my mind as we walked,
hand in hand, along the shore. Dusk was settling and the
waves that rippled over the sands had taken on a purple
hue. I looked at Jenore in the fading light and saw that she
was deep in thought. I took a guess at where her mind was
taking her.

"Are you thinking it wouldn't be so bad to stay here?"

She came back from a distance. "Not so much thinking
it, as wondering if I ought to be thinking it." She glanced at
me then away. "What about you? Could you live here?"

I let my shoulders rise and fall. "I couldn't be a confidential op," I said. "Nor could you." Then I followed the
thought. "Although we could commute to Olkney and off-
world."

She said nothing for a few steps. "No, it would be too . .

. strange. Too much of a clash, going out there among the hurly-burly of crime and nefarious doings then coming back here to peace and serenity."

"Perhaps we should just go back to chartering," I said.

But Jenore lifted her head and clucked her tongue in a motion that meant "No" on Thrais. "We'd get bored," she said. "That's not the same as peace and serenity."

'Then . . . what?" I said.

She squeezed my hand and brought it up to her lips. "Then we go on as we have. We get Ubrach back for Addeus Ing then we see what the next investigation brings."

WHEN WE GOT BACK to our room at the Mordene house, my traveling integrator was waiting on the dresser with a message from our client.

"The man you engaged to make contact with the sisters came by the Videlia Inn. He has succeeded."

"Tell him we'll be back in the morning," I said. I looked at Jenore. Her eyes were bright with anticipation.

Peace and serenity would have to wait.

"THEY WILL ARRIVE this afternoon on the *Williwand*," Imbry told us when we met in the lounge of our hostelry. The metallic-and-ceramic cube was on the table between us. "It's an independent freighter. I presume they prefer the informality of such vessels."

"How shall we handle it?" I said.

The fat man said the normal process for such encounters was for the seller to meet the buyer at a secure location, so that the goods could be examined and determined to be genuine.

"Bolly's Snug?" Jenore said.

"If they have done any due diligence on my background," Imbry said, "they will know that is where I usually conduct business. Suggesting anywhere else might give them qualms."

"I'll give them qualms," Addeus Ing said.

Imbry showed him the briefest possible smile. "I advise that you stay away. Far away. Any sight of you in the vicinity will blow the opportunity, and we will not get another."

"Bolly's it is," I said. I raised a finger. "But they have seen Jenore and me as well."

"It would not seem out of the ordinary for me, as the middler, to conduct the transaction on my own."

"No!" Addeus Ing's raised voice drew the attention of other persons in the lounge. I wondered how the voice-imitator handled his single syllable.

"Calm," I told him. Then, to Imbry I said, "I mean no offense, but I am not comfortable with leaving the business entirely up to you, either."

Jenore said, "An elision suit?"

Imbry waved away the suggestion. "Bolly does not allow them."

"Then some other form of disguise," I said.

The fat man thought for a moment. "I expect they will bring someone to protect their interests. They will not look askance if I do the same."

"A thug," I said.

"In the artifacts trade, the preferred term is 'ensurer'," Imbry said. "All you have to do is look quietly menacing."

I assured him I could manage that.

"No weapons," he said, "and no communications devices of any kind. Bolly's rules are strict."

"I would be interested to meet this Bolly," I said.

"You won't have the occasion," Imbry said. "No one meets Bolly. That is the strictest rule of all."

WHEN JENORE and I were alone again, she said, "Perhaps the simplest plan would be to intercept them on the way to the meeting and relieve them of the idol."

I gave it only a moment's consideration before saying, "That might be difficult. We don't want to draw the interest of the Bureau of Scrutiny. Weapons fire in the streets of Olkney would do that."

"They're not supposed to bring weapons to the meeting."

I corrected her. "They're not allowed to have weapons *at* the meeting. On the way there and back . . ." I spread my hands in a gesture of ambiguity.

"I don't like relying on Luff Imbry," she said. "He has the look of a man who is faithful only to his own agenda."

"Yes," I said. "Moreover, he looks to have been highly successful at fulfilling it."

"We need to think it through."

"We do," I said. I glanced at the chronometer. "And we don't have much time."

IMBRY CAME to collect me at the hostelry, arriving early to assist me into a disguise. He brought an upper garment of a style recently fashionable among Old Earth's second-tier aristocracy and those who imitated their ways: a padded jacket with a flared waist, slashed sleeves, and extravagantly wide shoulders. Beneath it, I was to wear baggy pantaloons, so loose-fitting that no one would be able to tell my gender. And to top it all, he produced a cloche headpiece that featured a veil of beaded strings that descended from a protruding brow-piece to the collar of the doublet.

I put them on and regarded myself from all angles in the room's reflector. "What do you think?" I asked Jenore.

"I wouldn't recognize you," she said. "And no one who knows you would ever expect you to go out in public looking like that."

"So it will do?" Imbry said.

"I think it will," I said.

IMBRY and I traveled to Bolly's in a ground car. Air cars were not welcomed there. Jenore followed along a short time later, after reiterating to Addeus Ing that he was to remain at the hostelry until we signaled that the idol had been recovered. He appeared anxious, pacing the room, and muttering to himself. Jenore told him, once we delivered Ubrach to him, he was at liberty to exact whatever revenge he wished on the women we had known as the Vauderoys.

"But we will not be part of that," she told him. "This case has already drawn official attention, and we have no intention of sharing a cell with you in the Archon's contemplarium."

Imbry and I arrived shortly before the time set for the meeting. We entered through the common room and made our way to the rear of the building, along a corridor lined with doors. Imbry touched his hand to a plate set beside one of the portals, and it swung open to reveal a small room with a plain table and chairs. Imbry went around the table and sat with his back to the wall. I sat beside him.

We waited.

Then a chime sounded. "They're coming," Imbry said.

Moments later, the door opened and the three women appeared in the doorway. The one I remembered as Shuriz leaned into the room and inspected it carefully, even bending to look under the table.

"Looks all right," she said and led her two accomplices into the room. Behind them came a large man carrying a wooden box that was big enough to contain Ubrach. The women sat and he placed the container on the table between us and them. Then he closed the door and stood with his back against it, arms folded. I judged him to be relaxed and capable.

There were no formalities or greetings. Imbry said, "Open it."

"Shuriz" touched a metal clasp on the box's top. Something clicked and the sides of the container fall away. There before us, in his familiar squat, was the idol that had first been found in the remains of an amphitheater on the world Thriffle, a statue judged by antiquarians to be a representation of some admirable specimen of the amphibian-like ultraterrenes who had abandoned their drying-up planet to pursue their destinies elsewhere—and judged by Addeus Ing and his fellow cultists to be worthy of their worship.

Imbry leaned forward and examined the object, as did I,

although my vision was somewhat occluded by the strings of colored beads hanging before my eyes. But it was surely the same piece that had been stolen from Ing's cabin on *Peregrinator*. I had had some concern that the three purloiners might try to pass us a copy, but if that were the case they would have brought us a polished, untarnished creation. The Ubrach before us had the appearance of a statue that had been gathering dust in somebody's storage room.

I clasped my hands before me on the table, the signal to Imbry that this was the straight goods. Then I leaned back in my chair and let him begin the haggling process, while I kept an eye on the hired bravo. If there was to be trouble, I expected it to come from that direction.

And so it did, though not the kind of trouble I was watching for. Something struck the door against which the hired muscle was leaning. He straightened up and managed a half-turn toward the door before it was hit again from the other side and swung in to strike the man hard. Off balance, he staggered back, giving me a view of the open doorway, through which now came Addeus Ing, his face full of rage, an iron bar in one upraised hand.

Ing struck at the hired guard, but the latter was worthy of his pay, because he caught Ing's wrist before the blow could land and delivered a counterstrike to the cultist's midsection that doubled my client over. The bar fell to the floor with a metallic clang.

And then the room filled with thick white smoke. The fight disappeared from view, as did the three thieving women, and the sound of coughing came from within the obscurity. I left my chair and dropp0ed to the floor, where the air would be clearer. I was conscious of motion beside me then a sudden draft swirling the smoke though it lasted only a brief span before the billows continued as before.

"Imbry?" I said, reaching toward the space where he had been sitting. My hand should have met his ankle, but found only smoke-filled air. That was when I knew what had happened.

I crawled along the baseboard, thrusting the chairs aside, struggling to keep from coughing while I struck the wall with my fist every few minims. I heard flatly solid thumps, one after another, until I heard a deeper, hollow sound. I put my mouth as close to the floor as possible, sucked in a breath of mostly smoke-free air then stood and threw my shoulder at the wall.

Something gave, though not all the way. I hit the panel again, and the disguised door crashed open inward. I threw myself through, entering a barely lit corridor, so narrow that it must have been a tight fit for Luff Imbry as he fled the smoke-filled room behind me, where a chaotic struggle to escape still occupied the three women, their thug, and my client. Trailing wisps of smoke, I hurried along the passage until I came to a blank wooden wall.

This was a more solid barrier than the one I had shouldered my way through. The poor light behind me made it too dark to see anything. I felt the surface in front of me, methodically quartering the wood, until my fingers found a narrow cavity at waist height. Inside was a metal ring. I slipped two fingers into it and pulled sideways, and a spring-loaded bolt moved aside.

I pulled, and the door came toward me. And then I was out into an alley at the rear of Bolly's Snug, windowless and doorless stone walls to either side. I expected, at best, to see Luff Imbry departing in some vehicle he had left there.

Instead, I saw the fat man himself, firmly held in the grip of two large and capable-looking individuals. At their feet, tipped over onto its frog-like face, lay the divine Ubrach.

A smaller man was bending over to examine the statue. At my appearance, he stood, and I recognized the anonymous fellow who had warned me that Imbry was not to be trusted. He made the little flicker of fingers, as if I might need reminding.

I approached Imbry. "I am your client," I said. "This was not appropriate."

He showed me an equivocal face. "Addeus Ing was the ultimate client," he said.

"Ah," I said, as the situation became clear. Rather than pay the cost of purchasing the idol from the thieves, plus Jenore's and my fees and expenses, Ing had opted to hire Imbry directly.

I stooped and picked up the idol, rested it on my hip. "Your malfeasance means our agreement is vitiated," I said, "as is our contract with Ing."

Imbry's captor spoke. "He has disrespected an Honored Associate of Green Circle. We need to make an example."

"It was only business," the fat man said. "Nothing personal."

I regarded him for a moment then spoke to the Green Circle force. "Lock him away somewhere with a very narrow doorway. Feed him only bread and water until he can get out on his own."

Imbry made an involuntary noise that bespoke misery. The Green Circle man smiled. "Imaginative," he said. "It's a shame you don't come into the orbit."

"I have other things to do," I said.

The door into Bolly's Snug had closed itself behind me. I

edged past the fat man and his captors and, carrying the idol, made my way up the alley to the street then found a route back to where Jenore was waiting in the ground car. She looked at Ubrach then peered behind me.

"Ing?" she said.

"He is no longer our client," I said. "But we seem to have acquired a god."

"We will not be able to collect the balance of our fee from Addeus Ing," I told Erm Kaslo, "nor recoup our expenses."

Apparently the eponymous owner of Bolly's Snug took a dim view of the cult leader's antics. Ing had not been heard from since.

Jenore added, "But we won't have to pay Luff Imbry the remainder of his fee."

Kaslo ran his hand over the smooth dome of Ubrach's hairless head and shrugged. "We can probably sell this for something."

But not to the cultists. Word had reached us that the Ubrachians had disbanded after their leaders were released from detention, having lost the object of the cult's veneration. Apparently Addeus Ing was the only one who retained an appetite for carrying on with the religion. The authorities on Meech's World took exception to practitioners of oddball sects that indulged in violence. The detainees had been subjected to intensive re-education methods, against which only Ing's fanaticism had survived.

"There are also rewards for the capture of the three women," Kaslo added.

"But we don't know where they are based," Jenore said.

"Actually, we do," the op said. He bade his integrator show us a map of the various star systems where the trio had carried out their successful thefts, and the network of whimsues that connected them. I saw the pattern immediately, but let Jenore make the point.

"They are all within easy reach of . . ."—she peered at the display—"a star called Ramilles."

"Home to a secondary world named Arthur," said Kaslo, "where no similar thefts were carried out by a trio of women."

"Because that's where they live."

Kaslo confirmed her conclusion and said that a routine canvass among who's-theres and public sensor percepts in the city near the world's only major spaceport soon showed us where the women rested between forays.

"I have an agent watching the addresses. When they show up, she will alert us, and we will advise the constabularies here at Indoberia, and at Carrigan, Manfredonia, and Tumbarumba. The cumulative rewards will more than amply cover our losses, yielding a decent profit."

"All's well that ends in the black," I said.

Kaslo gave me a wry look. "A common expression on Thrais?"

"It is. And a truth."

HAVING BEEN on assignment without time off for the length of the Ing investigation, we were granted several days of paid leave. Jenore had heard of a resort on an island not too far from Indoberia. She booked us a cottage and we traveled by omnibus and packet boat. The accommodations were at the midpoint between utilitarian and luxurious, but the scenery and relaxed ambience of the place were more than satisfactory. We swam, ate, lazed about, and indulged in intimate relations. Jenore tried to introduce me to dancing but, like everyone else who witnessed our efforts, I preferred to watch her.

"I think your handedness has grown over the years," I said when she returned to sit with me at one of the tables confining the dance floor.

She made a wordless sound of scoffing but smiled then graciously acknowledged the applause that had accompanied her to her seat.

While she danced, I had ordered us two of the complicated beverages that the resort offered its patrons. She took a sip to quench her thirst and made a pleased face. I raised my glass in a salute and smiled back at her.

"So," I said, "now what?"

She moved her head in a this-or-that equivocation. "So on we go," she said.

"Stay with Kaslo? Or go back to chartering?" I thought about it for as moment then said, "Or something entirely new. We could even retire and live on the Green Circle stipend, spend our time wandering among the stars."

Her sigh was one of contentment. "I'm happy enough doing what we've been doing. What about you?"

"If you're happy, I'm happy."

"Then we'll see what comes." She drained her glass and raised a hand to summon the server.

"Yes," I said, "whatever comes."

To Arthur Raisfeld, with thanks for help along the way

About the Author

Matt (Matthew) Hughes writes fantasy, space opera, and crime fiction. He has sold 24 novels to publishers large and small in the UK, US, and Canada, as well as nearly 100 works of short fiction to professional markets.

His latest novels are: *A God in Chains* (*Dying Earth* fantasy) from Edge Publishing and *What the Wind Brings* (magical realism/historical novel) from Pulp Literature Press.

He has won the Endeavour and Arthur Ellis Awards, and has been shortlisted for the Aurora, Nebula, Philip K. Dick, Endeavour (twice), A.E. Van Vogt, Neffy, and Derringer Awards. He has been inducted into the Canadian Science Fiction and Fantasy Association's Hall of Fame.

Web page: www.matthewhughes.org

Also by Matthew Hughes

Fools Errant

Downshift

Fool Me Twice

Gullible's Travels (SFBC omnibus of *Fools Errant* and *Fool Me Twice*)

Black Brillion)

The Gist Hunter and Other Stories

Majestrum

The Commons

Wolverine: Lifeblood

The Spiral Labyrinth

Template

Hespira

The Other

To Hell and Back: The Damned Busters

Song of the Serpent

To Hell and Back: Costume Not Included

To Hell and Back: Hell to Pay

Old Growth

9 Tales of Henghis Hapthorn

The Meaning of Luff and Other Stories

The Compleat Guth Bandar

Devil or Angel and Other Stories

Made in United States
North Haven, CT
15 September 2022

24141725R00174